# RENAISSANCE
# WOMAN

Like time-travel?

**Check out the Turning Points series**
at jodielane.com

The Siege of Masada
Transylvanian Knight
To Kill An Emperor
Renaissance Woman
Heart and Stomach of a Queen

**Turning Points Short Stories:**

Siege of the Heart
The Time-Traveller's Date
A Soldier's Love
A Soldier's Honour

# RENAISSANCE
# WOMAN

JODIE LANE

To Kate M.

# ACKNOWLEDGMENTS

Thanks go to, as always, my friends and family for your encouragement, curiosity and support. I'm well over halfway through writing this series, and I couldn't have done it without you all!

My excellent beta readers! Carolyn, Kate, Zane, Rebecca, Alicia and Jess—thank you so much for taking the time to pick out of the plot holes and ask the hard questions. I'm so fortunate and grateful to have such a terrific group of critically-minded writers and readers upon which to draw.

Barb and Mum—thank you for proofreading again. It's getting better, isn't it? And a special mention to Alan—the information you gave me on horse-riding gave me confidence to add those extra, accurate details. Feedback from you, David and Scott at North Lakes Writers' Group encouraged me greatly as you've listened to snippets of this book over the course of the year.

And Dee, whose editing was far sterner this time round. I feel like we've stepped up our game, which makes the praise all the more worth it. Not to mention another excellent cover design—this series has come alive because of you.

# *One*

**1492 AD**

"Stop her!"

"Demon!"

"Whore!"

Michelle bolted down the muddy alley, chickens squawking in her wake. The villagers were close behind. If they caught her she would be tried as a witch. She couldn't afford to time travel away—so many jumps had worn her out, muddling her wits. She needed food and rest—not an enraged mob screaming at her heels, determined to burn her.

If she hadn't been so tired she never would have walked directly into the main piazza where a crowd listened avidly to a preacher. She would have loitered around the edges, stolen a dress or begged a bite to eat. Instead she had strolled into the view of the ugly Dominican friar who fixed on her and cried indignation at her uncovered hair, her masculine attire.

"Sin!" He had pointed and the crowd had followed his enraged gaze. "Not only wanton with her hair uncovered, unbound, but flaunting her body in God's eyes. Such sin!"

Michelle had frozen in the face of his fury. Like a pack of beasts, the crowd roared and surged towards her. Michelle did the only thing she could think of doing.

She ran.

"She's getting away!"

She hoped so. Fit as she was, this unexpected sprint was unwelcome, and the fields around the Italian village provided no cover. A sideways lunge into a stable and a dash between stalls. She kicked open the back door then scrambled up a ladder into the hayloft. She flung herself behind some bales and hoped her hiding place was good enough.

"That way!" Angry men flooded the stable below, sending horses into panicked whinnies. Michelle forced her breath to slow and projected an aura of nothingness.

"Out here!"

Feet thundered on the flagstones below and out the door. Quiet returned. Michelle peeked out as a middle-aged man with a straggling beard emerged from a stall and petted his charges, calming them one by one. The groom circled the horses twice then stopped at the bottom of the ladder.

"I see you run up there, maybe you is agone now, but I don't think so." The musicality of his voice made him sound whimsical. "They is gone, they who is chasing you."

Michelle raised her head cautiously. "Thank you. I'm afraid the preacher in the piazza took against me."

The groom leant on a stall, stroking the head of the gelding that whickered over his shoulder. "That Savonarola. Don' take much to get 'im all a-riled up. I'll be glad when 'e goes to Florence."

Savonarola. *Just my luck.*

"You're not a fan of his?" Michelle slid down the ladder.

The groom shrugged. "I prefer looking after the horses—they is simpler." He patted the gelding affectionately, feeding it an apple from his pocket.

"Sensible of you." Michelle brushed stalks of hay from her trousers. "Now is there any chance you could tell me where I might purchase a dress, a place to sleep and some food?" She pulled out a small silver ring, one of those she'd been issued with for this perilous trip into the past.

The groom eyed the ring speculatively. "Si. Climb back up into the 'ayloft and I is bringing a dress and the food. You can sleep there—there is no rats."

Michelle smiled. "Thank you, signor."

\* \* \*

Kind as the groom seemed to be, Michelle still took precautions. She activated her tiny forcefield dome and stretched before she went to sleep. Footsteps below woke her and she deactivated the field seconds before the groom's head emerged at the top of the ladder. He brought her an old, moth-eaten brown dress and a pail containing lukewarm pottage.

"I'll be off and away at first light," Michelle said, managing not to pull a face at the taste of the pottage. "Thank you for your help."

"Si," The groom watched her eat, to her annoyance. She would wait until he was gone before she changed into the dress. "Where is you a-going?"

"France," she lied.

"Si. For another of those rings I could give you the direction?" he added hopefully.

"No thank you, I know the way." She didn't, but she wasn't about to burn through her funds when she could use the chronokinetor to guide her.

"Hmph." The groom didn't leave. "It was not easy, getting the dress and the food up 'ere. Folk in the village still a-riled up. Might be you need 'elp leaving without a fuss."

"I'll be fine." Michelle put steel into her tone. She ate faster, trying not to gag, and handed the pail back to the groom. "Thank you. You'd best get back to your duties."

"Hmph." He rubbed his beard and retreated down the ladder. Michelle waited until it was fully dark, snuck down and relieved herself just outside the door, then climbed back up the loft and set the forcefield before lying down in her bed of hay.

She rose well before dawn, knowing a groom's day would start early. With her own clothes stashed in her backpack, she concentrated on being inconspicuous in her shabby dress as she crept down the ladder.

"Folk still be a-looking," the groom's hoarse voice sounded by her ear.

Michelle whirled and stopped herself from hitting him. "I don't have any more money for you!" She strode to the main stable door, conscious that he was a step behind her. When she reached for the bar his bony hand grasped her wrist. Michelle dug her fingernails into his skin and twisted her arm free. She yanked his own arm up behind his back and pushed him against the stable door. "I said, I don't have any more money for you."

"I was just trying to 'elp!" he wheezed.

"Whatever you say, my friend. Now unless you want a broken wrist I suggested you stay in this stable while I leave. And don't think about telling anyone I'm heading to France, or I'll come back and break both your arms."

She waited until he grunted affirmation and let go, lifting the bar on the door and slipping out before he could say anything more. She hurried along the back laneways of the town in the black early morning. By the time the grey light of dawn crept into the sky, she was well on the road to Milan.

# Two

Squaring her shoulders, Gwyn marched to the entrance of the Borgia house. "I have word of a plot against His Eminence Cardinal Rodrigo Borgia," she announced to the astonished guards. "He would be most obliged if you advised him, as it will save his life."

They stared at her, then exchanged incredulous looks, not bothering to stop leaning on their pikes. Gwyn cleared her throat. "I'm not here to waste time," she warned.

Despite her confidence, her welcome had been less than cordial. One guard had reported to the mistress of the household, who had ordered Gwyn locked into the cellar. Dim light filtered in through a tiny grate at street level; it was getting dark outside. Gwyn closed her eyes and sank into the timepiece. The images she saw centred on a grim, grey-haired man, dressed in red robes, then white. Thankful for a subject of Renaissance Italy last semester, she recognised Pope Alexander VI: the Borgia Pope. Infamous for nepotism, lechery and corruption, yet his reign was critical in shaping Europe's future. Gwyn didn't care what vices the future Pope had. She just wanted to fix the turning point and go home.

Arrival in this year had been tumultuous. She had appeared in a haze of blue light in a wealthy home, heralded by screams of a maid. Two footmen had escorted Gwyn roughly out into the street and dumped her in the gutter. "It'll be broken fingers for you next time, thief! Begone!"

Gwyn brandished her decidedly unbroken middle finger then fled. A

5

street away she slowed to take her bearings. It was a very different Rome to the one she had left.

Renaissance clothing was garish compared to the simple tunics and dresses of Ancient Rome. Gwyn had made herself inconspicuous with the help of the timepiece and drifted through the crowd. She hugged her shawl tightly around her to hide the fact that her dress had neither ruffs nor slashes and petticoats didn't buoy her skirts. She was a drab sparrow compared to these peacocks—men and women both.

In just over a week there would be an attempt on the life of the new Pope, Rodrigo Borgia. Gwyn asked the way to the Borgia household, amused by the Italian spilling elegantly from her mouth. Her question had received appraising looks—some suspicious, some knowing—and she was advised by one old dear, "You'll never get anything out of them, lass. Best find someone to help you get rid of the babe and pray for forgiveness."

Now, left in silence and now darkness, Gwyn paced the stone floor of the empty cellar and brooded. Until the timeline was fixed, she couldn't escape. Even if she wanted to, all she had was a knife, brought with her from Ancient Rome.

At least this turning point revolved around saving a man's life rather than killing him. She could redeem herself from the part she'd played in engineering Emperor Domitian's murder. She shuddered, the memory too fresh in her mind.

\* \* \*

Keys jangled and the cellar door opened. A man stood there, clad in a black robe with a solid gold cross on a long chain around his neck. He held up a lantern and Gwyn threw up her hand against the harsh light. When her eyes adjusted, she examined his face. Black curls worn loose to his shoulders, inscrutable eyes set above a straight nose and hard mouth framed by a neat goatee. "My mother tells me you came to our gate speaking of plots against my father. He is currently in conclave, electing the next Holy Father. Are you telling me someone would breach the sacred trust of that state and commit murder?"

His words were sceptical but his tone was not. Gwyn frowned and shook her head. "No, sir. Not during conclave. After he has been made Pope."

She knew her words carried the impact she desired when the man flinched and gripped the doorway. "What do you know of this?" he hissed. "Speak!"

*Here we go again.* Gwyn cricked her neck. "I have been gifted with visions of the future. I know Cardinal Borgia will be made Pope, and I know that someone will try to kill him shortly after."

The man leant in close and gripped Gwyn's shoulder. She squinted against the lantern's light but held his gaze. "And why would you warn us?" His voice was laden with suspicion. "For gold? Certainly not for love—too many hate us because we're Spanish."

What would this man believe? Gwyn chose her next words carefully. "There is a greater power than you or me, my lord, and I must do the right thing. You don't have to trust me, just believe me enough to take precautions for your father. You can keep me here to ensure I don't speak to anyone else, though I'd prefer not in this storeroom." She glanced around and shivered. "In a week, you will know I speak true."

The man let go of Gwyn and examined her. Innocence wouldn't work here; practicality would, so she tried to keep her face blank. "If you are truthful, you shall be rewarded," he said. "If you lie, I will put you in a sack and throw you into the Tiber to drown."

Gwyn nodded. "I understand, my lord." She repressed a shiver, not wanting him to mistake cold for fear.

"Come." The man gestured to the door. "I'll have my mother prepare a servant's room and you will tell me everything you know. You will not speak to anyone other than her or me. You will not pass messages to the servants. If you try to leave, the guards will tie you up in this room and I will beat you." He gripped Gwyn's arm hard as she walked out with him. "You know who I am, don't you?"

Candles flickered in the corridor outside the storeroom. Gwyn could see now his black robes were those of a priest, augmented by the gold cross. "You are Cesare Borgia, my lord, son of the future Pope," she told the bishop.

"Correct." Bishop Borgia twisted his mouth into a grim smile. "And you belong to me now, girl."

# *Three*

**1492 AD**

"Father."

Cardinal Rodrigo Borgia paused at the low voice and sidestepped to the open hatch where his son hovered on the other side. "Cesare," he said.

"I have only a few minutes, Father—I bribed the guard to look the other way."

"Good, good—take these scrolls and see they reach the right families." He passed several tiny, tightly furled scrolls through the food hatch. Cesare accepted them.

"We delivered the gold as you instructed. How goes the voting?"

"Slow, my son. The Cardinal Orsini is my biggest enemy." Cardinal Borgia pulled his weathered face into a grimace and removed his red hat. "Della Rovere is no friend of mine either."

"We almost have the Sforzas on our side."

They continued to whisper of bribes, threats and promises until Rodrigo said, "I must not linger. Continue the good work, my son."

"Father, there is one more thing. You... you will succeed. God is on our side."

Rodrigo raised a thick eyebrow. "Of course He is, Cesare, but we must help Him wherever possible." He turned, hearing the hatch click shut behind him. Sweeping back into the Sistine Chapel, he gazed at the ceiling as if he had merely paused in contemplation.

*When I am Pope I will have something done about this ceiling—it needs some*

8

*colour.* He added it to his mental list of future edicts. Better to concentrate on gaining the papal throne first, then consolidate his rule.

He needed a two-third majority to win. An unlikely candidate at first, several rounds of voting and much discussion had eroded the support of his opponents and built up his own power base.

"Looking for dinner, Borgia?" It was Cardinal Ascanio Sforza, a po-faced, chubby man in his late thirties. No lightweight himself, Rodrigo chuckled in the pretence of good humour.

"You have to admit, Sforza, the food becomes more limited the longer we are locked in here. I dread going to bread and water."

"Oh, I think you and I will survive." Sforza fell into step beside Rodrigo and they paced the length of the Chapel, passing other cardinals clustered in small groups. The susurrus of whispers breezed its way up the decorated walls to the vaulted ceiling above. Pausing by one of the tall windows, Rodrigo considered his fellow cardinal out of the corner of his eye, wondering what secret messages had been smuggled in from that man's influential family.

"Yes, you and I will survive," Sforza repeated, gazing out the window, unaware of Rodrigo's intense scrutiny. "Bread and water do not frighten me; it's skinny fellows like Della Rovere who should beware the fast. And if it gets cold you and I can huddle together for warmth."

Rodrigo understood. "You know I would offer you my cloak if you needed it, Cardinal Sforza." He smiled to appear amiable.

Sforza turned to him. "You are too kind, Cardinal Borgia, and very generous. If you lent me your cloak I would have to see you received a new one."

This time Rodrigo's smile was genuine, if akin to that of a shark. "Oh I do love new clothes, Cardinal."

"Your attention, please!" The Master of the Ceremonies entered the chapel. "It is time for another vote."

\* \* \*

The poky servant's chamber was better than the dank storeroom, but only just. It was dark, draughty and Gwyn heard mice scratching behind the walls. The shutters rattled in the breeze but at least there was a window. Cesare ordered a tray be sent from the kitchen with her meals to prevent her from speaking to anyone but the silent maid.

She wiled away the hours in her room, lying or sitting on the narrow cot. The chest at the end of the bed was the only other piece of furniture—Gwyn would lean close and inhale the woody smell occasionally to calm her mind and settle into watching the shifting patterns of the past and future through the timepiece. Threads that dipped and spun then merged into a central river of time showed her how individuals' lives could change in a thousand different ways but the flow of history swept them on. In a few days the life of one individual— or his death—would impact the river of history enough to change the course.

After a day of this Gwyn waited until the maid came in to empty the chamber pot then, as she waited by the door, jammed the lock with a wad of fabric. The maid closed the door and turned the key but the bolt didn't fall true, so once she was gone Gwyn snuck out to explore the house.

Spying on the family proved fascinating. Cesare was often out, muttering politics with his mother over wine when he did come back. His brother Juan also spent most of his time away from the house and usually returned late at night, dishevelled and drunk. The youngest boy Joffre had lessons with his tutor or played in the garden with his teenage sister, Lucretia. She was not yet elegant like her mother but with the same creamy skin and blue eyes she was a beauty. Kind yet spoilt, she adored Cesare and the feeling appeared mutual.

Gwyn lurked on a balcony above the courtyard and peeked down at the siblings, seeing a different side of Cesare. He was attentive, seeking his sister's opinion though he mocked her gently if she said something naïve. He was also physically affectionate, kissing and touching Lucretia often. His black, high-necked Bishop's robe contrasted severely with Lucretia's light blue gown, square-cut over her décolletage and trimmed with lace. It was as if a crow had learnt to smile and sought to charm a singing bluebird.

Gwyn slid away from the balcony rail and ghosted back to her room. The Borgias were plagued with rumours of incest and fratricide. She could see how some of the rumours had begun.

"Just a few more days." She rolled onto her pallet and slept.

A knock at the door the next morning stirred her. The hinges creaked and Vannozza dei Cattanei peered in. Cesare's mother was gorgeous and poised. Age had added dignity and Gwyn's heart sighed for a moment at the sight of her hostess in a brocaded red gown, low-cut over the breast and adorned with gold necklaces. She would never be that beautiful but she could aspire to be self-assured.

"My lady." Gwyn got up from the pallet and bowed, then curtseyed awkwardly.

Vannozza smiled. "My son has not told me how long you are to stay, but I thought perhaps you might benefit from a walk in the garden. He cannot mean to keep you cooped up here forever."

Gwyn could have kissed her. Relief that she no longer had to sneak around brought a smile to her face. "Oh thank you, my lady, that would be wonderful." How was it Cesare's mother was so much kinder than him? She dreaded his visits. He quizzed her about her visions and often asked the same question in different ways, picking on every detail. Gwyn remained calm and answered honestly about what she saw but collapsed once he left, praying her nerves would hold.

"Come," Vannozza said. She led Gwyn down the narrow servants' stairs and into the airy courtyard. Gwyn blinked at the light. She breathed deeply of the fresh air then bent to smell the flowers.

"Mama!" Lucretia sprang up from the bench. Vannozza greeted her daughter and they wandered through the garden, chatting affectionately. Gwyn was left to soak up the sunlight and trail her fingers through the leaves of topiary. She closed her eyes.

"Who are you?" Lucretia surprised Gwyn. Her eyes flew open and darted, searching for Vannozza. The woman was over by the courtyard door, speaking urgently to a servant.

"I, uh, I'm a servant of your brother's," Gwyn replied, eyes flicking back to Vannozza.

"Which brother?" Lucretia demanded.

"His Excellency Bishop Borgia," Gwyn answered. "But he has ordered me not to speak to anyone save him and your honoured mother. Please don't get me in trouble, my lady."

Lucretia pulled a flower from its stem and plucked the petals idly.

"Cesare won't do anything—he's too busy trying to make sure Papa wins the election. I've been cooped up here while he and Juan go about having fun. I'm bored. What kind of a servant are you? Are you his mistress?"

Gwyn gaped. Not so innocent after all. "I, uh, can't say, my lady. I really should go." She gritted her teeth. She wanted to stay out in the sun a while longer.

"Lucretia." Vannozza returned, cheeks flushed. "Go and put on a better dress, your father will be here soon. They have made him Pope." She turned to face Gwyn, "You must return to your room."

Gwyn bobbed a mangled curtsey and obeyed, smiling. *One part down!* Now that Rodrigo Borgia was Pope she just had to make sure Cesare prevented the assassination that—by her reckoning—would take place in four days at a banquet. With the turning point thus corrected Gwyn could return to her own time and get back to normal life.

She fidgeted in her room for the rest of the afternoon. She stretched and did exercises in the cramped space and played with her knife. It was made for domestic use, but maybe she could find someone to teach her how to throw it. Meric, the Wallachian-born, Ottoman soldier she had befriended in Transylvania, had taught her some fighting moves. She wondered if he was still alive. Unlikely—he'd be in his fifties by now, an age most mercenaries didn't reach.

She sensed it was Cesare at the door when the key turned—he never knocked. She turned and bowed. His dark eyes were unreadable, as usual.

"Congratulations, my lord." Gwyn kept her voice steady. He was like a panther, poised, ready to pounce at any second.

"Your prediction has come true," Cesare said. "My father is Pope. He will take the name—"

"Alexander the Sixth," Gwyn interrupted, trying to keep the upper hand.

Cesare regarded her through narrowed eyes. "Alexander the Sixth," he agreed. "As for your other visions, tell them to me again. I want to be prepared. My father believes that now he has won he is safe. I know better. I want to know exactly who my enemies are, the enemies of my family."

Gwyn took a breath to sigh then held it. She let it out slowly. "Of course, my lord, My visions show me that four days from now you will dine with your father at the palace of Cardinal Orsini. You will be Cardinal by then." Cesare's lips tightened at this. He had reacted badly when Gwyn first told him Rodrigo would promote him from Bishop to Cardinal while making his younger brother Duke of Gandia. "I would make a better general than Juan," he'd raged, frightening Gwyn. She'd tried not to cower. While the timepiece helped her convince Cesare she spoke the truth, he didn't always like it, and he had a temper.

Gwyn continued with details of the assassination attempt. "Someone poisons the wine—a servant—and serves it to you and your father. In one of my visions he drinks it and dies at the table. In another vision you are there with a monkey on your shoulder and you let the monkey taste your wine and food. The monkey dies. You and your father leave, outraged."

"And the killer? Who orchestrated the plot?"

"I don't know, my lord—my visions don't show me." It frustrated Gwyn. The timepiece gave her the ability to focus on the critical event but it didn't make her omniscient.

"You spoke to my sister today," he changed tack, eyes narrowing.

Gwyn blinked. "She spoke to me, my lord. I am sorry. You mother let me walk in the garden and Luc–your sister wanted to know who I was."

"You should not have spoken to her! I told you not to talk to anyone save my mother and me!" he thundered.

"Please, my lord. I said I was your servant and I wasn't to talk to her. That is all. No harm was done. She thinks I'm your mistress or whore." Gwyn pressed her back against the wall. There was so little space in the room that Cesare and his anger occupied most of it.

"Spy. Whore. What does it matter?" Cesare glared. "How else could you know these things except by betraying your former master or overhearing a cardinal plot in a brothel?"

"Please, my lord. I'm neither." Gwyn drew strength from the solid wall behind her and stopped her shaking. *Keep it together.*

"Not a whore." Cesare's voice was quiet now but no less dangerous. "Would you like to be?"

Gwyn started shaking again. "No, my lord," she whispered. His dark eyes raked over her and he leant in, pinning her. Gwyn raised her hands and shoved—his chest was hard despite his slight build. "NO!" She tensed for another attack.

Cesare stepped back and watched her. "Not a whore then." His eyes ran up and down her again. She still wore her dress from Ancient Rome, with the addition of stockings, a petticoat and a sleeveless smock over the top—spares from another servant. She felt naked despite the layers. "Pity. But I will discover how you know these things. I don't believe in visions. And don't speak to my sister."

He left. Gwyn sank to the floor and hugged her knees. *Four more days,* she promised herself. *Then home.*

# *Four*

**1492 AD**

Michelle examined the tavern and decided it would do. Not as dingy as some of the others in Milan, The Duke's Head boasted a wide entrance and several unshuttered windows open to the street. It wasn't over-crowded, but as stars crept into the evening sky Michelle expected business would pick up.

She strode inside, projecting an aura of masculinity. No one expected to see a woman dressed as a man—knife on her belt, squared shoulders—so no one did, thanks to the chronokinetor. She had purchased clothes in a town on the way; dark tunic and wide-sleeved shirt belted over trousers tucked into knee high boots. She enquired about a room in a gruff voice and haggled over the price before ordering a meal. Halfway through her tankard of ale and bowl of stew a gaggle of local soldiers wandered in and spotted the newcomer.

"We 'ave not seen your face before," one young man declared.

"Just passing through." Michelle nodded and kept eating. The soldier sneered.

"Come on, Filippo! Sit down, 'ave a drink," his comrades encouraged. Filippo sniffed before stalking over to the soldiers' table, pinching the barmaid's bottom on the way. More people entered the tavern; jovial voices rose as a piper struck up a tune in the corner.

Michelle mopped up the last of her stew with bread and sipped her ale, then stood. An early night for an early start—a bustling centre like

Milan would have both horse and supplies to see her on her way to Florence.

"I think you should buy us all a drink." It was Filippo again, not drunk but fuelled by several cups of wine.

"Sit down, Filippo," a deep voice intoned. Michelle glanced at the speaker, a grey haired captain who sat with the soldiers, before returning her focus to the aggressive soldier.

"Sit down, Filippo!" the other soldiers chorused. "He is just pissed because his lover ran away with a Frenchman," one added. They chuckled.

"Sit down, signor," she said. "Enjoy the rest of your night with your friends." She concentrated on influencing him.

It might have worked, save for a passing drunk jolting Filippo into Michelle's arms. Automatically she steadied him but the realisation on his face as he felt the softness of her chest was damning. "A woman!"

Michelle tensed and forced out a laugh. "Have another drink, signor, and maybe I'll look like the Queen of Spain!"

Filippo wasn't fooled. "I'm not drunk," he hissed and leant forward, sniffing Michelle. "What kind of abomination are you, to dress in men's clothes?" He squeezed her breast. She snatched his wrist and twisted his arm behind his back. *Second time in a day.*

She put her mouth close to his ear and whispered fiercely, "Sit down with your friends, signor." With one last tweak of his arm, she released him and pushed him towards his table. He stumbled then rebounded with a roundhouse swing. Michelle dodged it easily. She tripped him and he landed face down on the grubby wooden floorboards. Michelle knelt on his back and wrenched his arm around again.

Stunned silence filled the tavern. Michelle wondered at it—surely they had fights here?

"Who would like to take charge of this young man?" she asked loudly. Pulling a coin from her belt purse with her free hand she flipped it to the gaping barmaid. "For the meal. I will seek accommodation elsewhere. I prefer somewhere… quiet." She waited to see if the soldiers would come to Filippo's aid. She'd have a real fight on her hands if that happened.

A small gesture from the captain removed some of the tension in the room. Two soldiers stood and approached. "We will take him."

Michelle nodded and got up quickly. She slung her bag over one shoulder and made a swift exit. "Well, shit," she muttered as she considered the darkening street.

"Signora." It was the captain from the tavern. His uniform strained across his shoulders and a gut crept over his belt, but to have lived long in his profession meant he knew how to handle himself.

"I don't want trouble, signor." Michelle held up her hands. None of the other soldiers had followed him out but she eyed him warily and kept a watch to both sides.

"Neither do I, signora, I just wanted to ask you about that." He pointed to her left hand where the chronokinetor lay embedded. Michelle was astonished. Most people didn't notice it or thought it a tattoo or strange scar. She clenched her hand.

"Just a birthmark." Was he trying to distract her so his lads could get the jump on her? She turned to walk away.

"Gwyn," the man said. Michelle froze. She turned back. The man frowned. "You look like her, but older. Not as old as you should be, but I suppose anything is possible with that thing."

Michelle spoke slowly. "No, I'm not her. But I think perhaps you and I should talk. Somewhere…"

"Quiet," he supplied and grinned, displaying broken teeth. "Take a walk with me, signora."

* * *

The barman silently served a flagon of wine and placed two cups beside it. Michelle sighed. Avoiding alcohol was hard in these times. "Water too, if you please," she asked. When that arrived Michelle's companion eyed it suspiciously.

"That won't be clean, not in this city."

Michelle smiled and dipped a tiny metal rod into the carafe. "I'll take my chances."

The man opposite considered Michelle, then held out his cup for her to pour water. "Spent my younger years drinking mint tea and water," he explained gruffly. "Miss it now and then. Now, you're not Gwyn, but you have a thing like she did. It was thirty years ago, but I remember." He sipped his water and looked distant.

*Thirty years ago.* Michelle calculated. "Transylvania? Wallachia?"

The man looked at her and nodded. "Aye."

Michelle settled in. This tavern was quiet, as the man had promised. Several other customers huddled in the dim light and appeared to be minding their own business but that was no guarantee. The man noticed Michelle glancing around and said, "What's said in this place won't go further, signora."

"Not signora, please. Just call me Michelle."

"Meric."

"So, Meric," she sat back and stretched her legs under the table. "How did you meet Gwyn? 1459 would have been the year, am I correct?"

"Aye, perhaps you can give me some answers first. You're not the first person I've met who dresses as something they're not, but others— like young Filippo back there—aren't so tolerant." He finished his cup of water and poured himself a wine. The rich red smell told Michelle, by no means an expert, that it wasn't the usual taproom swill.

"How about an answer for an answer? I sent Gwyn to Wallachia, to the year 1459, and I know she influenced some events there."

Meric chuckled. "That she did, though I don't think it was her intent."

Michelle's eyebrows drew together. "It should have been!"

Meric sobered but his grizzled face held the hint of a grin. "Aye, she fell in love instead and caused all sorts of trouble. My turn. Does that thing," he pointed at her left hand, "do the same as hers? Take you to a different time?"

Michelle was incensed. "Did she tell you that? What an idiot! Falling in love too! I knew sending her was a mistake. But..." She remembered the last report she'd read. "The timeline was correct. Vlad the Impaler fought against the Ottomans. She must have convinced him."

"I think it was more to do with her running off with his wife that tipped him over the edge," Meric replied, considering his wine. "Not that it would take much—bloody maniac. He slaughtered the Sultan's envoy." His casual tone juxtaposed the hollow look in his eyes. "I've seen many terrible things as a soldier but that bastard... he was something else."

Michelle didn't doubt it. She huffed and downed her water. Pouring a wine and topping up Meric's cup, she answered his earlier question about the chronokinetor. "Yes, it allows me to time-travel. Did Gwyn tell you what it did? And you believed her?" She didn't bother to hide her incredulity.

Meric guffawed. "Better than that, she took me with her on several damn trips. Made me sick in the gut but I've an extra three years of my life thanks to her."

*Unbelievable.* Michelle sat in silence for a moment. "Irresponsible little minx," she muttered.

"She was young," Meric said. "Tough though. Not much of a fighter but didn't complain, and could think on her feet."

Michelle shot him a disbelieving look. "So, despite her incredible foolishness she managed to bring about the desired result. And then she left you?"

Meric shifted and looked guilty. "Aye, we left her with Vlad and then the Hungarians arrested him. I think she escaped. Alina and I hightailed it to Moldavia and I served her brother for a while as a mercenary. Made my way here after some years—I'm in the service of the Duke of Milan now. Do you know if she survived?"

Michelle tapped her fingers on the table. "Yes, she survived. I'll have to rescue her later, wherever or whenever she is. Probably Ancient Rome by the latest report I received in my own time. I've got more important things to worry about right now. It's not my job to fish her out of every mess."

Meric frowned. "Forgive me, Signora Michelle, but are you not working with her? You both..." He gestured at the timepiece.

"Working with her! No—she's an accident. She shouldn't even have one of these." Michelle waved her left hand. "It was desperation that made us send her to Wallachia—I was against it. I'm here to make sure certain things happen—it's my job. Now, can you recommend me somewhere to stay? I need to buy a horse in the morning too. I'll pay for this." She gestured at the drinks. "Can I buy you a meal?"

Meric frowned. "They don't do meals here. I'll eat back at the palace guardhouse. Where are you going that you need a horse?"

"Nowhere you need to worry about," Michelle replied. "I won't be causing trouble here, if that's what you're asking." She sipped her wine. Tiredness trickled down her throat with it. She had walked all day to reach Milan and wanted nothing more than to go to sleep.

Meric frowned. "I can ask about a room—they won't ask questions if I tell them you're discreet."

"I'm discreet."

The old soldier got up and talked softly with the barman. A middle-aged man walked in and greeted Meric at the same time. Meric pointed to Michelle and the man joined her at the table. "I'm a friend of Meric's," he smiled. "Leonardo's the name."

Michelle ran her eyes over him. "You're a painter," she stated, noting the stained hands.

"And sculptor, and inventor, amongst other things." Leonardo smiled. "Buy you a drink, young man?"

# *Five*

**1492 AD**

"A monkey, Cesare? Why in our Lord's Name do you have a monkey? This isn't the university." Rodrigo Borgia sounded baffled and his son hid his exasperation behind a smile.

"They already think we're Spanish barbarians, Father. Let them be horrified and gossip and I will listen to see who is merely disgruntled and who plots treachery."

The Pope shook his greying head. "You worry too much. Our person is sacrosanct—they'll bicker and mutter but that is all."

Cesare looked out of the carriage window and petted the monkey on his shoulder absently. It nuzzled his fingers then hid in his curly black hair. "We're here."

The carriage rolled to a halt. Liveried footmen opened the door and gave flourished bows. Cesare waited for his father to exit then followed, watching the servants carefully as he padded in soft slippers—red to match his cardinal's robe and hat—through the arched entrance of Cardinal Orsini's home. The palace was even more sumptuous on the inside—frescos decorated the walls, elegant vases and urns adorned doorways that led from hall to hall. Servants glided between guests, offering refreshments from silver platters.

"Welcome, Holy Father!" Cardinals crowded around, kissing Rodrigo Borgia's ring, looking like bright parrots pecking at seed and equally noisy. Cesare listened to their squawking and smiled at the dismayed chuckles that met the appearance of his monkey. He stroked his chin, noting that Cardinal Sforza wasn't present.

A feast lay on a groaning table set for the dozen or so guests. Orsini himself ushered the Pope towards a seat. "Such an honour, your holiness. Please—this way. I've ordered the finest Spanish wine for you tonight—only the best for our Holy Father."

Cesare wanted to sneer at the sycophancy but displayed a congenial smile instead.

"A new pet, Cardinal Borgia?" A cardinal oiled over to Cesare and put a hand up to the monkey. It shrieked in outrage and bit. The cardinal snatched back his bleeding finger and sucked it.

"My apologies." Cesare threw him an insincere smile. "He hasn't learnt who his friends are yet."

The man harrumphed and skulked away. Cesare drifted through the crowd, exchanging greetings with the other guests. He noted who was there and who wasn't, who talked with whom and who kept apart. Cardinal Della Rovere hovered like a vulture, his bald head shining in the light of the chandelier. Orsini was jovial, patting the Pope on the back and gesturing broadly, but it was either too hot in the chamber (Cesare didn't feel overly warm) or Orsini had a sweat problem. Cesare eyed the hovering servants too. They poured wine and served bite size portions of cheese and pigeon-stuffed pastries. All their attention seemed to be on keeping their guests sated.

He sidled out a door and followed the trail of servers to the kitchen. No one dared question him as he wandered past dishes being prepared, breaking off titbits for his monkey. Finding nothing suspicious, he returned to the dining room and joined his father.

"Where have you been, Cesare? We are about to start," the Pope demanded.

"Oh, just talking."

"Would you honour us by saying grace, Holy Father?" Cardinal Orsini beamed. His forehead shone.

The Pope intoned the blessing and servants carved stuffed pheasants and dished out richly cooked vegetables. Several cup bearers poured more wine. The same man poured for the Pope and Cesare but no one else. Before his father could drink Cesare stood, raising his goblet. "A toast, your eminences! To our Holy—oh, the cheeky beast." The monkey, used to Cesare raising food and drink for it, lunged forward and stole a swig of the wine. Several cardinals laughed along with him. "Just keen to drink the Pope's health." Cesare smiled around at everyone. Cardinal Della Rovere sat silent—a foreboding expression on his face. Cardinal Orsini poured perspiration.

"You wanted to give a toast, Cardinal Borgia?" Orsini pressed.

"Oh, yes!" Cesare patted the monkey and handed it to his father. The Pope frowned but said nothing. "To our Holy Father."

"To our Holy—" Orsini chimed. Cesare held up a hand.

"We all have our differences, I know," he spoke kindly. "But our purpose should be God's purpose, and the work we do should glorify Him. We are but servants in His grand plan—even his holiness here is but a servant of the Lord." He looked at his father and smiled, eyes flicking to the monkey.

"Praise our Lord and His servant!" Orsini declared, raising his cup.

"Yet, my brothers, we bicker and squabble!" Cesare went on. "This is foolishness and part of our weakness as mere men. I, for one, pray to our Lord for the strength to move past my foibles and aspire to glorify His name!" He could have gone on, but a gasp from his father gave him the sign he'd been waiting for. He looked and the others followed his gaze.

Foam spewed from the monkey's small mouth and it writhed with awful, high pitched screeches. Within moments the animal twitched into silence and the Pope hastily dropped it on the table. "Poison," he croaked.

Cesare grasped his father by the arm. "Let us go, Father. It's not safe here." He glared at the white-faced Orsini and the stone-faced Della Rovere. Many of the other Cardinals looked shocked—Cesare memorised who didn't. He hustled his father out past them all amidst the cries of outrage and dismay and bundled him into the carriage. "Go!" he ordered the driver, who clacked the reins.

"Cesare, someone tried to poison me!" Rodrigo Borgia grasped his son's arm as they rattled through the streets.

"I know, Father. Our enemies are everywhere."

\* \* \*

Escaping the room to spy was the only respite Gwyn had from her thoughts. She drifted through the servants' quarters, the storerooms, the halls and courtyards, using the timepiece to stay inconspicuous. No one questioned her, their eyes glazed over if someone looked at her. Gwyn wished she could talk to someone. *I wonder if Michelle will ever come back to my time and find me.* As annoyed as she was at the Time-Space Agent for getting her into this mess, Gwyn rather thought Michelle would be quite proud of what she had achieved with Vlad, Domitian and now the Borgias.

*This mission has been easy compared to the others. But I'm over it now. I want to go home.*

Gwyn's dreams were full of murder, so she abandoned sleep to sit in the garden. The household was asleep—she heard the gate guards change shift at midnight—so she sat and waited. Tonight should be the night it was all over—the timeline would be fixed.

There was a clatter of hooves on the street. Gwyn straightened but didn't rise from her seat under a fruit tree. "Mother!" she heard Cesare yell as he bounded up the marble steps. Light flared above from hastily lit candles. Doors slammed and voices exclaimed as Cesare went from room to room, checking on his family.

"Cesare, what is it?" Vannozza demanded. Gwyn kept still and listened. The garden was dark and the fruit tree hid her from the balcony above.

"They tried to kill Father tonight, at the banquet." Cesare sounded out of breath. "They put poison in his wine. I had to know that you were alright. That Lucretia was alright."

"Who tried to kill him?" Fright abounded in Vannozza voice.

"Della Rovere and the other cardinals. Orsini, some others, I don't know all their names but I will find out. Go back inside, bar the doors. I will put extra guards on the house."

"But, Cesare!" Gwyn heard Lucretia protest before a door shut and the voices became muffled. Gwyn released a breath she hadn't realised she'd been holding. It was done. She would return to her room and gather her things, then jump back to her time and find her family. It would mean re-orienting herself in modern Rome but damned if she was going to try to find the ruins of the Colosseum in the dark, on a night of plots and murder.

She slipped out of the courtyard and into the passage that led up the stairs to the servants' quarters. Back in her room she cricked her neck and smiled. *Time to go home.*

The door opened behind her. Gwyn whirled. Cesare loomed, looking like the devil in his cardinal's red, hat missing and eyes alight. "It happened." He advanced. Gwyn backed up and thudded against the wall. *Calm, stay calm, get ready to jump—never mind about your things.*

"I know," she told him.

Cesare sagged, putting his head in his hands. He raised it again and stared at Gwyn, puzzled. "How did you know, really? Were you a servant of Della Rovere? Of Orsini? Did you hear them plot?"

Gwyn shook her head. "No." She didn't care enough to try to convince him anymore. "Look, it's done, your father is alive, he can go on Poping or whatever it is he does." Her words slipped back into casual speech, no 'my lords'—she was done with that.

Cesare's expression was incredulous. Gwyn suppressed a laugh. "Do I sound like a servant? No. Why don't you go get some rest? I'm sure you'll be busy chasing plotters and planning your revenge. You're not a nice person but you're essential it seems. So I wish you all the best." She gave a half wave. Would he just go so she could concentrate?

His eyes boggled. She risked enraging him but didn't care. She'd had enough. "Go on, go!" Flapping her hands she herded him back into the hall and shut the door.

A soft knock had her rolling her eyes. She opened the door a crack. "Yes?"

Cesare fiddled with his sleeve. "May I speak with you in the morning?"

"It's morning now," Gwyn pointed out. "Don't bother me too early. But sure." She'd be gone so it hardly mattered but she was on an assertive roll. Cesare nodded and left. Gwyn shut the door.

Her things—which were few—went into a cloth bag that she slung over her shoulder. She closed her eyes and sank swiftly into the meditative state that connected her with the timepiece. Gwyn expected to feel ahead on the timeline and rush past the centuries to her own year.

She barely made it a month.

"What?" Gwyn opened her eyes, breaking the trance. She tried again.

A few weeks from the moment she was in, the timeline diverged again. Nothing was certain from then on. No clear path led her into the future.

"Shit!"

# Six

**1492 AD**

Gwyn slept late and woke cranky. She was not going home. She was stuck in this time until she sorted out another turning point.

"Signorita." A maid opened the door. "Please come with me—my lord wishes you to breakfast with him."

Gwyn looked at her creased dress—she'd slept in it—and decided she didn't care. It wasn't Rome she had to stay in, so Cesare could go hang. She wasn't going to try to impress him.

The maid showed her into an airy parlour with east-facing windows. Cesare entered from another door, looking as fresh as she was rumpled. She hid her scowl. She wanted a bath and fresh clothes. "What can I do for you this morning, my lord?" Her words were deferential but her tone was not.

Cesare looked as nonplussed as he had the night before, though a high-necked doublet and soft breeches that ballooned above his boots lent him an air of elegance. "Uh... sit down. Please. Have something to eat." He hovered until Gwyn sat and helped herself to some fruit. She was confident she could jump herself into the night and escape if need be, though she'd have to fetch her bag from her room.

"I'll have the maid move your things to a better room."

Gwyn shot Cesare a look. "I'm afraid I can't stay, my lord. I have to go to Florence."

"Florence! Whatever for?"

Gwyn sighed and kept eating. "Another vision. Another man's life

27

needs saving. I know I said I didn't want money but if you could advise me the best way to get there I'd very much appreciate it." She hoped the hint would be enough. He owed her, after all.

Cesare looked alarmed. "No, no. You cannot go to Florence. You must stay and tell me what you see for my father, for me. Even my sister—my father is arranging a marriage for her and I want to know she'll be happy."

Gwyn frowned and said sharply, "I'm not a fortune-teller."

"But it was true! Just as you said! I took the monkey; it drank the wine and died right there and then! Orsini was guilty—Della Rovere too. Who knows how many others were in on the plot but I'll have my vengeance! What's to stop them from attacking my mother or sister?" He was agitated now, rocking back in his chair and clutching the table. Gwyn poured herself a juice and swallowed contentedly.

"Look, I don't know what will happen to you, or them." Why couldn't he see it was useless? He could threaten, bribe or cajole—she couldn't see what he wanted her to see. She saw the events surrounding a turning point in history—how, she didn't know, but it was what it was.

Cesare's eyes narrowed. He stood and grasped a knife from the table. Gwyn paused and watched him. "You will stay and scry for the future of my family. I command it."

He was dangerous—she was stupid to have forgotten it. And while she was faster connecting with the timepiece to make a jump these days, she might not be fast enough to escape. Better to placate him now and jump later with her things. "Fine," she said flatly. "But on two conditions." She wasn't ready to give him the upper hand completely— he was suspicious enough to disbelieve her if she gave in too easily. She barrelled on before he could interrupt. "One: I assume you will pass me off as your mistress or similar? A mistress should bathe, and have a new dress perhaps. You shoved me in that rat-hole for over a week and I stink."

Cesare opened his mouth. She kept going. "And two: you might pretend I'm your mistress but it is that only—a pretence. You don't touch me. That's all I want: to be clean and to be safe."

Cesare sat down slowly. He tapped the knife menacingly. Gwyn held his gaze. She was quaking inside but didn't dare show it. Had she pushed too far?

"Very well," her captor murmured. "And in return, you shall not try to escape and you shall read the future for my family and me."

"You already threatened me about escaping when I first came here," Gwyn pointed out. "And I will do my best, but that is all." Her nerve threatened to fail. The tension was palpable.

Cesare shot out a hand and Gwyn jerked backwards, but he was only reaching for the servant bell. The maid came in and he ordered, "Draw a bath for the Signorita, and send the seamstress to her new chamber with fabric for a gown. Something… pretty."

"Yes, your eminence."

"Thank you," Gwyn said to the maid and Cesare. He stood.

"Come this way."

She pocketed a pear from the platter and followed him.

"This is your new room." It was a chamber adjacent to the breakfast parlour. "My chambers are through there but the door will be locked. You may go into the parlour and the courtyard down the stairs. If my sister finds you there you may speak to her, but yes, I will tell her you are my mistress."

*Lucretia will be satisfied,* Gwyn thought. "And your mother?"

"My mother knows you have information but not how. You will not speak of visions to anyone but me. I'll not have our house accused of witchcraft."

"No problem."

Her casual response made Cesare frown. "I will come to you tonight after supper. I suggest you have something to tell me then."

"Of course." Gwyn wobbled between sarcastic and deferential. *I need to wash and sleep some more. I'm not smart when I'm tired.*

Cesare sniffed. "Very well. I'll see you tonight." He stalked from the room.

Gwyn slumped onto a chair. The maid came in, holding her bag. "Thank you. What's your name?"

"Maria, Signorita. Your bath will be here shortly."

"Thank you, Maria"

Gwyn relished the bath despite the fact the tub was only hip deep.

She scrubbed ferociously with pumice and cloth, giddy on scented oils. Her hair she attacked with a comb and the towels felt ever so soft when she climbed out. The portly seamstress measured Gwyn's hips, breasts, arms and legs, clicking her tongue and muttering about scrawny wenches. She curled her lip when Gwyn requested plain fabric instead of silk. "I wouldn't waste silk on you anyway, girl. I dress my mistress and dear Lucretia and they deserve the finest gowns money can buy. You'll be out of here in a week and no doubt you'll sell any dress I make you."

"Whatever," muttered Gwyn.

She lounged on the bed the rest of the afternoon, dressed in a fresh shift and enjoying the luxury of dozing in a state of cleanliness. When darkness fell the maid returned with the dress, whispering that the seamstress had cut down an old dress rather than stitch a whole new one. Gwyn didn't care. The dark blue gown had lightly-puffed sleeves and a square-cut neck with a narrow band of brocaded material that ran down the centre to the hem. It was simpler than Lucretia's and Vannozza's dresses, but Gwyn was grateful for that. She didn't think she could pull off a more elaborate outfit, especially with the minimum curling and pinning of her hair as done by the maid.

*Alright, Gwyn, don't get distracted. What's the plan? Cesare wants visions and you can't give them to him. Do you jump into the night and escape the house somehow? Or do you bluff your way through and buy more time?* She was tired, that was the problem. Not just physically, but emotionally. Another escape, another challenge to get to Florence and prevent Lorenzo de Medici's death. She was sick of it. Here she was almost comfortable. Getting to Florence meant stealing a horse and disguising herself as a man for safety.

"Ugh," she groaned and flopped onto the bed. "I just want to go home!"

* * *

Several days passed. Gwyn drip fed Cesare what she knew of the Borgias, avoiding anything too controversial or political. She told him that Lucretia would marry but the union would be annulled, and that there would be conflict between the powerful families of Italy. She touched on the extremism of Savonarola without naming names.

The longer she stayed, the worse the pressure to divulge important information became, but she couldn't muster the energy to escape. She told herself she was gathering information and making plans, rather than rushing into things.

Lucretia sought her out, as Cesare had ordered his sister confined to the house while he sought the plotters who would have poisoned him and his father.

"I'm bored," the girl complained to Gwyn, lolling on a half-couch in the breakfast parlour. "I want to go out riding."

Gwyn perked up. "Me too. I wonder if I could convince Cesare to let us go out with guards."

"I'll take you out riding," a male voice said.

Both females turned. Juan, the dashing soldier brother, stood in the doorway. He walked over to his sister and drew her up off the couch. "Sister, dear, you are like an exotic bird trapped in a gilded cage. We need to let you out to show off your plumage."

Lucretia preened at the flattery. "What kind of bird is Gwynia, then? She's not nearly so pretty as me."

Gwyn laughed, unoffended. Lucretia *was* gorgeous. "A drab sparrow, my lady."

Juan was surprised at the repartee. Then he tapped his nose. "Birds that look dull often have the loveliest song. It is clear that something attracts my elder brother to you. I'd like to know what that is." He leered, obviously thinking he was being charming. Gwyn gave him a false smile.

"So will you take us riding, Juan?" Lucretia demanded, oblivious to her brother's lechery. "We are ever so bored with being cooped up here like chickens." She laughed at her own wit. "Cesare says it's for our safety, but surely with you we are safe?"

"Pfft. Cesare is always so gloomy," Juan said derisively. "No one would dare molest you with the Duke of Gandia, commander of the Papal armies, at your side. Let us go, and let Cesare skulk around hunting shadows."

*Unfair. Cesare has reason to be paranoid.* But Gwyn recognised the opportunity. "Oh," she exclaimed, then kicked herself mentally when

Juan and Lucretia looked at her. "I don't have a riding dress," she finished lamely. *Who cares what you wear? You don't want them to leave you behind.*

"I have skirts that might fit!" Lucretia dashed off to find a maid.

"Would you be so kind as to order the horses?" Gwyn pressed Juan. She didn't want to lose the moment.

"Uh, of course." He walked from the parlour and Gwyn threw herself into her room and locked the door.

Her bag was necessary but would look out of place on a short jaunt. She took out what she could and pressed it as flat as possible, tying it under her petticoat. When the maid Maria arrived with Lucretia's riding habit, she frowned at Gwyn's bulky appearance but said nothing.

The horses were saddled and ready when Gwyn burst into the stable yard.

"What's the hurry?" Juan asked, already astride his black stallion. Lucretia sat side-saddle on an elegant bay mare.

"Just didn't want to miss out," Gwyn answered breathlessly as she located her mount, fitted with a side saddle. She halted, realising her dilemma. *Don't cause a fuss! Just get on the horse and get out of here!*

"A hand to mount, my lady?" a stable hand asked.

"Yes, please." Gwyn tried another simpering smile. The stable hand blinked but kept a blank face. He showed her where to place her foot and boosted her onto the horse. Gwyn wiggled, prompting the horse to shuffle and whinny. "Sorry," she whispered. *Side saddles are so stupid! How does Lucretia look so elegant on one?*

"Ready?" Juan asked, sounding impatient.

"I'm ready!" Lucretia sang out and kicked her horse into a trot. Juan cursed and urged his mount after her, leaving Gwyn to bring up the rear. A groom swung up onto a horse and followed, and the four of them clattered out through the entrance arch to the street.

Jolted by her awkward seat on the horse, it was all Gwyn could to do hold on and follow the Borgia siblings. *Why didn't I stay put and work out another way to escape?* She considered turning around but her sensible side knew that to get to Florence she needed a horse and this was the best way of getting out of the house with one. The opportunity might not come again.

"Ow!"

"My lady?" the groom reined in beside her. Just ahead, Juan and Lucretia had stopped racing and were chatting animatedly. Gwyn tried to orient herself.

"Just not used to riding side-saddle," Gwyn grumbled.

"As you say, my lady." She heard no hint of judgement but Gwyn wondered what he really thought of this awkward mistress of Cesare's. Not that it mattered. She'd be gone soon.

"Where are we?" she asked.

He told her but it was no help. She needed a signpost to Florence. Escaping might be harder than she had thought. Another reason to go back to the house and make a plan.

"Juan!" Gwyn's eyes flew up at the shout. She spotted Cesare riding towards them, his face like thunder. He was magnificent in a slashed black doublet and high boots, a rapier at his side.

"Uh oh," Gwyn breathed. She pulled on the reins and slid to the ground. "Can you please help me?" she begged the groom. Confused he dismounted and took her horse's reins.

"Juan, what are you thinking?" Cesare demanded. "Don't you know how dangerous it is for Lucretia to be out on the streets?"

Juan's face was mulish, but Lucretia tried to keep the peace. "Don't be angry, Cesare. I begged him to take us out riding. Gwynia and I were so bored!"

"Gwynia?" Cesare's head swung around.

*Oh shit.* He was less than ten metres away and the horse didn't fully shield her from his furious gaze. Cesare could reach her in a moment if he wanted to.

She stomped on the groom's foot and shoved him as hard as she could. He cried out and fell backwards, still holding the reins of both horses. They whinnied and shied. Gwyn wrenched the reins for the groom's mount from him before placing a hand firmly on the animal's warm neck.

*Don't go too far.* She reached within her mind. One day she'd learn how to time-jump with her eyes open but for now the best option was still to shut out the world as best she could, ignoring Cesare's command to halt. Ignoring Lucretia's cry of dismay, she felt along the timeline twelve hours and jumped.

*Flick!*

It was night-time. Gwyn staggered as the horse leant against her. "Woah, it's okay," she told it, recovering. Weariness pressed upon her. She breathed deeply as she patted the animal, the rich smell of horse sweat filling her nostrils. "Sorry, horse. I couldn't take the other one—side saddles are useless. Let's get out of here." Not having the energy to mount, she led the animal along the cobbled streets, tense and wary of any noise.

*Hang on, what am I doing?* She would waste hours trying to work out which way to go. The stars were no use to her—she didn't know how to navigate using them in this hemisphere.

The horse stood patiently as Gwyn sank back into the timepiece and searched for the aberration in the timeline that kept her here. She had done it so many times in the last week it took but moments to locate the turning point and its location in Florence. She compared it to her current time and place.

"Right," she said, opening her eyes. They had adjusted to the dark as much as they could. "Come on, horse, it's that way."

# *Seven*

**1492 AD**

Michelle rose early and found the horse trader Meric recommended. He had told her she should get change from a florin for a good quality beast, but the process still took time. She needed to look as though she knew what she was doing, and that meant haggling.

"Too bad you can't just buy one from a list." She ground her teeth in frustration and tried to appear unconcerned by the back and forth. Anyone in too much of a hurry to leave town would receive unwelcome attention, but she chafed at the delay.

"Come on, Giovanni, I told my friend here you were honest and quick! You've made a liar out of me!" Meric rode up on a sturdy gelding. "He and I want to get on the road but it'll be noon before you finish dickering."

Michelle bit her tongue. What was he doing here, and dressed for a journey too? She didn't need or want company but refrained from arguing in front of the horse trader. "Took your time," she joked, raising an eyebrow at Meric. He threw her a significant look. She had no idea what it meant.

Giovanni shrugged and settled on a price, displaying yellowed teeth. Michelle returned the smile and shook hands on the deal. She would have happily paid more to get moving but the need to be circumspect won out.

"What are you doing here?" she asked Meric as they rode south towards the gate.

He didn't take his eyes off the streets. Shopkeepers opened shutters and stallholders shouted their wares—nothing strange about that. What was he looking for? "I'm coming with you to Florence. I have to leave Milan."

"What?"

He kneed his mount past a wagon full of horse manure. Michelle was forced to trot to catch up, holding her breath. The gate loomed ahead. "Tell you once we're out of the city," he said.

She was forced to stay silent as he tipped the gate guards and they navigated against the stream of people entering the city that morning. "What the hell?" she demanded once they were clear. "This isn't an invite-yourself-along jaunt. I need to get to Florence in a hurry and I've business there once I arrive. I don't need you slowing me down."

Meric eyed her. "Aye, I might be an old man but even I can see by your seat you're not a rider. It's a few days to Florence—I know the way and I won't get saddle sore. Chances are *you'll* slow *me* down. If your amulet is like Gwyn's then you can't magic us there, which is why you need a horse. I've a bit of money but the way I see it you can pay for our food in exchange for me being your guide. As I said, I have to leave Milan."

"How come?"

Meric looked shifty. "That young soldier who wanted a fight last night—Filippo—he followed us to the tavern. Normally I go there alone and don't let anyone see me."

Michelle could understand why. She gathered fairly quickly after Leonardo da Vinci had hit on her that it was a bar for men who preferred other men. "So he decided to cause trouble for you?"

Meric grimaced. "He's a young idiot but he's ambitious. He doesn't like me. Taunted me when I got back last night. Said that the Duke wouldn't stand for a sodomite training his soldiers into cowards and weaklings." He snorted. "Idiot. Like a man's company in bed determines his courage on the battlefield. I fought with Mehmed the Second and no one would call him a coward."

Curious, she asked, "How did you know I wouldn't judge you in the same way? That's a big assumption to make of someone you've just met."

Meric shrugged. "Gwyn never found it an issue—she wanted to sleep with Alina, Vlad's wife. I thought perhaps people from your time were more tolerant."

"I'm not from her time!"

He gave her a quizzical look. "But you have the amulet like her."

Michelle growled. "It's a chronokinetor, and she took mine when she shouldn't have. You were born closer in time to her than me. Her society is nowhere near as advanced as mine!"

Meric raised an eyebrow. "If you say so. It's this road up here—we take the left fork."

They rode most of the day, crossing the Po to the south and following the river valley southeast towards Bologna. The land was rich—farms and villages abundant, fat cows grazing in meadows and golden fields of wheat ready for the late summer harvest. The sun shone hot, with the occasional cloud idling on the horizon. Even as the Alps faded behind them the hills to the right grew into the Apennines.

Michelle decided to keep Meric as a travelling companion even though his story about fleeing a homophobic court in Milan didn't add up. Considering the proclivities of many artists she would be surprised that a soldier would be persecuted. Or perhaps it was because he was a soldier. Still, he was competent, quiet and knowledgeable—she could do far worse. She'd leave him in Florence and fix the turning point there before moving onto the next one.

Her mind drifted to Gwyn. *Stupid girl. Messing around with things she doesn't understand.* Michelle would find out what happened in Transylvania and Ancient Rome—how the girl had managed to fix *that* turning point was beyond her. *Luck. Sheer luck.* Not hard work, skill and experience—all the qualities that made Michelle the best.

"Ease up on the reins," Meric said sternly. "You'll harden the mouth and we won't get a good resale in Florence."

Michelle relaxed her grip and her mount shook its head. "We should probably stop for the night soon." A couple of pigeons waddled across the path, fluttering into a tree with a trill as Michelle's horse approached.

"There's a place just up here if you're happy to camp?" He pointed to a low hill, lightly covered in trees. "There's a spring there and I don't want to waste money on an inn. My bones might be old but I can still sleep rough."

*You're not that old*, Michelle wanted to say but bit back her reply. In this time it was incredible that he'd lived into his fifties, particularly as a soldier. "You've looked after yourself well," she said cautiously.

He barked a laugh. "I learnt good habits in the Empire. Cleanliness, eating well. And I was smart enough to get away from the battlefield—training soldiers is a lot less hazardous than being one."

Michelle grunted agreement.

They camped the night and rode on the next day, following the road south.

* * *

Meric was talkative at first but took the hint when Michelle gave him short answers, to her relief. All too often she had to pretend to be interested in people to garner information, but with him her questions received direct answers then they would fall silent.

He was right about her as a rider. Competent but never comfortable, she hid her groans every time she dismounted and took the time to stretch. Meric insisted they lead the horses on foot every hour, to give both themselves and the animals a break. Michelle was silently grateful, particularly late in the day.

*What was it that writer said about horses? Dangerous at both ends and damned uncomfortable in the middle. Too bad they're essential to the success of humans as a species.* Horses were prolific on many agrarian colony planets in her time, but on Earth they had dwindled in favour of hardier species like camels and goats. Her world Vivaldis was heavily industrialised, with air and rail transport the preferred mediums.

Thinking of Vivaldis made her ache for home. She missed its cosmopolitan atmosphere—aliens and humans mingling with colour and flair. It was easy to be anonymous there—no one looked twice if your outfit was different to theirs. She missed Brrrys having her back. Here she was on guard, constantly at risk of being exposed as an outsider. Fifteenth century Italy might be less insular than many other countries, but interlopers were still viewed with mild suspicion at best, outright hatred at worst.

*This is what comes of running so many missions without a break. Still, it's all up to me.* Her stomach clenched at the thought. Billions of lives depended on her—the Shift had been engineered to weaken the Allied Planets in the war to come. She steeled herself to concentrate on her immediate surroundings. Brooding would not get the job done, distraction could get her killed.

Her hand strayed to the knife on her belt. It must have caught Meric's attention, because he asked, "You can fight, then?"

Michelle smirked. "I can handle myself. Why hasn't Filippo made trouble for you before?"

"Hmph. Young idiot never had cause to follow me before. I'm usually a lot more careful before going to that bar. He must have seen us talking outside."

Michelle shrugged. That was Meric's problem, not hers. "And things will be better in Florence?"

"My days in Milan were numbered anyway. I can't drill guardsmen forever. I've got money in a bank in Florence. I'll buy a little shop and retire—pay some young fool to do the running around. Buy a wife, maybe, to look after me in my dotage. Some sensible widow who'll be discreet in her affairs and appreciate a husband who doesn't yell or hit or make demands in bed."

Michelle looked at him, surprised. "Sounds like you have it all worked out."

He snorted. "Better than dying on the battlefield or drunk in the streets like many a crippled soldier. I saved my money and invested it with the Medicis."

*Oh really? That* is *handy to know.* "That was astute of you. You'll have to show me their banking house—I've heard it's very grand. Have you seen any of the Medicis before?"

He shot her a look. "Some of them. Thought you were ditching me as soon as the gates were in sight."

She smiled. "Maybe I'll keep you company a while longer. If that's alright? Buy you a few meals to thank you for guiding me."

Meric's expression didn't change. "As you say."

# *Eight*

**1492 AD**

Getting out of Rome was the tricky part. The gates didn't open until dawn and Gwyn feared Cesare would somehow find her. She used the shadows to steal breeches from a clothesline and belted her Roman tunic over the top. She stuffed the pretty dress and riding skirts into a bundle and tied them to the saddle.

The pull of the turning point directed her north. She tethered the horse in a clearing out of sight of the road and had a nap. Shortly after mid-morning she kept going, hoping to find a village or farm to buy some food. Instead she rode for hours, envying the horse as it grazed periodically.

*Ugh, at least I knew where my next meal was coming from with the Borgias.* She let the horse have its head as they ambled down another hill. As the road crossed a stream at the bottom she turned to follow the waterway, needing another break.

She rounded the bend and stopped as several dogs barked a warning. A group of brightly dressed women washed clothes in the stream while children played nearby. They all paused and looked at Gwyn, while the dogs growled.

"Uh, don't mind me. I'm just watering my horse," she said.

"Is that a man or a woman?" one lady asked another. That woman laughed and called to the dogs, who wagged their tails and returned to cavorting with the children. Gwyn understood them even though they weren't speaking Italian. It sounded familiar, though she couldn't place it.

"Sorry to bother you!" she called out in the same language. "I'm just passing through."

They all stared. The first woman rose slowly from where she had been squatting on the bank. "You're a gadje. How do you speak our tongue?"

Gwyn tried to place it. She had heard and spoken so many languages in the last few months; why was this one familiar? "Oh!" They were gypsies. "I travelled with…" What did they call themselves? She searched her memory. "Secani! I travelled with Secani in Transylvania— a long way northeast of here."

"Is that so?" No one spoke for a few moments—the only sounds were the children laughing and the splash of the stream.

"Well, I won't keep you." Gwyn turned the horse's head.

"Wait." It was a command. "Water your horse here," the woman said. "I would know how our cousins to the north fare."

*Okay.* They didn't seem threatening and Gwyn's legs and butt ached. She slid out of the saddle and led the horse to the water's edge. The women returned to beating clothes on the rocks. The spokeswoman shook her item of laundry out—a loose white shirt—and draped it over a bush to dry. She sat down on the tree stump and gestured for Gwyn to join her. Gwyn glanced around and looped the reins over a branch where the horse could graze. She sat opposite the woman on the ground.

"I am Rosa."

"Gwynia."

"How long were you travelling with Secani in the north, Gwynia?"

Gwyn thought about how she, Alina and Meric had been taken captive by gypsies. "I was travelling the same way as them for a while." Not by choice, but there was no need to say that.

"And they taught you our tongue? It is said to be difficult for gadje to master." The faintest hint of an accusatory tone lingered in the air. Gypsies were renowned for keeping their customs and language secret. Gwyn concentrated on projecting friendliness.

"I pick up languages fast."

"Hmm. And today, where do you ride?"

Gwyn thought about lying but saw no point. "Florence. Well, I'm heading that direction. I'm not sure how long it will take." Hopefully no longer than a week.

"You're taking the coast road, so that will take longer. You should have taken the fork several miles back if you wanted to be there quicker."

"What? Oh, shit." Gwyn sagged. Following a general direction wasn't the same as knowing the right road.

Rosa chuckled. "You can cut through the woods back to the road. Come take a meal with us and tell me of our cousins. We'll be done here soon."

Gwyn hesitated. She was hungry, and the gypsies seemed kind. "Thank you."

The Romani camp wasn't far, but it was well hidden in a gently sloping meadow bordered by tall trees. A lad helped Gwyn unsaddle the horse, making her glad again she hadn't taken the fancy ladies' riding horse. It would have been obvious that mount was stolen. Rosa insisted Gwyn sit and offered her wine and water. Gwyn opted for water, which brought a smile to Rosa's face.

"Gadje always choose wine," she told Gwyn. "You really did travel with Secani."

Gwyn didn't tell her that fresh stream water held much more appeal than wine on a hot day. They sat in the shade and she explained how the gypsies she had met in Transylvania were fleeing the lowland wars and sought work from the Hungarian king. Rosa and several other older women nodded sagely. Men of the camp drifted up and Gwyn was introduced to them as a friend of the Secani, travelling to Florence. They didn't question her story, thanks to the influence of the timepiece, but weren't overly welcoming either, the suspicion of outsiders strong. She overheard one man mutter, "She may be a friend, but a gadje girl travelling alone is trouble. Best she is gone as soon as hospitality allows."

Gwyn bit her lip, trying not to be offended. It made sense; she didn't know what trouble she might bring down on these people. And they were hospitable; they'd fed her a meal of cheese, roast rabbit and greens and she wished she could travel with them. *Stupid,* she told herself, *even if they wanted you with them they're still heading south, not north.*

"Stay the night, and we'll see you on the right road in the morning," Rosa told her.

"How can I thank you?" Gwyn was embarrassed she had nothing to offer. A niggling voice in the back of her head warned her to be more cautious, that they might steal her horse and keep her prisoner, but the comfort of being with people who fed her was simply too good to miss. *I really need to get home,* she told herself. *I'm over these adventures.*

"Tell us a story," Rosa instructed. "After the meal tonight."

* * *

Gwyn told several stories that night. She was nervous at first, but the encouragement of her audience let the words flow and she told them a story about Masada. The Romani sympathised with the plight of the Jews but shook their head at the mass suicide. They applauded the bravery of the girl who hid in the water cisterns with the old woman and the children.

A tale closer to home for them was the war in Wallachia. Gwyn painted a fearsome picture of Vlad—the children squealed in delight at his bloodthirstiness, though Gwyn kept an eye on the parents to see if she was being too gory. They appeared to approve of the lesson that gadje princes were dangerous and couldn't be trusted.

Then other story-tellers told their tales. The firelight flickered and danced as a cool breeze trickled down through the treetops to the ground. Leaves rustled and the smell of animals, wood smoke, roast meat drifted through the air. One of the dogs sat by Gwyn and she stroked its fur. The dog rumbled contentedly, leaning its weight into her as it dozed.

Two cups of wine soothed her throat but after eating such a tasty and satisfying meal Gwyn became sleepy. She would have joined the dog in drifting off, but the storytelling ended and her host appeared.

"Rosa," she said as children were hustled off to bed. The men continued to chat by the fire. "I need to tell you something." She yawned. "It's about the next few years in Italy."

Rosa took Gwyn's arm and led her to the edge of the camp. "Let's go to the latrine. What do you want to tell me?"

They relieved themselves and nodded to several other women making a last trip before bed. Under a tree Gwyn paused and lined up her fuzzy thoughts. She needed to be careful how much she said. "War is coming to Italy. In the next few years the French will invade and march on Rome. They'll go as far south as Naples but have to retreat due to plague, I think." Cesare's demands on her had brought up memories of Italian history. "The Pope will war against various Italian families—the Sforzas, and, um, the Medici perhaps? Crap, I can't remember." She needed to sleep.

Rosa stood unmoving beside her. "You have the Sight?"

Gwyn yawned again. "Just visions from time to time. I'm careful about who I tell. You've been kind to me and I know your people often suffer worst in times of war. I don't have anything more specific than that, unfortunately. No dates or locations of battles."

An owl hooted and leaves rustled. "Thank you, Gwynia. Any warning is better than none. We will spread the word and watch for the signs."

"Oh good. I hope it helps." Gwyn sighed contentedly. Her limbs were relaxed, her stomach pleasantly full and the satisfaction of knowing she would soon be horizontal made her smile. Tomorrow's problems could wait.

Rolled in a blanket and lulled by the sound of people shuffling quietly to bed, Gwyn drifted between wakefulness and sleep. A warm snuffling startled her, then she relaxed as the dog from earlier curled up alongside. It gave a great huff and rested its nose on its paws. Gwyn smiled and slept better than she had in weeks.

Rosa shook her awake at dawn. Birdsong drifted into the lightening sky. "Come, have some breakfast. One of the lads will ready your horse and guide you through the woods to the road."

"Thank you." Gwyn stumbled after her. Her heart ached at the prospect of leaving these brief friends. Tears threatened to spring from her eyes when Rosa enveloped her in a warm hug, but she bit her lip and smiled thanks. Rosa handed a small bag of food and cloak to her.

"God go with you, Gwynia," Rosa said. "Thank you for your words."

"Thank you for being so kind," Gwyn managed, then turned her horse to follow the mount of the lad escorting her. He spoke few words, merely led the way through the woods. Her horse ambled along, picking its path carefully. Several rabbits startled Gwyn at one point as they dashed across her path, and squirrels chattered in the branches above.

The sun was clear of the horizon when her guide left her on the road north. He rattled off a series of towns and villages she should pass through so she would know she was still on track. It was the most he'd spoken to her. He rode back into the woods, disappearing like a shadow, as Gwyn's words of thanks stumbled after him.

* * *

Gwyn rode all that day and the next, supplementing her rations with fruit she stole from orchards and meals she begged at farmhouses. Guard geese attacked her at one farm—she then found out how quickly she could mount a horse. Wary of strangers, she maintained her disguise as a boy. Her weary, hungry demeanour was enough to ensure most people paid her little attention, and despite the rapidly cooling nights she slept outside away from villages and towns. She did her best to look after the horse but cursed her lack of knowledge when it came to readying the animal. Saddling up took far longer than it should have thanks to her clumsiness and only luck kept her from being stepped on by heavy hooves or falling hard from a loose saddle.

"Thank you for bearing with me," she murmured on the third day. A cold shower of rain had them sheltering under a large tree—a hint of winter to come. Several mushrooms grew between the roots at its base—Gwyn didn't know what kind. *Be handy to have a guide to what's safe to eat and what's not.* The horse snuffled at her tunic as Gwyn fed it an apple. "I think we're halfway there." She stroked its broad nose, listening to ducks quacking in puddles nearby. "God, I'll be glad when this is done, and I can go home." *Then the only thing I'll have to decide about mushrooms is whether to buy sliced or whole.*

Another week and she'd told the horse all her adventures, from Masada to Rome. The horse was an excellent listener, punctuating Gwyn's tales with the occasional snort or headshake. They clopped up and down hills, spent over a day making better time in a wide valley full of farmlands, then ascended into hilly country again. Gwyn often dismounted and walked behind, holding onto the horse's tail as it plodded up steep ascents.

Traffic on the road increased with the hills and as she topped each rise, she could see a great dome. Gwyn stared at it for some time, mind idle.

"Oh!" She dredged the name from memory. *Cattedrale di Santa Maria del Fiore. I'm almost there!* Energy surged through her and she straightened in the saddle. "Right. Just once more. You can do this."

If this wasn't the last turning point, she didn't know what she would do.

# *Nine*

**1492 AD**

Stabling the horse somewhere would have been nice, but Gwyn needed the cash more. "I hope you go to a good home," she whispered as she patted the animal and blinked away tears. The horse sneezed and whinnied to other animals in the yard. Manure and hay scented the air, along with the aroma of unwashed human—a pungent smell after the clean air of the countryside, but one that signalled civilisation.

The fellow who bought the animal winked at her as he handed over the small purse. "It's all in there, lad."

"Thanks." Gwyn counted it regardless. She suspected she'd been ripped off but she had no idea how much a horse cost and was too tired to ask around. "Where might I find the house of the Medicis?"

The man guffawed. "They won't bank your money, lad! It's a pittance." He stopped. Gwyn glared at him.

"I'm tired and hungry and I've just ridden from Rome. You've paid me a pittance for my horse; you can at least tell me where I'll find the house of Lorenzo de Medici!"

With fresh directions, Gwyn tried to recall the burst of energy she'd felt upon seeing Florence. Food perked her up a bit, but lethargy threatened to overwhelm her as the warm afternoon lingered. Summer had given way to autumn but the weather didn't appear to have noticed.

She wandered around the Medici house pretending to be a country lad lost in the city sights, gawking at the dozens of arched windows and impressively large cornice that lay just below the roof line. Somewhere safe to sleep would be critical. She debated whether to abandon her plan of gaining entry as a messenger and try again the following day.

"Ugh, just do it!" She received an odd look from a passing man. *Got to stop talking out loud. Too many days of just me and the horse.*

She marched up to the servants' entrance of the Medici home. "I have a message for Signor Medici, Il Magnifico, if you please." She threw confidence into her tone. It wasn't as hard as it usually was, despite her weariness. *I've lost count of how many times I've had to bluff my way through things now.* She smiled slightly. She was getting good at this.

"Il Signor is not receiving visitors," the footman said. "He is not well." He sneered down at Gwyn from his place on the step.

Gwyn wasn't deterred. "I've just ridden from Rome, from the home of a very important cardinal, whose name I will not bandy around in the street. Surely there is someone with more authority than you who can pass on the message to Signor Medici. It concerns the very future of Florence." *So there.*

Her lofty words combined with the timepiece caused the footman to waver, then concede entrance. Gwyn followed him to the kitchen where she was seated with a bowl of vegetable soup and yesterday's bread. "A bowl of water and a cloth, if you please," she said to the maid. "The dust of the road has made me filthy." Washing her face, neck and hands improved her mood, as did the food. She soaked the bread in the soup, softening it to an edible state and savoured the taste of the broth, flavoured with thyme and garlic.

The footman reappeared with an imperious valet in tow. He, too, sneered at Gwyn's appearance but to a lesser degree. "You have a message?"

Gwyn looked around the large kitchen. Servants bustled about carrying, chopping and cooking at various hearths, stoves, tables and shelves. Utensils hung from hooks, serving dishes and food were laid out in various stages of preparation. The servants weren't close but she lowered her voice to be safe, forcing the footman and the valet to lean closer to hear her over the clatter. "An attempt will be made on Il Signor's life tomorrow night. He is already unwell, this is known. The attack will take the form of poison so his death seems natural."

The footman and the valet gaped at her. Their rich livery and sophisticated attitudes placed them as her social superiors but Gwyn held the upper hand. "Watch for an assassin in the household," she advised them in a whisper. They looked apprehensive. "Put only your most trusted servants in Il Signor's rooms, and watch any who handle his food and drink." Her visions of the future hadn't shown her who administered the poison, only that in one future Lorenzo drank from a cup, choked and died, and in the other, the cup was knocked over and he lived.

The footman and the valet exchanged looks. "We have so many staff in this household," the valet breathed. "How can we watch them all?"

Gwyn nodded. "Let me stay in the kitchens and watch tomorrow for suspicious behaviour. Tomorrow evening, admit me to Il Signor's rooms and I can watch from the shadows if I have not found the killer already."

"But..." The valet's brain was ticking over. "What if *you* are the assassin?"

Gwyn rolled her eyes. "Then I'd scarcely be drawing attention to myself by alerting you to the plot because even if I succeeded, you would have me arrested in a heartbeat, and I'd be executed for murder."

"That's true," the footman chimed in. "Not even Niccolo Machiavelli could get him off those charges."

Gwyn started.

"He's a lawyer," the valet explained. "Making quite a name for himself."

She suppressed a laugh. "Right. Well, is there somewhere I can stay out of the way and keep an eye on everyone?"

A swift discussion took place. The valet swore the footman to secrecy and disappeared to consult with Lorenzo's doctor. The footman dragged a pallet into a small storeroom and showed Gwyn the servants' washroom. She sighed, not wanting to give away her gender but aching for a bath. Then she had an idea. "I'll blend in more if you have spare livery I can wear?" The footman nodded and dug out a spare tunic and hose with the braided vest in the Medici colours.

A gong sounded. "I have to go wait table now," the footmen said. Gwyn shooed him away then barricaded herself in the washroom. She hoped all the servants would be too busy with dinner to come in.

Her luck held—she was belting up her tunic just as someone hammered on the door. "Sorry," she muttered as she slipped around an irate pair of maids. Back in the kitchen she loitered on a bench in the corner, idly scratching skin that had been irritated by the harsh soap. She ate with the rest of the servants and deterred conversation with grunts. She projected an air of unapproachability, concentrating on munching through the pastry of her leek and onion pie.

The following day was a painful mixture of tension and boredom. She watched servants, drifted about the house and generally made herself inconspicuous. She didn't see anyone acting suspiciously, not even in the kitchen which was a hub of activity and full of people all day long. Visitors came and went, including the priest Savonarola who spent some time in with Lorenzo.

The evening drew in. Gwyn pinched food from the kitchen and stashed it in her pockets. The valet fetched her at suppertime and installed her in the drawing room next to Lorenzo's bed chamber. She waited in the shadows with the door cracked open, watching any who came and went while she nibbled quietly. The doctor performed his evening examination on the great man, who lay on his four poster bed beneath pierced metal globes filled with smouldering coals and frankincense.

"Continue with the milk puddings and wine for a few more days, Signor, and I feel you will be strong enough to leave your bed. You've many years left in you yet!" The physician smiled through his white beard and nodded encouragement. "Keep the window shut—the outside air is full of dangerous miasmas."

"Thank you, doctor," Lorenzo rasped.

"I'll send them in with your meal now," the doctor told him, and left. Gwyn tensed. The fug of incense in the air made it hard to draw a deep breath—her nostrils felt clogged and she swallowed to try to clear the smoky taste from her mouth. *Didn't think to pinch something to drink.*

The footman had been dispatched to the kitchen to oversee the preparation of Lorenzo's supper, and the valet himself bore it into the room. His eyes flicked towards Gwyn hiding in the dark next room, then focussed on his ill master.

"Are you hungry, my lord? I have suet pudding made from almond milk and sugar—very tasty."

"No, but the doctor says I must fortify myself. Help me sit up."

The meal tray was placed on a table beside the bed while the valet propped up Lorenzo with pillows. Gwyn couldn't tear her eyes from the wine—a burgundy liquid in an elegant Venetian glass goblet.

"Here, my lord." The valet balanced the tray on Lorenzo's lap and dipped the spoon in the pudding.

"Lorenzo! I must see you!" A woman hammering at the door caused Gwyn, the valet and Lorenzo to jolt. The valet swore under his breath and placed the spoon down.

"I'm sorry, my lord, I'll send them away. We gave orders that you were not to be disturbed."

Lorenzo gestured weakly and Gwyn frowned. The woman's voice was familiar. Was it a family member who dared impose? Did Lorenzo have a wife or daughter who had been kept from him during his illness?

She registered a thump and looked up, startled, as the valet hit the floor unconscious and a figure strode in. Disregarding pudding and wine, the intruder pulled a glass vial from a pocket and reached for Lorenzo's mouth, trying to force it open.

"No!" Gwyn lunged forward and grappled the assassin—they tripped and fell. The vial flew into the air then smashed on the floor. Gwyn was too shocked to attack further—she stared up into Michelle's face.

"Oh, you are fucking kidding me!" Michelle yelled, and slapped Gwyn so hard her head snapped around and smacked the floorboards.

"Stop them!" Three footmen, including the one who'd admitted Gwyn to the house, barrelled into the room and launched themselves at the women. It took two to restrain Michelle, but Gwyn just gaped and did not resist as she was marched from the room.

# *Ten*

**1492 AD**

"What in the name of stardust are you doing here?" Michelle hissed in Gwyn's face, using the torch function in her wrist computer to cast a glow. Gwyn stumbled back and fell against the stone wall. Michelle's lip curled.

"I... uh, I came to fix..."

"You just ruined my opportunity to fix this timeline! Do you know how many turning points have manifested here? The Shift has gone crazy! I need to fix these as fast as I can and get back to the present before we're all doomed."

The bafflement on Gwyn's face caused Michelle to slam her fist against the solid wooden door of the room.

"Oi!" One of the footmen who had dragged them into the cellar thumped the other side of the door in response. "Pipe down in there! You'll be up before a magistrate afore you know it and you won't like what's coming for you then."

"Shut up," Michelle spat back. "Right." She advanced on Gwyn. "You are coming with me and I am going to fix this thing."

"Wait, what? Can you please just tell me what's going on? How did I mess up the timeline? I came to fix it!" Gwyn raised her palms, eyes wide and pleading.

Michelle stopped and let the appearance of calm wash over her. She looked about—the cellar contained furniture covered in dust sheets. She dragged a sheet off a three-legged stool and seated herself in the centre of the cellar, placing her hands neatly in her lap. Dust coated the floor, except for where it had been disturbed by Michelle and Gwyn. A dank chill hung in the air. "And who sent you to fix this particular turning point, may I ask?" Her tone was pleasant, but she could see Gwyn wasn't fooled. The girl remained pressed against the opposite wall and showed no signs of relaxing. *Good. Little idiot needs to know how much trouble she's in.*

Gwyn mumbled something.

"Pardon?"

"I worked it out."

Michelle stared at her. "There are highly qualified technicians with extremely complicated algorithms scanning historical timelines constantly for fluxes and turning points and you just *worked it out.* Do you care to explain your methodology?"

She saw Gwyn set her jaw. *Ah. Teenage belligerence.*

"I was trying to get back home," Gwyn stated defiantly. "I went to Ancient Rome and fixed the timeline there. When I went to jump home I found a turning point in this year, with the Pope. So I fixed that. Then I found this turning point, so I came to fix it. Just like I fixed your problem in Wallachia. I've done a few of these now, no thanks to you. But you're welcome!"

Michelle filed the information away and let the silence fill the cellar. The only light was cast from the candle a footman had accidentally left, stumped into the old wax of a holder. When she spoke, her voice was quiet. "I don't know what you did in Ancient Rome, but I will find out. As for Wallachia, I heard you ran off with Vlad the Impaler's wife and nearly ruined everything instead of focussing on the task at hand. The Borgia Pope—who knows what you've messed up there, but as for *this* turning point," her voice grew louder, "may I ask why you thought preventing the death of Lorenzo de Medici was the right thing to do when the history texts state that he died in his bed of illness on this very night?"

"What do you mean, died?" Gwyn's voice quavered. "I thought I was meant to save him."

"And what gave you that impression?" Michelle asked in a clipped tone.

Gwyn opened her mouth. Her forehead creased. "Because I had to save the Pope?" she whispered.

Michelle crossed her arms and waited.

Gwyn's pace of breath increased. "But… you can fix it right? I mean, I was so sick of the murder and the betrayals I thought that surely saving someone was the right thing to do…"

"You. Thought."

Gwyn stared with annoying, puppy-dog eyes. "I just wanted to go home," she whispered.

A disaster, that's what this was. Michelle sighed and thought about how she could fix this. Escape from the cellar was the first thing but that would be simple enough when someone opened the door. The little window at the far end opened onto the street but had bars. Wouldn't keep rats out, but there was nothing but the old furniture and that wouldn't attract rodents.

"What are you going to do?" Gwyn piped up.

Michelle swung her stare back to Gwyn. "I'm thinking. When I'm done I will let you know." Michelle could have sworn Gwyn rolled her eyes. "This is serious, Gwyn. There's no room for your teenage romantics or stupidity."

Gwyn bridled. "Look, I stuffed up, I'm sorry, but it's the first one and I think I've done pretty well up until now!"

"Running off with Vlad Dracula's wife?" Michelle's voice dripped sarcasm.

Gwyn frowned. "How do you even know about that anyway? Did you, like, watch through a wormhole or something?" Her blush was visible even in the dim light.

"I ran into your friend, Meric, when I arrived in Milan. Someone else you just told all about time-travel? How many people have you revealed our secret to?"

Different emotions crossed Gwyn's face too rapidly for Michelle to read them, then Gwyn said, "Meric? He's alive? That's awesome! Wait, how old is he?"

"In his fifties, he's the one who brought me to Florence. Now be quiet, I still have to think about how to sort this mess out."

Gwyn subsided. Michelle brooded. Gwyn shuffled. "Be quiet!" Michelle barked.

Gwyn sighed. "Too bad you don't get a phone call in this day and age."

"What?"

"A phone call. In my time when you get locked up you get a phone call—to get a lawyer or a family member to come bail you out."

Michelle stared, then shook her head. "Be quiet." She closed her eyes and slowed her breathing, hands loose in her lap. What would happen now Lorenzo lived? Could she rectify the damage tonight? She'd always had algorithms and backup plans, but the further they went timewise from the turning point the more unpredictable the timeline would become. "Right," she declared, opening her eyes. "We are going to escape from here, then jump back to several moments after you interfered. Once everyone is gone from the room, I'll take care of Lorenzo."

"Um. Won't they put on extra guards or something?"

"You can bare your breasts and distract them." Michelle was matter of fact.

"No way!" Gwyn said, horrified.

"I can't leave you anywhere because then you'll be in the wrong timeline, so you might as well be useful! If you hadn't gotten in my way I would be gone by now."

Gwyn hung her head. "How are we going to escape?"

"They have to move us in the morning to take us before a magistrate presumably. Stay close to me and I'll jump us out then. Get some sleep for now. I'll take first watch and wake you."

"Do you have any water?"

Michelle growled and pulled a flask from the bag she wore over one shoulder. "Just sip—that's all there is. Now go to sleep."

Gwyn accepted the flask with a dark look and took several swallows. She sighed, looked around, then handed the water back. Maintaining her baleful glare, Michelle tapped her fingers impatiently as Gwyn dragged several dust sheets from an ornate chair and shook them out near the window. Folded, one sheet made a pillow, the other a blanket, and the girl settled on the floor. Within minutes her breathing was steady and even. Michelle shook her head at how quickly Gwyn had fallen asleep. *No sense of danger. How has she survived this far?*

\* \* \*

Michelle woke when the door rattled. "Gwyn!" she hissed. The girl jerked awake lurched out of her chair. Michelle growled, "You were meant to be on watch!"

"Sorry!"

"Stay close to me," Michelle said, shifting her bag to her back as she stood.

Two men stomped into the room and grabbed Michelle by the arms, dragging her outside. She dropped her weight but they compensated. She turned her head to see Gwyn being hauled out behind. *Dammit.* They were not close enough to touch.

Urgency pressed on Michelle; she wanted to jump while they were still in the house. It would be easier to reach Lorenzo and rectify Gwyn's mistake that same night, but she couldn't afford to leave Gwyn behind. She would have difficulty finding a rogue element once she'd ensured Lorenzo was dead. *It's got to be now.*

"Gwyn!" She lunged, twisting one arm free. The girl looked startled and reached out. Before they touched, a blinding pain struck Michelle's head and her vision went black.

# *Eleven*

**1492 AD**

Gwyn hung her head as she was hurried along the cobblestone streets. Ahead of her Michelle hung limply over the shoulder of a guard. Gwyn hoped she was only unconscious.

The events of the previous night replayed in her mind. According to history, Lorenzo should have died. Gwyn had saved him. *How was I meant to know?* That was the problem—she hadn't known. She'd guessed. *Ohh, this is not good.* Even though Michelle was arrogant and high-handed, she would be able to fix it, wouldn't she?

As they hustled along in the dewy dawn light, a surge of panic threatened to swamp Gwyn. It was like her first time-travel all over again, when she knew nothing and was terrified. She tried to calm herself, but as early-rising Florentines stared at the little procession, she was aware of how conspicuous she was. Two women dressed as men under arrest and being marched to a magistrate or a cell. One older man frowned so deeply as they passed that Gwyn flushed. They were judging her, she could feel it. A tremor ran down her spine. They still burnt people as witches and heretics in this time—Savonarola ended up that way, she remembered. Bile rose in her throat. She forced it back down with an acidic swallow.

They entered a grim building, manned by more guards. She had to do something. She couldn't jump away—the guard holding her would come too and Michelle would be left behind. Gwyn would be alone again. She bit her lip.

As they marched down stone steps, fetid air washed over them. "In you go!" The guard gripping her forearm shoved Gwyn into a large cell, walled in stone on three sides with the fourth made up of thick iron bars from ceiling to floor. Gwyn gagged and stumbled as Michelle's slumped form was thrust at her and the door clanged shut.

"Working late?" Several women lolled on a wooden bench, cackling. Prostitutes, Gwyn guessed by their revealing necklines and brightly coloured dresses, not to mention their attitudes. She ignored their comments and, breathing through her mouth, dragged Michelle to the opposite wall, propping her up and kneeling down to check for a pulse. It was strong.

"Please wake up, Michelle." Gwyn was mortified to hear the quaver in her voice.

"Hmm?" Michelle's dark eyes fluttered open. "What the fuck hit me?"

"One of the guards," Gwyn gushed. "Oh thank God you're awake. I couldn't reach you, I'm sorry, then he hit you on the head." Her shoulders sagged in relief. Michelle would get them out of here.

A baleful stare encompassed her. "You should be sorry. If it weren't for you I could have jumped away. But I can't afford to leave you hanging about to make more trouble. Now, where are we?"

Gwyn rocked back. She had thought Michelle's harsh words from the night before had just been from shock, but the resentment she heard now kicked her right in the gut. *I didn't mean to stuff things up! This is so unfair!*

"Oh, don't cry!" Michelle glared even more fiercely, while the three prostitutes catcalled.

Gwyn couldn't answer. Humiliated, she brushed hot tears from her face and turned away.

"Be nice!" one of their cellmates advised, the sincerity of her words undermined by the heckling of the other two.

"Shut up!" Michelle roared, and a guard strolled up to rattle his sword on the bars.

"Be quiet, the lot of you! You'll get what's coming soon enough! Don't make me cut out your tongues in the meantime!"

The prisoners fell silent, except for the sound of vomiting in a cell nearby. The cold from the stones seeped into Gwyn. With difficulty, Gwyn repressed her snuffling and wiped her face on her sleeve. "We're in prison, if it isn't obvious. Guards took us from the Medici house and shoved us in here. I don't know what will happen now." *So there.*

Michelle sighed gustily. "This is even worse than being locked in that room. Look, I might have to go, and come back for you."

A black pit of terror opened up in Gwyn. "What? You can't leave me!" *Please don't leave me alone again!*

"You'll just slow me down!"

Gwyn felt the tears return. "Can't we, you know, try talk our way out of it using these?" She waved her hand with the timepiece, hearing her voice rise in pitch. "I've done stuff like that before." Granted, the only time she'd been locked in gaol she'd been bailed out, but Michelle would be able to do it, surely?

"Really?" Michelle's tone was sceptical.

"Well, kind of," Gwyn said in a small voice. Right now she didn't feel like as though could talk anyone into anything. A cockroach scuttled by her foot. She cringed, then wished she could follow it into its hiding place.

"No, there's nothing for it. Unless you can magic up one of your lawyers to argue us out of here, I'm going to have to fight my way out, and you're a liability."

"If you have money, I may be able to find you a lawyer," a soft voice spoke from the door of the cell. Gwyn and Michelle jerked around. It was the man from the street, the judgmental one.

"What are you doing here?" Michelle demanded.

"I saw you in the street," he replied. "I recognised Gwyn."

"Meric?" Gwyn gasped. She stared through the bars at the middle-aged man.

Meric shook his shaggy grey head. "You look just the same, Gwyn. How is that possible? Unless… it hasn't been that long for you? You escaped Vlad?"

Nothing about him looked the same, but the voice she knew. A tearful smile broke onto her face. "I did. The Hungarians arrested him and I escaped. It's only been…" she calculated mentally, "two months or so for me. It's been…"

"Thirty years for me."

*Thirty years.* She couldn't imagine it. *He still remembers me.* Her smile widened. "How are you? What are you doing in Italy? Is Alina...?"

Michelle cut in. "Look, this reunion is very sweet, but you two can reminisce later. You mentioned a lawyer?"

Gwyn bowed her head. "I only have a few coins."

"I have money. Meric, can you find us a lawyer? There'll be something in it for you." Michelle spoke authoritatively.

Gwyn glanced up and was gratified to see Meric give Michelle a long, cool stare. "I'll do it for Gwyn. You don't need to pay me."

\* \* \*

The prostitutes were released several hours later, when their pimps were finally roused to pay the exorbitant fine. Michelle stretched and meditated. Gwyn didn't want to imitate so settled for doing the exercises Meric had taught her—strengthening and self-defence.

"Here." Michelle got up and corrected one of Gwyn's moves. "You're not much of a fighter, are you?" The tone was mocking.

Gwyn flushed and glared. "No, I'm not. I've managed to talk my way out of most problems without killing everyone who gets in my way."

Michelle barked a laugh. "I don't kill *everyone*. But I can defend myself. You look like you'd fall over if someone breathed on you."

"I just..." Gwyn stopped. Her lip quivered. Michelle was right—she wasn't a fighter. She thought about all the times she'd been attacked— she'd only survived through someone else's intervention or by fluke. She hunched her shoulders and changed the subject. "Where do you suppose Meric is?"

"He'd better not have run off with my money." The threat in Michelle's voice was clear.

"He's a good person!" *He wasn't always,* a treacherous voice whispered. Gwyn tried to ignore it. *He'll be back. He won't leave me.*

"Hmph."

It was in fact, after noon when Meric returned with their lawyer in tow—a slight, dark-haired man dressed in black robes and cap. The man wrinkled his nose—the cells were filthy and no one had changed the buckets—but otherwise wore a blank expression as he greeted his newest clients.

"I have secured your release on the condition that you leave Florence immediately after paying a fine for the inconvenience of the city guards and compensation for distressing the House of Medici. If you follow me, I will sign such documentation as there is on your behalf, unless, of course, you can read and sign it yourself."

He sounded bored but Gwyn didn't care. She wanted to breathe a great sigh of relief except worse aromas had overpowered the smell of vomit. She felt sick and ached all over. *Just get us out of here!* Michelle, on the other hand, replied swiftly and courteously, "We can both read and sign, thank you kindly, Signor. We appreciate your services."

"I've brought your bag of clothes, Michelle." Meric proffered it. "Might be as well to change into something more seemly. We'll find something for you too Gwyn."

"My dress is back at—"

"We'll sort her out later," Michelle ordered. "If you would lead the way, Signor?" she continued in a more friendly tone.

Gwyn pulled a face at her back as they exited the cell, passing the guard who unlocked it with an outstretched hand. The lawyer dropped a coin onto it with a nod. "Until next time."

Upstairs, a guard captain signed off on the lawyer's scrolls with a sigh and held his own hand out for payment. "Isn't her husband or father here to sign on her behalf?" he asked, dismayed when Michelle stepped up and took the quill.

"No," she replied, scanning the document and scrawling an illegible name at the bottom.

"Hmph. Witness, please Signor Machiavelli." He jabbed a bony finger on the parchment.

"Machiavelli? As in Niccolo?" Gwyn asked, curiosity piqued. Michelle glared her into silence.

"The same," the lawyer replied dourly as he signed their paperwork, blowing on one of the documents to dry the ink then furling it up, leaving the other for the captain to file. "Might I enquire as to how you know my name?"

"Uh, just heard you were a good lawyer," Gwyn stammered as they trooped outside.

"I take my work where I can." He managed to imply that trash such as their selves was at the bottom of his desired list.

"Gwyn, can you keep your mouth shut for five minutes?" Michelle snapped. "I'm going to change. You'll pass as a boy for now if you concentrate. We must be on our way out of the city and I'm sure we've taken up enough of Signor Machiavelli's time." She stepped into an alcove and dragged a skirt out of her bag. Gwyn and the others stepped away to give her privacy.

"No wonder she likes you," Gwyn muttered to Machiavelli.

He raised thin eyebrows. "And why, pray, would that be?"

"Oh, no reason. She's just ruthless and respects that in others," Gwyn remarked bitterly.

Machiavelli smiled coldly. "She sounds like a sensible woman, if there is such a thing." He bowed and strolled away.

"What was that about?" Michelle wanted to know as she re-joined them. Meric shrugged. Gwyn didn't answer. "Then let's go. I'm starving. Meric, can I repay you with a meal?"

Gwyn brightened at the prospect of food and the chance to talk to Meric more. They found a quiet tavern and ensconced themselves in a corner of the courtyard. A fountain trickled nearby—they ordered food and a barmaid poured ale for them all. The lunch rush was over; only a few other tables in the courtyard were occupied.

"So," Michelle began. "Tell me about Wallachia. How did 'convince Vlad to go to war with the Ottomans' turn into 'run off with his wife'?"

Gwyn coughed ale, setting her tankard down. Blushing furiously, she clenched her jaw. Meric laughed loudly. Gwyn glared at him. "Look," she said. "I tried my best. I tried to convince his wife to persuade him for several weeks, but then I just had to get out of there. He kept trying to…" Her frown deepened. "Look, I'm not like you. He scared me."

"He tried to rape her twice, three times?" Meric interjected. "Alina, Vlad's wife, intervened once, I saved her the second time. She's right—he was frightening. He cut half my ear off when we were barely more than boys." He displayed the sliced appendage, normally hidden under his grey hair.

Michelle was silent. Gwyn expected a lecture on how useless she was at self-defence and how she, Michelle, would have kicked Vlad's butt. *Or simply slept with him to get what she wanted.*

"I'm sorry to hear that," Michelle said after a pause. "It is one of the dangers of time-travelling as a woman, which is why I was loathe to send you to Wallachia in the first place. Why did you choose to go to Ancient Rome?"

Gwyn was baffled but tried to hide it. "Well, uh, I made it back to my own time, and I was in Rome with my family when… something happened. A weird feeling—the landscape changed, people changed. I knew something had happened in history, so I concentrated on the timepiece and found the spot where it had gone wrong. For some reason Emperor Domitian didn't die when he was supposed to, so I went back and fixed it."

Michelle's expression was inscrutable.

"You killed a Roman emperor?" Meric asked, wide-eyed.

"Well, not exactly." She shuddered. "I found the people who were plotting and just helped them along a bit. Made sure they talked to each other and said the right things. And it worked! But then when I tried to go home I hit another turning point, in this year, in Rome. Someone tried to kill the Borgia Pope, so I went and warned them. Then I hit another turning point, here in Florence, so I tried to come fix *it.* I'm just trying to get home!" Her voice cracked.

Michelle sat back and put her hands behind her head and closed her eyes. "What I would give for an Agency computer and the right algorithms."

"The right what?" Meric asked.

Gwyn perked up. "You said that before—computers and algorithms and stuff. So you don't just concentrate and see what might and might not happen?"

Michelle gave her an incredulous look. "I'm astonished that it's taken you this long to screw up if that's how you've been operating! What a haphazard, inaccurate, inefficient way of doing things!"

Anger burnt inside Gwyn. "How was I supposed to know any different? You threw me in there blind!"

"You threw yourself in there when you took my chronokinetor at

Masada! It wasn't yours and the fact that you have it makes my job harder now!"

"It's not my fault it's stuck in me! Why is it stuck in me? Or do you still not know?"

Meric slammed both palms on the table and frowned at both women. "I'm not sure what exactly you two are talking about, but you're attracting the attention of everyone in this tavern and you're supposed to have left the city by now. So calm yourselves and tell me if you're staying, going or what, because I'll not bail you out twice." He spoke quietly but commandingly. Both women fell mutinously silent and he laughed. "My God, if you could see yourselves. Are you related? Because you sure look alike."

"I'm an orphan," Michelle stated.

"She's born, like, six hundred years after me," Gwyn added. *And I'm not a bitch like her.*

"Aye, maybe it's the light. You could be sisters when you glare like that. Anyway," he paused as a waiter brought food out to them. "Anyway, are you coming or going after this meal?"

Michelle broke off a piece of bread and dipped it in her soup. "Going. I have to finish up here in Florence and find the next turning point. There are dozens of them."

"Dozens!" Gwyn cried, aghast.

Michelle turned a critical eye on her. "Yes. I'm afraid you won't be going home just yet."

# Twelve

**1492 AD**

Meric never slept through the night these days, so he sat up against the bedhead and let his thoughts drift. Beside him in the wide bed Michelle was serene, snoring slightly, while Gwyn twitched and muttered her way through a dream. What fate had brought these two to him? Who knew? Taken as a boy to fight in the Sultan's armies, then sent back to his homeland an enemy, fate had set him on the path of life as a mercenary, marching from land to land in search of war.

Meric frowned and shook his head. He had outlived most of his contemporaries. It was foolish to get involved with Gwyn and Michelle, but he was curious.

What did they plan? Michelle spoke of turning points, of fixing history. *Huh.* History was an accident of great men befriending and killing each other as it suited them. How did one fix that?

He stretched and cricked his neck. Michelle twitched awake.

"You'd be a good soldier," Meric spoke softly. "Always at the ready."

"Hmph. Been in a lot of fights." Michelle sat up and glanced at the sleeping Gwyn.

"What do you intend to do?"

Michelle sighed. "If I may, I'll leave her with you, then go and sort out this Florence turning point. I'll pay you to keep her safe."

Meric shrugged. "Very well. She can pretend to be my daughter while I look for a shop to buy. What is it you have to do here?"

Michelle frowned. "Does it matter?"

"Will it affect me?"

She was silent. "Of course it will. It will affect the whole of Italy. But you, directly? Not so much—not for a few years."

"Then tell me. I might be dead in a few years. I won't try to stop you."

Michelle smirked and he realised she believed he couldn't stop her even if he wanted to. *Look like Gwyn she might, but she's a blade forged in a different fire.*

"Lorenzo de Medici should have died two nights ago. He's ill—it'll come as no surprise to anyone. The calculations I have show that for some reason he didn't. So I went to correct that."

"Kill him, you mean." His words bore no judgment.

"Correct. But she," Michelle jerked a thumb sideways, "had some stupid notion that she was meant to save Lorenzo, and got in my way."

Meric absorbed this information. "How do you intend to fix it? Go back to that time and stop Gwyn?"

"No. The problem with being in the same time as one's self is proximity sickness. You become unbearably nauseated and can even pass out. I intended to jump to a few hours after that, possibly just before dawn, when the servants are more likely to have let their guard down. But that was while we were still in the house. I couldn't reach Gwyn before they knocked me out." Michelle grimaced. "I can't afford to leave her alone to wreak even more havoc."

"You're awfully hard on her. She's young."

"She's immature and thoughtless."

"Hm, aye, weren't we all once?"

Michelle grimaced. "If you were training a soldier that endangered his comrades, would you be so kind?"

Meric shrugged. "Maybe not. But it seems as though you can fix what she's done, so ease up. She'll learn."

Michelle shrugged down under the blanket again, muttering, "Soft."

\* \* \*

Gwyn woke depressed. The conversation she'd overheard when Meric and Michelle had thought her asleep left her in no doubt as to the regard in which she was held by the Time-Space Agent. *Immature and thoughtless.* The words stung.

Michelle was already up and dressed, while Meric snored. Gwyn could see dust motes floating in the strip of sunlight that crept in through the shutters. Gwyn watched Michelle surreptitiously as the older woman stretched. Too lethargic to do the same, she closed her eyes and sank her mind into the timepiece.

She was aware of them now, the other turning points. She hadn't thought to look past Lorenzo de Medici because the timeline split and became fuzzy. But now she traced dozens of threads dotted with aberrations and splits—so many choices and events that changed how the future would look.

Gwyn opened her eyes.

"Meditation?"

Gwyn glanced at Michelle, surprised at the question.

"It's a good habit. Part of every Agent's training." Michelle pressed her palm against the wall for resistance and leaned away to stretch her arms. Gwyn got up and looked for her shoes, shuddering at the feel of grit on the floor.

"It's such a mess," she muttered. "There are turning points all over the place. I can't find the right timeline."

Michelle frowned. "What do you mean? You said before you concentrated and found the turning points. How do you do that?"

Gwyn located her shoes and dragged them on. "I just sort of relax my mind, and it's like I can see the timeline. I could feel where it had gone wrong in Rome both times—it's like a zig-zag or a bump. I found if I focussed hard I could see images and hear stuff, but it took a bit of practice. It doesn't tell me which way is right or wrong, just shows me where it starts to split. I knew Domitian was supposed to have been assassinated, and that Rodrigo Borgia was supposed to live because I've studied both those times. I didn't know enough about Lorenzo de Medici, which is why I stuffed up." She blushed and shook out the skirts of the cheap dress they'd bought her yesterday, waiting for Michelle's abuse.

The other woman frowned. "So erratic," she said. "But fascinating all the same. I've never heard of an Agent using a chronokinetor in such a way. We concentrate and connect with it on different levels, for language, direction and to access data stored in it for a mission, but the calculations have already been made before we even leave our own time. Then again, we also only ever fix one turning point at a time. This situation is unprecedented."

"Oh." Gwyn didn't know what to say to that. Not wanting to be criticised again, she kept quiet.

"What can you see now?" Michelle asked.

Gwyn shrugged. "It's all a mess, I told you."

"Try."

Meric snorted in his sleep. Early street sounds drifted in—Florence was beginning its business for the day.

Gwyn sighed and sat on the edge of the bed, closing her eyes. Her mind opened to the timepiece. "I can still see Lorenzo," she slurred. "But it's like he's been blocked off, I can't feel how to go there. If I look ahead, it's a mess. Letters being handed to lords. Cesare Borgia gets one. He reads it and curses. An ugly French man—I think he's the king—laughing. Blue banners—it's his army. Italian nobles meeting and discussing defence plans. I don't recognise any of them except for Cesare Borgia. A woman in armour, she's there too. It keeps changing. The Pope is blessing the Italian armies. There's fighting. A city is burning. The French king is frustrated—he's ordering his armies home to regroup. They've got artwork and gold and stuff." She opened her eyes. "That's weird, I thought the French kicked the Italians' butts and got all the way to Naples... Uh oh."

"Yes. Uh oh." Michelle said grimly. "Lorenzo de Medici is famed as a great diplomat. Him being alive means he must have convinced the Italian lords to unite against the French. I have to get back and fix that as soon as possible."

"But... if you go back and leave me with Meric, you'll be in a different timeline to me!" Gwyn couldn't keep the edge of panic from her voice. Then she realised what she had said.

"You heard us talking." It was a statement.

"You were going to *leave* me here?"

Michelle gave her a cool look. "Perhaps not. Your little visualisation trick might come in useful."

"Oh *good.* I'm glad I might be *useful.*"

"Don't be a child," Michelle snapped. "The fate of billions rests upon me fixing this mess before the Shift closes off all possibility of time travel. If I have to leave you, I will."

Gwyn bit her lip.

"You can't leave her here, that would be cruel," Meric joined in the conversation, swinging his legs over the side on the bed.

"To you or her?" Michelle asked.

"Hey!"

"To her." Meric ran his hands through his hair. "Is breakfast part of our immediate future or are you disappearing now that you've had a night's rest?"

Michelle smiled wryly. "We'll do breakfast. Then Gwyn can come with me to the Medici house and we'll jump back and fix this thing."

"Excellent." Meric rubbed his hands together and pulled on his boots. Gwyn followed them downstairs to the taproom and mulled silently while Meric ordered food for them. She pointedly ignored Michelle and quizzed Meric about his doings since she had seen him last. Learning Alina had died after a decade safe in a convent was a sad relief, but she sighed audibly when Meric confirmed the death of Vlad Dracula in battle some twenty years before.

Gwyn noticed Michelle listening. "You probably would have liked him," she said snidely.

Again that cool look from the older woman. "He was a murderer, a rapist and extremely cruel according to both historical record and your own account of him. He served a purpose in history, but I don't respect or like people like that. These times are so barbaric." She waved a hand.

Gwyn frowned. *She has an answer for everything.*

"I'll walk with you to the Medici's," Meric said. "I have to go that way anyway, and I'll be sorry to see you disappear again, Gwyn. You've made me feel young again, reliving those days." He smiled, and Gwyn couldn't help but smile back.

"I'm really glad I got to see you again," she said.

"How touching." Michelle stood. "Let's go."

# *Thirteen*

**1492 AD**

"I guess this is it," Michelle heard Gwyn say to Meric. They loitered down the street from the servants' entrance of the Medici house. Michelle assessed the people who came and went to determine the best way to gain entry.

"Take care of yourself, Gwyn. It was good to see you again." He gave the girl a back-cracking hug and nodded to Michelle. "Look after her, please."

"Of course." Michelle pursed her lips. She wasn't a monster—she would do her best for Gwyn, but the fate of the Allied Planets rested upon her. From the way Gwyn looked at her one would think Michelle was going to dump her with no heed to her safety.

"Alright." Meric nodded briskly and strode away. Gwyn gazed after him mournfully.

"Come on," Michelle tapped her on the shoulder. "We're going to go inside, get as far upstairs as we can manage and then jump. Stay right on my heels—actually, holding my hand would be best—because when I jump I may not have time to give you any warning. We'll jump to the early hours of the morning and we'll have to be *quiet*. I'll take care of Lorenzo—if there are guards I expect you to do whatever it takes to distract them, then I'll jump us out of there and we'll escape the house. Got it?"

Gwyn nodded mutely and Michelle gripped her shoulder. "I mean it,

Gwyn—it is so important we fix this, and then we'll sort out the other turning points."

"I get it!" The girl shook Michelle off.

"Right." Michelle had to be satisfied with that. "Concentrate on being unremarkable."

"I'm good at that," Gwyn muttered and took Michelle's hand.

She was good—to the point that Michelle was glad they were holding hands as they approached the house or she might have forgotten Gwyn was beside her. *I suppose that's how she survived—blending in. Too bad she isn't a bit smarter, or she might have made a good Agent.* The thought irritated Michelle; she shook it off as she addressed the footman who answered the door.

Bluff gained them entrance; Michelle's influence using the chronokinetor sent the footman off to fetch the housekeeper. Other servants scuttled past them carrying wreaths and black drapes. There was wailing from somewhere further inside the house.

"Michelle…"

"Not now, Gwyn."

With the footman gone, Michelle marched up the stairs and made for the private chambers of the house, Gwyn in tow. The house was almost as dark during the day as it had been two nights before, and a fug of incense choked the air.

"No wonder Lorenzo has been sick for so long," Michelle muttered. "You would think they could open the shutters and let fresh air in."

"Michelle, I think someone has died."

"What?"

"Who are you?" A voice addressed them. The valet, stern and sallow with bloodshot eyes stood in the doorway leading to Lorenzo's chambers. Michelle squeezed Gwyn's hand.

"No one," she replied to the irate valet, and went to jump.

Nothing.

She tried again.

"I asked, who are you? What are you doing upstairs? Have you no respect?" The valet strode towards them.

"Michelle," Gwyn whispered nervously.

"I know! I'm trying!" But while the connection to the timepiece was there, it was as though a glass wall had sprung up between Michelle and the moment she was trying to get to. She could see it, but when her mind tried to take them there nothing happened. In desperation she let go of Gwyn and tried again.

"Michelle!"

Still nothing. The valet was yelling. Footsteps thundered on the stairs as men rushed up in answer to the valet's call. Michelle cast about, not knowing what to do. *Why the fuck isn't it working?*

"Oh hell!" Blue haze rose up and she felt Gwyn grab her arm.

*Flick!*

The house was dark and quiet. Michelle blinked, trying to see. "What did you do? This isn't the right time?"

"We couldn't go back," Gwyn babbled. "It was blocked, I could feel it."

"What?"

"It was like a glass wall! I could see where you were trying to take us but it was blocked off. I've never felt that before. I've slipped in times, but never been able to see but not go. What does that mean?"

Michelle digested Gwyn's words silently, then connected to her own timepiece again. She encountered the same resistance as she sought to take them to the night of Lorenzo's death.

"Michelle? What does it mean?"

Michelle growled softly. "It means the Shift has arrived. We are blocked off from going back. We can only jump forward."

"Huh?"

"Don't you listen to anything I say? We can't go back in time, only forward. We are stuck in this timeline!"

"Don't shout! Someone will hear us and I don't want to get arrested again. Can't we just get out of here and then you can work out what to do?"

Michelle waved her hand angrily. "I can't—oh, fuck. We're really screwed now."

"Come on, let's just go!" Gwyn grabbed Michelle's hand and towed her down the stairs in the dark and past the silent kitchen.

"Wait," Gwyn said, and ducked into the cavernous room, emerging with a bulging cloth bag. "I'm sick of being hungry," she said. "No idea where my clothes got to, but there was a cloak and a few other things, so I grabbed those. They'll come in handy."

Michelle clenched her jaw at the girl's initiative. She was meant to be the resourceful one, but right now she couldn't see past the immense dilemma thrust upon her.

"Let's go before we get caught," Gwyn whispered.

They slipped out of the servants' door and into the night.

\* \* \*

Meric considered his options as he left the tavern and strode into the dark street. A cat yowled and hissed nearby. Several rats scuttled across his path. Florence was still alive at this hour, but it wasn't always the kind of life one wanted to encounter. Wealthy folk rode in carriages, protected by footmen or guards. Any who walked the cobbles—as he did—kept their wits about them.

Earlier that day, he had found several shops that might suit him. Two of the owners even seemed interested in selling, but at prices Meric couldn't afford. He'd work on those. Asking around his contacts in Florence gave him the name of a few men who had more daughters than they could marry off. He'd visit those tomorrow and see if any of the wenches had common sense. He didn't care how comely they were.

"Meric!" a voice hissed. He whirled.

"Gwyn? Michelle?" He spotted them in the entrance of an alley. "What are you doing here? I thought you were…"

"Can't explain now," Gwyn answered. "Look, Michelle's a bit out of sorts, have you got somewhere to stay?"

"I am *not* out of sorts! I don't know what the hell you hope to achieve. We're fucked. The future is fucked. We might as well give up now."

Gwyn gestured helplessly. "Like I said, out of sorts. I didn't know where to go."

"How did you find me?"

"Um, hard to explain. Turns out if I concentrate hard with my timepiece it can give directions. I thought of you. Handy, hey?"

"It's got geo-locative functionality within a certain range!" Michelle snapped.

"Yes, that," Gwyn said.

Meric shrugged. "I've taken a room near here. Landlord doesn't seem too strict and it can't hurt my reputation having two women spend the night. You'll have to take the floor though."

"That's fine."

They walked with him several blocks and up the outside stairs to a pokey second-story room. Meric lit several candles and sat on the bed, offering Gwyn the chair. Michelle sat in the corner and sank into a trance-like state.

"I think she's meditating," Gwyn whispered.

"What's meditating?"

"Er... kind of like resting the mind, and training it to concentrate. She's pretty agitated."

"What happened?"

"I can hear you!" Michelle snapped.

"We tried to go back to fix... the mistake I made, with Lorenzo. There's some sort of force stopping us. We can only jump forward, but we're in the wrong timeline now."

Meric sighed and pulled off his boots. "Gwyn, I've seen a lot of the world and I'm not stupid, but I don't understand all this about timelines and forces and jumps. Are you saying you've changed things from what they are supposed to be?"

"She fucked it. Now we're all fucked," Michelle snapped.

"Er... yeah," Gwyn re-joined lamely. "I changed things. We can't fix that, but I thought maybe we can find out what needs to happen to take history back in the direction it should go. And now Lorenzo is dead. But it seems he had time to send some letters that will change the minds of some Italian lords and stuff. That's why it was so important that he died the other night, but I didn't know." Her face flushed. "I thought you might be able to tell me who is in charge of the different cities and whatnot of Italy. I need to know how the politics work here."

Meric sat on the bed. "Gwyn, I can't help you with that. I don't know much about Italian politics except it's like dancing with snakes. They backstab and poison and smile and marry each other. The new

Pope is accused of simony, and he's brought his sons and daughter and mistresses into the Vatican!"

"Yeah, I know." Gwyn's eyes slid sideways. "Look, tell me what you know, and I'll do my best from there. And… I also needed somewhere to stay, and she wasn't really in decision-making mode. You're the only friend I have."

At that they both considered Michelle. She was silent now, breathing steadily and face relaxed.

Meric sighed. "I'll try help as much as I can. But I'm here to retire, Gwyn. I'm too old to go riding around Italy trying to convince dukes and lords of anything."

"Of course, totally understand. Thank you." Gwyn pulled a tiny leather book from a pocket in her skirts, then rummaged further and produced a stick of charcoal.

"You can write?" Meric asked, surprised.

Gwyn stared at him. "Of course."

He chuckled. "Pity you're not looking for a rich, older husband. You'd make a good wife if you were from this time."

The sour look she shot him baffled Meric, so he shrugged and began to recount what he knew of the Italian dukes, lords, kings and doges.

# *Fourteen*

**1492 AD**

By morning Gwyn had a plan. She knew Michelle would sneer at it but she had nothing to lose. She squinted at the notes she had hastily scratched by candlelight the night before.

Naples was run by King Ferrante, who had a reputation for practising taxidermy on his enemies then sitting them around a table. The Doge ruled the Republic of Venice. The Papal States were ruled by the Pope, but his new rule was shaky. There were the Republics of Florence, Sienna and Lucca, the duchies of Milan and Savoy, and then some strange little territories called Marquisates of other places Gwyn had never heard of, and a Bishop ran a place called Trent.

Size didn't equal power. Florence was smaller yet far wealthier than the Papal States. The Duke of Milan was powerful in name only—he was kept prisoner by his uncle, called Il Moro, who ruled the territory with an iron fist.

"I trained soldiers for Il Moro," Meric said. "He's a better ruler than his nephew. All the Duke is interested in is hunting and feasting and not much else. Il Moro keeps the duchy strong, and his wife patronise the arts. But the Duchess is a princess of Naples, and writes to King Ferrante constantly to depose Il Moro and support her husband's rule."

"Uh huh."

They were sitting around a courtyard table of a nearby inn, eating breakfast. Other patrons sat nearby on long tables, munching their way through bread, cheese, milk and ale.

"Il Moro is the one who invites King Charles of France to invade," Michelle chipped in. She had been reticent all morning.

Gwyn looked at her in surprise. "Why would he do that?"

Meric frowned. "Yes, why would he?"

"Oh he regrets it later, by all accounts, but to shut Duchess Isobel up he reminds King Charles that France has a claim to the throne of Naples. It's his way of preventing King Ferrante from acting against his interests. The Duke dies in mysterious circumstances later too."

"What a... stupid, dangerous, arrogant thing to do!" Meric stabbed his knife point first into the table. "The French army is a professional army! They've been fighting for years against the English. Milan has the best soldiers of any Italian province but if they don't fight the rest will be torn to shreds!"

"Yep." Michelle chewed on her bread slowly. "That's what happens."

Gwyn looked at her, horrified. "Is there anything good that happens out of changing history? All I've seen so far is a siege that ends in mass suicide, a psychopath rapist go to war against a more civilised culture, an assassination—alright Domitian wasn't the nicest guy—and now you want to unleash hell and chaos on an entire country where they get their butts kicked and thousands die!"

Michelle straightened and stared at Gwyn coldly. "Humans are despicable, Gwyn. They were doing this anyway and it created the modern world. My job is not to make peace and stop progress. My job is to fix these aberrations so the Allied Planets has a chance of defending itself against the enemy that seeks to destroy us all. Humans must play their part in that defence or the other species will die. The Shanista, the Mayash, the Rilaans and the Nolii—none of them deserve to be eliminated and if saving humanity is what it takes to save them too, then I'll do whatever I must!"

Gwyn gazed back at Michelle, eyes wide.

Meric broke the silence. "Are you going to finish that cheese, Gwyn?"

\* \* \*

They finished their breakfast in silence. Michelle continued to brood and

Gwyn tapped her fingers on the table until Meric placed his large hand over hers. "Stop fidgeting. What are you thinking?"

Gwyn sighed and frowned at Michelle. She started to chew her lip then stopped. "We need to sabotage any alliance the Italian lords form against the French. Lorenzo may be dead, but those letters he sent influenced enough of them that it's changed how the various city-states will react. Or maybe it was just Milan? Could we go there and try talk to Il Moro? Maybe you could introduce us, Meric?"

"Er, I left Milan in rather a hurry," Meric said. Then the story of how he and Michelle met came out, and Gwyn deflated.

"I wouldn't ask you to go back there then."

"That plan is inherent with flaws. Chasing letters that say who knows what to who knows whom?" Michelle tapped her own fingers on the table until she caught Meric glaring and stopped.

"Well what's *your* plan then?" Gwyn snapped. "Unless you really have given up, 'cause that's what it seems like."

She defied the stare Michelle turned on her, glaring back despite the blush creeping up her cheeks.

"I have not given up," Michelle stated. "I overreacted last night and lost my temper. However, I said your little visualisation trick might be useful, and I'm formulating a plan that is far more robust than yours." She leant back from the table and stretched. "First of all, thank you Meric for all your help thus far. I don't want you to feel as though you need to chaperone us. I know you have your own affairs to conduct."

Gwyn turned to Meric, worry creasing her face. "But there's a war coming. Do you want stick around?"

Meric shrugged. "By the sound of it nowhere in Italy will be safe if you two have your way. I may as well delay my retirement plans until I know what the future holds." He chuckled, then stopped when he saw that neither woman returned his smile. "If you want to me go, I'll be off."

"No!" said Gwyn.

"You aren't a hindrance," said Michelle, "but we have no claim on you. I can't pay you as a mercenary—I need to keep funds for essentials, and I can protect Gwyn."

Gwyn snorted. Michelle ignored her.

Mollified, Meric patted Gwyn's hand. "I've got funds myself, here in the bank. But with war coming, mayhap I'll be as well to take them out."

"That… would be wise." Michelle nodded. "When the French army comes, they force Florence to pay for their billeting. You'll probably lose all your savings. But I can't guarantee safety or security, and it's not your job to do this."

Gwyn shifted. She had manipulated Meric into helping her when they had first met, by promising he could kill Vlad even though she'd needed him alive. Michelle was a contradiction of ruthlessness and honesty—or was that a contradiction at all?

Meric sighed. "Michelle, I'm a soldier to the bone. I'm not one to wait for the war to come to me, like these poor sheep." He gestured at the filling courtyard—Florentines chatting and breakfasting at the inn. "A siege is a terrible thing to endure. But I'll ask one thing as payment, and for that you'll have my service if you'll take it."

"What's that?" Michelle asked.

"When all of this is over, if I survive, can you find me a place in time where there is no war, no plagues and no upheaval, and set me down there to live out my days?"

Michelle considered. Gwyn held her breath. She didn't want to be left alone with Michelle, to be dragged all over the countryside and told she was a hindrance and a liability. She trusted Meric.

"Very well." Michelle nodded. "Assuming we succeed, I'll do my best to find you somewhere peaceful." She stared at the hand Meric put out for her to shake then gripped it firmly. "As much as I prefer to work alone, it'll be easier to look after Gwyn if I have another set of eyes on her."

Gwyn rolled hers. "So what's your brilliant plan then?" she asked rudely.

"First!" Michelle thumped the table and Gwyn and Meric jumped. "You'll follow my instructions exactly and do your best to stay out of trouble."

"Whatever," Gwyn huffed. "Yes, fine—you're a brilliant super-ninja-woman and I'll listen to your every word."

Meric half-covered a smirk. Michelle went on. "Second, my understanding of this time is that while the Italian houses don't trust each other, they mistrust outsiders even more. So which family rules a significant province and isn't Italian?"

Gwyn stared. Meric nodded and said, "The Borgias. The Pope."

"Exactly. So any conflict would do well to originate from there." Michelle sighed.

Gwyn shifted unhappily. "Cesare will be your man, then. Cesare Borgia—he's… cunning is the best word I can think of. He frightens me. But he's far more interested in politics than his brother, Juan. His only weakness is his sister."

Michelle put her hands on her chin and rested her elbows on the table. "Was it he you warned about the Pope's assassination attempt?"

"Yeah." Gwyn shivered. "He kept me prisoner and pretended I was his mistress to keep me around—he wanted me to predict the future for him. I told him I couldn't control my visions but he threatened to hurt me so I told him as little as I could, and then I escaped."

Michelle covered her face with her hands, then looked up. "We'll leverage that. We can pretend I'm a more powerful fortune-teller—you just have to introduce me. I'll handle him from there."

"If you're not buyin', you're not sittin'!" It was the innkeeper, red-faced and irate. "I've got customers waitin' for tables—unless you want more, clear off!"

Michelle stood. Slight as she was, she managed to look taller and more imposing than the innkeeper. "We're going." She spoke softly as she herded Gwyn and Meric out. "I'll take Gwyn back to your room, Meric. Can you organise horses for us to go to Rome? Take your money out of the bank too but use this for what we need." She passed him several coins and a silver ring.

He tucked them into his belt pouch. "How quickly do you need to get to Rome? Is it a mad gallop you're after, or can we take our time?"

Michelle shuddered. "No mad gallop—my arse won't handle it."

"Aye, then—I'll find beasts that can take us at a steady pace. What will you be doing?"

"I'll sort out travel clothes for Gwyn and food supplies. She can fill me in about Cesare."

"How about weapons?"

Michelle smiled. "Knives are good. Are there rules about commoners carrying swords?"

"Leave it to me." Meric straightened his shoulders. "I'll find us some crossbows too. We'll practise on the road."

Gwyn trailed after Michelle, feeling superfluous and very much alone.

# *Fifteen*

**1492 AD**

Cesare waited in the antechamber to his father's room, pacing and snapping his fingers.

"Sit down, brother," Juan yawned. "You've been edgy as a cat since Lucretia went away."

Cesare tensed at the mention of their sister. He had not been in favour of her marriage to Giovanni Sforza, a peevish widower with a sour face, but their father had deemed it politically expedient. With Juan wriggling out of marriage commitments, Lucretia had been the first to go. "I don't see why I can't be in there. I'm a cardinal. It's Vatican business—I should be there," he complained.

"Perhaps Father finds you too abrupt." Juan lounged on a settee and idly scratched his nose. "He's wooing the Austrian delegation—you know how prissy they are. Can't be seen having the Pope's children in the room."

Cesare snorted. "He would if it suited him."

There was no doubt which child had inherited Rodrigo Borgia's sharp mind and devious methods. Juan was too lazy, Lucretia too naïve, Joffre too young. Mutterings of military movements in the north made Cesare nervous, and he disliked being nervous. He and his father had quelled dissension in the College of Cardinals after the initial poisoning plot. Della Rovere had fled into exile and Orsini had mysteriously fallen ill and died. Cesare cracked his knuckles. *Pity I can't poison the French Army.*

The door to the Pope's reception chamber opened. "His Holiness wishes you to attend him now," murmured Cardinal Sforza. Juan leapt up and sauntered past while Cesare locked eyes with Sforza. He hated the man's obsequiousness but knew him to be a valuable ally who could turn into a dangerous enemy.

Inside the reception chamber the Austrians had already left. The Pope sat on his throne, chin on hand, resting his elbow on the arm of the ornate gilded chair. Cesare curbed his impatience and waited for his father to speak. Juan helped himself to a cup of wine from the decanter on the side table. Cardinal Sforza stood silently. Rodrigo Borgia brooded for several more moments.

"The Austrians claim to be unconvinced that King Charles of France bears any warlike intent on our land." Rodrigo slowly rubbed his chin. "They assert that even if he did, our Holy state would be sacrosanct and we would have nothing to fear."

Cesare could contain himself no longer. "Charles is an animal—he has no respect for the Papacy or any Italian state. My spies tell me he's fixed on a claim he supposedly has to the throne of Naples. He will plough through any Italian who stands in his way."

Rodrigo sighed. "And I have just signed an engagement contract for Joffre to King Ferrante's bastard granddaughter, so it would seem we must defend Naples unless I annul the contract and seek a marriage elsewhere. I should have looked for a French princess."

"Joffre is ten!" Cesare exclaimed.

"Hmm, you're right. Perhaps I could use his tender years as an excuse to break off the engagement," the Pope mused.

"But then you'd marry him to France." Juan seemed less outraged than his brother.

Rodrigo glared at his second son. "It is not as if you are volunteering to step up to the altar, Juan! You ought to do your duty to this family."

"Unmake Cesare as a cardinal," Juan drawled. "You know he hates it. Then marry him to whomever."

Cesare simmered but said nothing.

"I need Cesare where he is," snapped the Pope. "Why God has cursed me with ungrateful sons is beyond me. Everything I do is to glorify His name."

*I didn't know God was a Borgia,* Cesare thought blasphemously, then crossed himself. "Either way, Father, an invasion of Italy is imminent. If the Austrians won't come to our aid and Spain is too busy burning heretics we must look within for allies. Savoy and Milan are the first lines of defence, then Florence. Let me go to them and learn their minds, offer your blessings."

"I am the Duke of Gandia." Juan glared. "I should be the one to coordinate any military alliance."

"I need you here, Juan," the Pope soothed. "Overlooking our armies and marshalling our strength. A strong leader must be seen leading."

Juan preened. "Yes, well, I suppose that *is* more important than chit-chat in the north."

Cesare hid his sneer. Juan was useless at diplomacy—too hot-headed. Cesare might lose his temper amongst family but maintained his control with outsiders. Their father knew that and played to their strengths. Cesare loved and hated him for that.

Juan was dispatched to determine the current strength of the Papal army and outline a plan for defence. Cesare waited until the door closed behind his brother and, with a hard glance at Cardinal Sforza who remained to the side of the chamber, said to his father, "If Charles gets this far it will be dire for us."

Rodrigo flapped a hand in dismissal. "I know that, Cesare, which is why *you* must convince Savoy, Milan and Florence to block France. Venice we might ask for arms, though our Lord God knows they only ever look to the sea. The other duchies and republics and marquisates will follow suit if we stand together. I suppose that means I'll have to honour Joffre's engagement, then Naples can send arms."

Cesare sighed. "Yes, Father. Would you have me leave straight away?"

"Not just yet, but soon. It is autumn already and I'd have you back before winter. There continues to be dissent in the College of Cardinals. Sforza, read to Cesare the list of names of those we think who might still plot. We will cut off their support from their families. It's time the Papal throne tightened its grip on the Romagna."

\* \* \*

Cesare rode north. His loyal servant, Michelotto rode beside him but kept silent as his master thought. The finest horses saw them make good time to Florence, where Cesare passed on his condolences to Piero de Medici on the loss of his father. Now they ventured north again, crossing the River Po by barge, and with the mountains looming in the distance approached the gates of Milan.

"Welcome, Cardinal Borgia!" Ludovico Sforza, known as Il Moro, was loud and expansive in both voice and gesture, filling the great hall of the castle with his presence. His wife, Beatrice, a gracious lady dressed in immaculate fashion, sat beside him at a table that ran the length of the hall. A bitter-faced young woman sat next to her. Cesare guessed the young lady was Isabella, the Duchess of Milan and granddaughter to King Ferrante of Naples.

"It is a pleasure to attend you, Lord Sforza." Cesare bowed, elegantly sweeping his red cardinal's robes under him. "Your nephew the Duke is not here?" He kept his tone light but the question was loaded. Everyone knew that Il Moro coveted the title of Duke himself. He kept his nephew chained like a hawk, permitted to fly and hunt—within reason. Cesare's spies had intercepted several letters from the Duchess to her grandfather in Naples complaining that her husband had no real power and she was sidelined as a lady of the court. Cesare intended to leverage this discontent if need be.

"My nephew is out hunting! You know what young men are like!" Il Moro boomed.

Being a young man himself in a position of great responsibility, Cesare turned his sneer into a smile. "One would think the Duke would attend to Italian politics a little more closely, considering the current threat of France."

Lady Beatrice twitched and fluttered her ornate fan. Il Moro walked around the end of the table and came to clap Cesare on the shoulder. "He is lucky his loving uncle works tirelessly on his behalf to manage affairs of state. I have encouraged him to take an interest." He spread his hands and looked mournful. "I confess," he said, dropping his voice, "he is something of a feckless youth, interested only in horses, hunting and whores." He chuckled at his assonance. Cesare saw Duchess

Isabella's lips tighten. Il Moro might have spoken quietly, but his voice still carried in a hall that hung on his every word.

Cesare kept his smile pasted on. "Then perhaps you and I can discuss the matter of France, Lord Sforza."

"Pah! France. Charles is nothing but a posturing idiot with dreams of grandeur."

"I have word that he means to stake his claim to the throne of Naples—unfortunately the rest of Italy lies in his way. Do you not feel this is cause for concern?"

Il Moro shrugged and turned away. Cesare caught the warning look Lady Beatrice shot her husband. "Very well," Cesare said. "You are much closer to his borders. I imagine you have a more accurate grasp on his intentions than we do in Rome."

"Very true! Come, sit and tell me how the Medici boy fares in Florence now his father is gone. A sad loss for all of Italy."

Cesare sat, ignoring the stare Duchess Isabella gave him. He would deal with her later.

* * *

Michelotto slipped back into Cesare's guest chambers and joined his master in front of the crackling fire. Autumn came early this close to the mountains, unlike in balmy Rome. "I've found letters, my lord," Michelotto breathed, "from King Charles of France."

"What do they say?" Cesare's voice was equally hushed.

"Charles thanks Ludovico for his offer, and assures him that Milan will not suffer any repercussions from the movement of the French armies through the Duchy."

Cesare cursed. "Is he so threatened by King Ferrante that he has to use France? Does he not see the hell he would unleash upon Italy?"

Michelotto shrugged.

"I fear it is my doing that Ludovico invites France in," a soft female voice spoke from the doorway. Cesare and Michelotto whirled, stilettos out and ready. They stared at Duchess Isabella who clutched her fur wrap tightly around her shoulders.

"How did you get in?" Cesare demanded.

Isabella fluttered her eyelashes. "I am the mistress of this castle, though you would not think it. I hold the keys." She lifted a large ring of keys on her sash.

Cesare appeared to relax, though his eyes remained sharp. "Come sit, your grace, and tell me why you visit me in my chambers at night. Michelotto, you may go." The manservant bowed and made himself scarce.

"Wine, your grace?"

"Please." Isabella fluffed out her skirts and perched on an armchair by the fire. Cesare poured wine and passed it to her with a flourish. She accepted it with a nod but Cesare noticed her hand was shaking. He lit a taper from the fire and set it to a hanging brazier. The scent of sandalwood drifted down.

"So," he sat opposite and his eyes raked over her. More conservatively dressed than Lady Beatrice, it added to her careworn demeanour.

"You are young to be a Cardinal," Isabella broached the silence.

Cesare raised his eyebrows. "You are scarcely older than me and you are a Duchess. You know power does not only come to those with age."

She clenched her fist and scowled, a most un-Duchess-like expression. "I have no power here, as you can well see. Ludovico and Beatrice rule Milan. My husband is told to keep his nose out of political affairs and I am shunted into a dank apartment with none of the ladies and consequence my station demands."

Cesare sipped his wine, letting the silence build. Isabella did not wait long to fill it.

"I have written to my grandfather of this insult. Many times. He may be old but he is conscious that *we* are royalty, and Ludovico is just jumped-up nobility. He promises he will send an army to restore my husband to his duchy, but he has not said when. He says my husband must prove himself a man."

"Ah." Cesare let the single syllable roll around the chamber. He understood now why Il Moro sought to steal a march on Naples. Lust for power was a strong motivator, one Cesare understood and respected. But that did not mean he would watch the rest of Italy burn for one man's ambition.

Isabella looked at him. Cesare saw a mixture of fear and defiance in her eyes. She had ambition too. He smiled.

"Your eminence?" She shrank back.

"Fear not, your grace." He rose and knelt beside her, taking the wine from her and setting it aside. He clasped her hand. "Our Holy Father is also most keen to see your husband restored to his rightful power. Why, my brother Joffre is due to marry the Lady Sancha of Naples next month. King Ferrante is our ally, and his family is our family. Nothing is more important to the Borgias than family," he said with sincerity.

Isabella relaxed. "So, you will help us then?"

"Of course! With these letters, we have evidence of Ludovico's collusion with the French. Our Holy Father will be most upset and may even threaten to excommunicate him." She gasped. "I know, an extreme measure that may not come to pass, but it demonstrates the seriousness with which the Church takes these matters. You must be ready though."

"Ready?"

Cesare patted her hand. "Il Moro will not give up power easily." *He'll not give it up at all, I'll wager.* "But perhaps I can speak sense to him. Will he be in his chambers now?"

Isabella looked askance. "He stays late in the hall, drinking and feasting, but even he should return to his rooms soon."

Cesare kissed her hand, looking into her eyes all the while. "We shall wait for him. I'll send my man to find your husband the Duke so he can join us in our discussion." He smiled again.

Isabella blushed and rose, smoothing her skirts. "Of course. Let us go."

# *Sixteen*

**1492 AD**

"Lord Ludovico."

Il Moro halted stomping into his chambers and stared at Cesare and Isabella standing by the fireplace, its blaze more generous than the one in Cesare's guest chambers. By rights these apartments should have belonged to the Duke, but along with everything else in the duchy, Il Moro gave himself precedence. He barked, "What? Who let you in here?"

Cesare noticed Isabella trembling again and put a hand on her shoulder. "Her grace the Duchess said you would be kind enough to grant me a private audience," he said smoothly, no hint of tension visible on his face.

Il Moro grunted. "She did, did she?" His glance at Isabella was baleful. "Should have been damned guards on the door but everything's gone to horse manure since my captain disappeared."

"Of course, I'm very grateful to your lordship for seeing me so late. The matter is urgent."

Il Moro frowned. He was drunk, Cesare observed, but not stupid. "What matter is so urgent that could not wait until morning?"

Cesare approached, hands open. "I considered approaching the Duke directly, but since you said he had no interest in matters of politics I thought it best I spoke first to you. The Duchess here gave me most disturbing news," he smiled back at Isabella, who looked increasingly nervous, "and I wanted to consult you to make sure that the Vatican's interest is aligned with Milan."

A soft gasp came from Isabella. "You... you... Pope's bastard!"

Il Moro looked at her and chuckled. "Did she come running to you with some sob story about her feckless husband having no power? Interfering little wench. Did she spread her legs to get your attention?" He smirked at Isabella.

"My lord, despite what you may have heard about my family, I am a man of God." Cesare halted just before Il Moro and painted contriteness on his face. "Yes, the Duchess came to me, but as I said, I thought it best I speak to you." He put a hand on Il Moro's shoulder and smiled gently. "We men understand these things, after all."

"Too right!" Il Moro laughed, eyes fixed on the fuming Isabella. Cesare half turned and let his hand drop to the back of his belt where a stiletto hung. Ludovico was still laughing when Cesare stabbed him in the back, clasping his hand over Il Moro's mouth to choke the shouts. He held the dying man tightly until the struggles stopped, lowering the twitching corpse to the floor.

The Duchess was pale but upright. "Put your head down if you feel faint," Cesare ordered sharply.

"I'm alright," she whispered, eyes bright with shock.

"Well done, your grace," Cesare saluted her with the bloody knife. "This is how you take power."

"Quite so," she breathed.

"Now," he said, "we await your husband."

It was not long before Michelotto arrived escorting a disgruntled Duke. "Found him in the nearest whorehouse, my lord."

"What is the meaning of this? What has happened to my uncle?" The young Duke stared in horror at Il Moro's corpse, lying in a pool of blood.

"A fit of madness overcame his lordship," Cesare replied. "He attempted to rape the Duchess and I was forced to defend her honour. I may never atone for such a sin, but I could not stand by and watch such depravity take place."

"He... tried to rape you?" the Duke asked, stunned.

Isabella nodded, lips tight. "I will testify before a court to that effect, husband, but we must act swiftly to prevent any act of revenge by the lady Beatrice."

The Duke stared at Il Moro's body, then at his wife.

"If I may make a suggestion?" Cesare interrupted. "My man Michelotto here has experience in advising those in politics. He was at university with me in Lucca. Perhaps I should leave him to serve you—I fear I cannot remain with such a sin on my conscience. I must return to Rome and confess to our Holy Father. But Michelotto will help you stay the course." He looked meaningfully at Isabella, who straightened her shoulders and lifted her chin.

"I shall be grateful for his advice while I support my husband. Come, my dear, there is much to do. We are under threat of invasion from France. You must act quickly."

"Of course," the Duke replied absently, eyes still fixed on his dead uncle. He permitted Isabella to guide him from the room, Michelotto in tow. At the door she glanced back at Cesare.

He nodded once, and smiled.

\* \* \*

Cesare carried letters signed by the Duke addressed to the Doge of Venice and various other rulers of northern Italy. Michelotto would keep the Duchess in check and Milan would stand against the French. The other states would follow.

It took him many weeks to accomplish his mission; by the time he finished winter chased him home. It was there that he discovered that his brother had butchered their father's plan to take control of the Campagna. The Papal armies had been defeated and Juan had slunk back to Rome.

"What happened? You idiotic, self-aggrandising fool!"

Juan withered under his brother's fury but set his jaw. "That bitch Caterina Sforza corralled the Orsini and the Gaetani and the Savelli and the Colonna—all the great families of the Campagna. We were betrayed by these Italian snobs. I will wreak vengeance on them!"

"You will do as I say." The Pope strode into the room, his beautiful white embroidered robes flapping in his wake.

"No Cardinal Sforza?" Cesare asked ironically, checking his temper in anticipation of their father's scolding. The glare he received stopped him from engaging in further wit.

"Sforza professes his loyalty to the papal throne but right now I trust my thoughts only to my family and to God," Rodrigo Borgia snarled. He plumped himself down on the velvet covered chair that took pride of place in the room.

*And not all of them even then, I'll warrant.* Cesare kept his thoughts to himself.

"Father, I will take back the Campagna," Juan declared. "You did not have to summon me back to Rome."

"You needed reminding who rules this family, Juan, and if you had followed my instructions instead of dallying with that Sforza whore the other families wouldn't have had time to muster their forces against us! She played you! And in doing so she made *me* look like a fool!"

Juan had the sense to keep quiet this time, offering no further defence of his actions.

"What do you want done, Father?" Cesare asked quietly.

The Pope's glare swung to him, then became calculating. "Since you have proved yourself most adept at diplomatic missions, you will engage another ally."

Cesare frowned. "The northern states will be too busy organising a defence against France for the spring to send us troops."

"Not north, my son, but south."

"Naples?" Juan interjected. "Aren't they already our ally?"

Rodrigo shot him a look of scorn. "In word, only. King Ferrante won't attack us, but he won't send troops either. But now that Cesare has tied up the French threat in the north I want him to convince Ferrante that he can afford to spare the men and horses to strengthen the Papal States as a secondary line of defence against Charles."

Cesare tried not to splutter. He did not want to go to Naples.

"What's the matter, brother?" Juan smirked. "Aren't your diplomatic skills up to creeping up the backside of the corpse-kisser king?"

Cesare shuddered and beseeched his father. "Not Naples, please, father. It's a cultural backwater. And with what should I bargain?"

"I'm not sending you to enjoy concerts and art! And Ferrante isn't a necrophiliac, he simply stuffs corpses and places them around that ghastly banquet table of his, or so I've heard. As for bargaining, well, we have his lovely granddaughter Sancha, married to our dear Joffre."

Cesare looked at his father's smug countenance and a horrible shudder seized him as his mind leapt to the next thought. "Father, you told me Lucretia was safe, but… is Giovanni Sforza holding her hostage?"

Rodrigo Borgia scowled. "Not in so many words, but he writes that he fears the countryside is too dangerous to send her back to Rome as I've requested. Damn him. That is why you will not return to Rome until you have a Neapolitan army at your back. Once Lucretia is safely returned I'll annul her marriage to that treacherous Sforza and negotiate something with Ferrante. That is the other half of your bargaining chip. See that you achieve our interests *without murder* this time."

Cesare was gratified to see Juan appear shocked as the Pope swept out of the room. "Murder, eh, brother? I didn't think you had it in you."

Cesare approached the sideboard and poured himself a glass of wine, downing it before replying. "The problem with you, Juan, is that you don't think. Now I have to leave Rome again, and Lucretia is a prisoner."

Juan snatched the wine glass from Cesare and poured himself a drink. "Some of us think, brother, and some of us do."

"Well try not to *do* anything too stupid while I am away, *brother.*" Cesare scooped his hat from the table and left. Damn their father and damn the Sforzas! He'd done the world a favour by ridding it of Ludovico Sforza—there were far too many of them.

As if summoned by his thought, Cardinal Sforza appeared from an alcove in the hallway.

"What are you doing, skulking around here?" Cesare snarled, grabbing the Cardinal by the collar and thrusting him against the wall. "Hoping to hear our Holy Father's plans so you can write to your treacherous cousins? You lowly weasel!"

Cardinal Sforza appeared shaken, but when he spoke it was measured enough. "Calm your ire, Cardinal Borgia, you hold my name against me. Family may be everything to you Borgias, but believe me when I say that power is what interests me."

Cesare dropped his hands but kept his face close to. "And what power do you seek now? The power of the papal throne? Is that your cousins' plan? To make you Pope?"

"If your father truly saw me as a threat he would dispose of me without a thought. Or instruct you to, as you did with Ludovico Sforza. No, his holiness knows that I will be the avenue to persuading my cousins Caterina and Giovanni and all the other noble families to acquiesce to the Vatican's eventual return to dominance. The Italian states will never unite under their petty leadership, and united Italy must be, to resist the French."

Cesare breathed heavily, staring into his rival's eyes. "The French will be stopped by Milan."

"The French will be *slowed* by Milan. And Charles will not be in a good mood to have wasted time subjugating the north when his real goal is Naples." Cardinal Sforza narrowed his eyes. "That is where his holiness is sending you, am I correct? To Naples for an alliance? I may not be in his confidence but I have known your father for many years and I know his mind."

Cesare didn't answer, merely schooled his face into a courtier's blankness and stepped back. "My father's plans are no concern of yours. If you are sincere in your rejection of your family's treachery, you should concentrate on getting back into his good graces."

Sforza's smile was sardonic. "That is exactly what I am doing, Cardinal Borgia. His Holiness refuses to see me right now, but upon your return from Naples perhaps you would speak for me."

"Why in God's good name should I do that?"

"For information." Sforza tapped his nose with one finger. "Beware King Ferrante and his son Alfonso. They are slipperier than snakes and more... more devious than Borgias." His smile broadened.

"Hmph. You mistake me for my brother. I will be wary."

"I mean it, Cardinal Borgia. Do not trust the word of King Ferrante or his son Alfonso."

"*Thank you*, Cardinal Sforza. Now I must prepare for my journey. I am not even permitted to celebrate Christmas in Rome, but I know my duty. I suggest you save your concern for yourself."

He felt Sforza's eyes bore into his back as he marched swiftly down the hall. The gall of the man, to warn him against Neapolitans when the Italian families of the Campagna conspired against the Vatican. He knew where treachery lay.

# *Seventeen*

## 1492 AD

Gwyn fired the crossbow. The bolt hit the tree with a thwack and sank into the wood. "I hit it!" She jumped up and down.

"Not bad," Meric said, lifting the weapon from her hands and examining the sights.

"Too bad it wasn't the tree she was aiming for," Michelle muttered, raising her own crossbow and aiming carefully. The bolt hit the target tree an inch above the scrap of cloth Meric had pinned there.

Gwyn glared at Michelle but refrained from retorting. *You can't help rubbing in that you're better than me at everything.* She smiled gratefully at Meric when she saw the frown he sent Michelle's way.

"Relax your shoulders when you fire," he told Gwyn. "You're so tense it jerks the crossbow up."

"Of course I'm tense," Gwyn shot back. "I could kill someone with this!"

"Only by accident," Michelle commented.

This time Meric responded forcefully. "Michelle, it was but two weeks ago you weren't hitting anything either. Be grateful for that talent and ease up on Gwyn!"

"I have trained with weapons and unarmed combat for years, thank you very much!" Michelle responded. "This style of crossbow may be new to me, but it's hard work that is paying off in mastering it."

Gwyn sighed. "Yep, you're just amazing," she mumbled.

"Either way, keep quiet while I'm training Gwyn," Meric ordered.

Michelle gazed at them both, an unreadable emotion in her eyes. She loaded another bolt, placing her foot in the stirrup and pulling back the string. Gwyn watched the bolt hit the target centre and turned away.

"You're improving, Gwyn," Meric handed her back the crossbow. "It's not as though we're drilling for hours a day."

"I just want to reach Rome." She fumbled the bolt into the notch.

"Aye, as do I. All this shilly-shallying about the countryside, avoiding armies and whatnot is wearisome. Alright, now cock the string. That's good—breathe slowly when you aim. You want to at least look as if you know what you're doing." Gwyn glared. He laughed. "It's true. At least if you can bluff you might buy yourself some time."

*Now why doesn't his teasing upset me? Oh that's right, because he's not a complete jerk like she is!* Gwyn breathed, aimed and fired. The crossbow bolt flew through the trees and disappeared into the stream beyond.

"Maybe that's enough for today," Meric said tactfully. Gwyn waited for an outburst of laughter from Michelle. When none came she turned to see the older woman staring at the trees and frowning.

"The birds have gone quiet. Someone's coming," Michelle said.

Within seconds Meric readied another crossbow and handed it to Gwyn. "Keep it facing the ground unless I tell you." He took hers, loaded it and strode to the horses. Michelle was already halfway up a tree. The smattering of brown leaves did little to conceal her—Gwyn hoped no one would look up.

A trio of horsemen trotted into sight on the road. They wore light armour over brightly coloured doublets and breeches; one carried a pole with a banner—the heraldry was meaningless to Gwyn—but she guessed they were knights. They spotted Meric and Gwyn and the lead rider raised a hand. The knights reined in.

"Ho there! What business have you on the road, good people?"

*Who actually talks like that?* Gwyn tried not to look up at where Michelle was hiding. Instead, she concentrated on holding the crossbow as though she knew how to use it effectively.

"Good day to you, signors. My daughter and I are travelling to Rome, to visit family." Meric answered smoothly.

"Dangerous times, these, to travel without a group," one knight commented, resting his hands on his pommel and leaning forward for a better look at Gwyn. She tensed, wishing she could tell him to get lost.

Meric smiled, his crossbow hanging loosely from one hand. "Aye, that it is, but I know how to handle myself, and my daughter here is a fair shot. I'd be a fool to go about unarmed, with robbers and deserters about. But I feel comfort in seeing good Christian men such as yourselves, keeping our lands safe."

"Safe from the Borgias!" the other knight declared and his companions cackled.

"Ah, you are honourable Italians!" Meric bowed. "Please do not let me detain you, signors, for I'm sure there are battles to be fought!"

If Gwyn hadn't been so nervous she would have giggled at his sycophantic tone. It worked on the knights—they puffed up with pride and informed Meric, "Not anymore, we have that cowardly Borgia on the run, and the alliance of the Campagna is secure. It'll only be a matter of time before an Italian Pope sits upon the throne again."

"Well then, good signors, hasten to the honours which surely await you for your noble endeavours. It cheers me to know the war is done— we have been up and down these hills skirting armies for weeks and pray that we will soon reach our destination unharmed."

His flowery speech obviously amused one of the knights. "Come now, let us be off. This man has a pretty tongue and his daughter's too skinny for amusement—let us leave them be." He kicked his horse into a trot and the other two followed. Gwyn released a breath she hadn't realised she'd been holding and let the crossbow swing down. Her leg bumped the trigger and the bolt thudded into the dirt next to her foot.

"Oh shit!"

"Easy now." Meric unclipped his own crossbow and holstered it on his saddle. "After what you've been through, Gwyn, I'm surprised you don't have better nerves. You were bolder when I first met you. But I suppose that was a long time ago."

*It was and it wasn't.* She dared not look at Michelle as the other woman leapt down from the tree. Had she been bolder back then? Yes—and more stupid. Now she knew she had been freakishly lucky. Next to Michelle, she was just a kid mucking around with forces she didn't understand.

Michelle came to stand next to them. "I suppose that means we can ride straight to Rome now," she said.

* * *

Poor weather slowed their progress greatly. The roads were muddy and finding a place to ford swollen rivers and streams sometimes took them far out of their way. Meric told stories of his many campaigns as they spent one rainy afternoon holed up in a barn. The farmer's wife was reluctant at first to shelter them—her husband was away fighting—but the coin they offered mellowed her. That evening she appeared at the barn door bearing a pot of hot soup and a loaf of bread.

"Which lord is he fighting for?" Meric asked Gwyn, who had accepted the food. She'd hopped up to accept the food and set it down between the three of them for sharing.

"Dunno," she shrugged, setting the pot down and stuffing a chunk of bread in her mouth. "Wam me oo ars?"

"Aye, maybe later. Where was I?"

"Telling us about when you went to Vienna."

"Oh, aye." He carried on.

After supper Meric encouraged Gwyn to elaborate on her tale of Ancient Rome. Michelle finished her stretching routine and joined them to listen. He was wary, ready to cut in if the older woman made disparaging remarks, but for once Michelle seemed content to keep her opinions to herself.

"God must have guided your footsteps, to meet your friends from the Holy Land again so many years later." *Perhaps Allah guided me to her this time too.*

Gwyn shrugged. "I don't know about that."

Meric continued in earnest. "Well the Jews are people of the Book, and your friend Adi was a Jew, even if she married a Roman." He faltered when he saw Gwyn and Michelle exchange sceptical looks. "Aye, just a thought," he muttered.

"Most humans aren't religious in my time," Michelle explained. "I believe many still are in Gwyn's."

"Some." Gwyn looked uncomfortable. "My parents aren't though, so I'm not really."

Meric felt his jaw drop. "You mean, don't believe in God? Or worship false gods?"

"Don't believe in a god full stop," Michelle said. "We tend to believe you make your own future, and random chance makes up the rest."

*What a lonely, terrible way to live.* He bit off the thought. Michelle smiled sardonically.

"So no, neither Gwyn nor I are any sort of chosen one. If we have a physical resemblance it's because we possibly are related, though until I return to my time and can check with the scientists who took a sample of her blood, I won't know. That would explain why we are both natural time-travellers—it's genetic."

"It's what?"

"Means it's in our family, if we are related." Gwyn's mouth twisted as though she'd bitten something sour. "I'm going to bed." She got up and went outside to relieve herself.

Michelle raised her eyebrows. "We should all go to bed. Even if it's still rainy tomorrow, we should ride on. I'd like to reach Rome. It's been quite a few weeks since we left Florence—time's getting on."

"Aye." Meric gathered their bowls and the soup pot and stacked them neatly. He watched Gwyn surreptitiously as she came back into the barn and made herself a bed on some hay. Then he noticed Michelle watching her too, and wondered what the older woman was thinking.

\* \* \*

The rain rolled off the hills and chased them lazily into Rome. By the time they found a boarding house the water was flowing off rooftops and into the street, dowsing the horses' hooves and washing away some of the odours of people and animals living in close quarters.

"God, I miss hot showers in winter," Gwyn sighed, handing her reins over to the stableboy in the courtyard.

Meric shot her a quizzical look. "It rains hot in your time?"

Gwyn was halfway through explaining modern plumbing to him when Michelle returned from arranging rooms. "We are husband, wife and daughter investigating marriage prospects with a cousin," she advised, grabbing her saddlebags from Meric.

"Hey!" Gwyn protested.

Michelle raised her eyebrows. "It'll keep the landlord or any other young men from sniffing at your skirts. Meric looks fierce enough to break the heads of anyone who interferes with his precious daughter. Just stick close to him."

Gwyn wanted to say she could look after herself, but she knew how many close calls she'd had. Trust Michelle to make her feel more helpless than she already did. Gwyn stomped the mud off and followed the others up to their room.

"Let's get clean and fed, then once the rain lets up, we'll scout out the Borgia household."

"Sure," Gwyn sighed and kicked off her shoes. She wore the stays of her dress much looser than strictly appropriate, but even so felt constrained by the linen garment. It wasn't as nice as the dress she'd lost in Florence, the one she'd been given at Cesare's behest, but Michelle insisted that if she was dressed as a woman, Gwyn should be too.

Several hours later, the sun was out but the air remained chilly and the cobbled streets were slippery underfoot. "That place there," Gwyn pointed. They examined it—an arched tunnel with guards at its entrance led through to a large brick courtyard. The street-facing windows were small and high, an irony considering the Pope's family was no secret.

"What do you intend?" Meric asked.

"First we need to find out if Cesare Borgia is even there, or when he'll be back. Servants are usually the best for obtaining gossip like that. You two loiter out front, I'll pretend to be a travelling herb-woman and knock at the servants' entrance."

"Okay!" Gwyn was more than happy to hang about with Meric. They found a wall to lean on and chatted, surprised when Michelle returned after only a quarter of an hour.

"That was quick."

Michelle glared. "He's not in Rome. I spoke to a maid. He was sent north on some diplomatic mission and isn't back yet. Do your visualisation trick and tell me what the future holds."

"Why don't we move down the street a ways," Meric suggested. "It would look less suspicious."

Gwyn was grateful for the chance to prepare herself. The way Michelle ordered her about put her on edge. "Here's good." She pointed to an empty alcove in a nearby piazza—the stallholder having closed up shop when the rain came in and not bothered to reopen that afternoon. Closing her eyes, she merged with the timepiece and explored the timeline.

Her heart sank and she reluctantly reported to Michelle. "Milan is preparing an army—it looks like Cesare convinced the Duke to stand against the French—who are marching, by the way. The other states in the north are raising men. So I guess we missed the boat on that one— we'll have to disrupt their alliance somehow—Cesare was the one who orchestrated it."

"What else?"

"He's riding—definitely not in Rome right now—but the setting sun is on his right."

"He must be riding south to Rome then. That's good," chimed Meric from his position as lookout.

"Look into the future, Gwyn. When will he be back in Rome?" Michelle wanted to know.

"Er… You know this is not an exact science?" She was finding it difficult to concentrate with Michelle standing over her.

"The way you do it isn't, I know that."

That was it. Gwyn's concentration broke and she glared at Michelle. "Look, I need quiet and you aren't helping! He's riding south. Surely he'll be back soon."

Michelle's mouth worked, as though she wanted to say something, but she pursed her lips instead.

"What are we doing?" Meric asked. "It's getting dark, and curfew will begin soon."

"Let's go back to the boarding house," Michelle replied. Gwyn sagged in relief.

"Excellent, I'm hungry," she said. Meric's stomach rumbled as if in agreement.

"We only just ate!" Michelle protested.

"A good soldier learns to eat when food's aplenty," Meric declared. "A carafe of wine wouldn't go amiss either now we're here. Come on, ladies, my treat."

Michelle followed them silently, and Gwyn couldn't help but feel uneasy, as if she had failed yet another of the Time-Space Agent's tests. *She thinks I'm useless anyway. What's one more thing?*

\* \* \*

There was still no sign of Cesare Borgia a week later. Christmas came and went—chill winds wrapped themselves around the buildings and chased those who braved the streets. Michelle continued to infiltrate as a herb-woman while Gwyn and Meric wandered Rome, listening to gossip about the Pope and the war in the Campagna.

"I really don't want to tell Michelle that the lords of the Campagna are actually marching on Rome," Gwyn grimaced as they hurried through the streets. It had rained again that morning and the cobbles were treacherously slick.

"Aye, I doubt she'll be too happy." Meric huffed in surprise as he slipped on a wet stone, saved from falling by Gwyn. She released his arm.

"Careful, old man." She grinned.

"Old man! Have some respect, wench!"

They continued to tease each other as they hurried on towards the Borgia house. Rounding a corner they almost slammed into Michelle. The woman looked furious.

*She knows about the war. Oh crap.* "We were hurrying to tell you! We only just found out ourselves!"

"How did you find out? It's a secret mission!" Michelle grabbed Gwyn's arm firmly. "Or did you finally apply yourself and use the timepiece to locate him?"

"Huh?"

"What?" Meric asked. Michelle looked from one to the other.

"Cesare Borgia. He's gone to Naples."

"Naples? No, I was talking about... oh, shit, Naples, really?" Gwyn felt sick.

"What were you talking about?" Michelle demanded.

"The war," Meric answered.

"All the great Italian families have united against the Borgias," Gwyn said unhappily. "Those knights we met, who told us it was over? Well, it isn't—they are marching on Rome to demand the deposition of the Pope."

Michelle's jaw worked. Gwyn wondered if she was going to lose her temper again.

"And you're saying Cesare Borgia has gone to Naples?" Meric asked. "So we must ride there?"

"No," said Michelle. "It'll be too late for that. My understanding is that he's gone to fetch an army to fight the Italian lords, but if what you say is true he won't return in time."

"And we can't jump back and change it." Gwyn fidgeted. "So what do we do? We need Cesare. He's the best person to cause dissension between the lords."

"Not the best." Michelle tapped her fingers thoughtfully. "From what you've told me he's one of the best, but not the only one."

Gwyn frowned. "Who else? Juan's an idiot, Lucretia isn't here. Vannozza?"

Michelle smiled grimly. "Who do you think taught Cesare the art of realpolitik? The Pope, of course. We'll take this all the way to the top."

# *Eighteen*

**1493 AD**

Rodrigo Borgia groaned with pleasure as his mistress massaged his aching feet. "I'm too old and stiff to be traipsing around the city walls in this weather, Julia. But I can't trust Juan to see to the defences all by himself. I wish Cesare were here."

"He'll return soon, my lord, with soldiers and weaponry and he'll drive these pesky lords back to their rustic castles in the hills." Julia Fornezi dipped her hand in the bowl of warm scented oil and worked her hands up the Pope's calf muscles. Frankincense and myrrh burned in braziers and a large fire blazed in the hearth. The bedchamber was warm and cosy.

"Ahh, that's heavenly. What would I do without you, mi belleza?"

"I do not wish you to fret, my lord, though there is something I wish to share with you."

"Hmm? What is that, my love?"

"I met a woman today who claims to know a little of the future, and she said she must warn you." Julia switched to the other foot.

"A seer? Hmph, more likely just some charlatan trying to extort money from me. How much did this crone want?"

"She said she wanted nothing, only to be granted a private audience with you. I do not know why but I found her strangely compelling. And she wasn't a crone, but a woman as young as I."

Rodrigo grunted. "She'll start demanding money or favours as soon she gets in front of me. Besides, I don't have time to see mysterious seers, young or old. I must see to the defence of this city."

Julia paused. "I really feel you should see her, my lord. Please? As a favour to me?"

Rodrigo considered his mistress. She was as intelligent as she was stunning—he couldn't abide stupid women—and she wasn't called La Bella Fornezi for nothing. As ridiculous as this request was, he would humour her in case something useful came out of it.

"Very well, my love. Tomorrow I'll receive her, after the noon bell. My poor feet will need a rest by then anyway."

* * *

"Keep up, Gwyn," Michelle ordered in Turkish as they strode through the Vatican's bewildering array of over-decorated halls. She tried to keep her frustration with the girl in check—they could not afford any internal bickering upon meeting the Pope. They had one shot.

"You don't want to appear rushed," Meric reminded in the same language. They had selected one he spoke that was unlikely to be understood by anyone in the Pope's employ. Michelle and Gwyn had listened to him say a few sentences, then memorised several words to speak that language with the help of their chronokinetors. Meric was dressed as a man-at-arms, while the women wore neat dresses with square cut necks in the style of the day, complete with puffed sleeves and lace edging. They had rented the outfits specifically for the Papal audience. Michelle hated the heaviness of the skirts. Gwyn looked surprisingly comfortable in her cream and blue dress, and Michelle knew that her order to speed up stemmed from a twinge of jealousy.

More than a twinge, if she was honest. While Gwyn's ineptness in most things irritated Michelle, it was the girl's occasional competence that sparked that uglier feeling. That a simple human girl had not only an inexplicable talent for seeing through time, but somehow thrived where Michelle could not.

Now was not the moment to dwell on that, though.

They reached a tall set of double doors, beautifully carved wood with gold filigree and large brass handles. The escorting footmen knocked and a servant opened a door from within. Michelle, Gwyn and Meric entered the audience chamber and saw a figure in white on the Papal throne.

Jowly, was Michelle's first thought, but with piercing eyes, giving the overall impression of a well-fed vulture. They approached, knelt and rose when the gloved hand motioned for them to do so.

"La Bella Fornezi said I should receive you," Rodrigo Borgia began. "It is a mark of my esteem for her that I do so. However, I am extremely busy, so be swift with your petition."

Michelle cleared her throat. "No petition, your holiness, we are here to serve you, with any recompense for our services to be decided by the value of the information which we impart."

"Yes, yes, get on with it." The Pope's mouth twisted.

"Very well. I will be swift. My name is Michelle and this is Gwynia. She is a seer. She has visions of the future. It was she who warned your son Cesare of the poisoning attempt on your life, and told him to bring a monkey to test the wine."

Up until that point Rodrigo Borgia had looked bored and unimpressed—but at the mention of Cesare and the monkey his eyes snapped to Gwyn. "You play a dangerous game, signoras. You come into the holiest house of God, to His shepherd on Earth, and claim magic and visions. Do you wish to be burnt as witches?"

"Your holiness," Michelle claimed his attention with a sharp tone. "This is no game. The future of the world is at stake. Yes, we come at great personal risk, knowing we could be misunderstood and persecuted, but we come because it is the truth! Even now your enemies intend to knock at Rome's gate to remove you as Pope. Your son Cesare will be betrayed by Naples and no army will come to save you."

She was winning the Pope over, she could tell—he was a cynical man but her persuasion was aided by the timepiece. Then Gwyn spoke up. "Since Cardinal Borgia isn't here to vouch for recognition of me, your holiness, you could ask the mother of your children, since it was she who first received me when I delivered warning of the poisoning attempt." Her small voice didn't carry but her words resonated all the same. The Pope stood no chance against the two of them working to convince him. Teamwork had never happened before in any of her missions because Agents were too few and turning points too many.

Michelle sniffed. *I'm still better off working alone.*

"Naples… will betray us," Rodrigo Borgia repeated, thunder gathering on his face. "I have received a letter from King Ferrante detailing how delighted he is to have Cesare as a guest and how he looks forward to assisting Rome in any way he can."

"That letter is a lie," Michelle said. That knowledge had come to light the day before when Gwyn finally connected to the timepiece and searched for Cesare. Her visions were disheartening; Cesare imprisoned in a tower, Naples doing nothing save for reinforcing their defences. The Pope forced to step down. "You will receive a letter from Cardinal Borgia in three days' time, smuggled out by a loyal servant of your son's, telling you that he is the victim of treachery and any official word from Naples cannot be trusted."

The storm that was the Pope's mood swirled, filling the chamber. Michelle remained calm and stared him down. Here was a man used to getting his way, through charm, threats or bribery, but he hadn't reached his position as the head of the Catholic Church by ignoring useful information, welcome or not. He signalled a flunky. "Fetch Vannozza dei Cattanei here!" Then he rose in a flurry of silk.

Michelle shared a small smile with Gwyn and Meric as they were ushered into a side room to wait.

\* \* \*

"I don't care, cancel their audience; I have more important matters to attend to!" Rodrigo Borgia's roar resounded through the hall and Michelle crooked a smile.

"I think we're finally getting somewhere. Vannozza was pretty emphatic that your warning had saved the Pope and Cesare's lives, and he seems to trust her." She poured herself a small glass of wine and sipped. "Now, Gwyn, I expect you'll be questioned in more detail, so be ready."

Gwyn didn't reply straight away. She sat with her eyes closed beside a tapestry. For a moment she looked as tranquil as the angel depicted in thread behind her.

"Gwyn?"

"Gwyn, are you alright?" Meric asked, turning from the window where he had been staring out at St. Peter's Square.

"It's changed," Gwyn murmured, eyes still closed. "Just from us coming here, the possibilities have changed."

Michelle set down her glass with a clink. "You're saying the future has already changed? What do you see?"

"The Pope in a round castle. Armies around Rome. If I look north, the French are burning Milan. If I look south, Cesare falls sick in a cell. There's more, but..." She blinked and focussed on her companions. "My head hurts if I try look too far."

Michelle handed her cup of wine to Gwyn. "Here, have a sip. Good. This is incredible. I wish I knew how you are doing it but I won't say no to information."

"Burning Milan, you say?" Meric looked troubled. "I have friends there."

"And it's not supposed to happen," Michelle added.

Gwyn looked at her, expression worried. "Have we made things worse?"

Michelle clapped her on the shoulder. "Perhaps, but perhaps not." Her eyes flicked to the door. "We will wait to speak with the Pope."

The door opened several minutes later. The same flunky who had attended them before gestured for them to emerge. "His holiness will see you now."

Michelle led them out, while Meric offered an arm to Gwyn, who was pale and sweating.

"She has had another vision, your holiness," Michelle announced. One glance at Rodrigo Borgia told her he already knew, that her suspicion that they were being spied on had been correct. She was pleased, because it would work in their favour.

"Tell me," the Pope commanded.

Gwyn drew herself up and repeated haltingly what she had seen of the future.

"A round castle... Castel Sant'Angelo. Of course. But you say Cesare will fall ill?"

"A pox, your holiness." Gwyn swayed.

"Michelle, she's not well." Meric steadied Gwyn. Michelle agreed—

the girl looked terrible, but the Pope continued his barrage of questions.

"Does he die? How soon will this happen? Is it God's will that I let my son die?"

"I fear her visions tax her, your holiness," Michelle said, anxious that Gwyn would faint.

"I must know!" The Pope stood and advanced on the trio, eyes fixed on Gwyn. She dragged her gaze to meet his.

"Weeks from now," she slurred. "There is time to save him. But he cannot come here. He must go to Milan. If they don't fight, King Charles will pass through unhindered and come to Rome's aid." Her knees buckled and Meric caught her, holding her upright. "You must send us to save him."

Rodrigo Borgia straightened and nodded slowly. Gwyn's face relaxed and she took a deep breath. Michelle was fascinated. Was it all an act?

"You will send us to save him," Gwyn repeated, her voice quiet but now clear.

"I will," the Pope replied, then a glimmer of hardness entered his eyes. "As soon as the letter from Cesare arrives."

# *Nineteen*

**1493 AD**

"Are you feeling better, Gwyn?" Meric answered, putting his hand on her forehead. "Michelle, pour her some of that wine, there's a good lass."

Michelle raised her eyebrows but complied. "So… that was all real?"

Gwyn shot her a dirty look. "Of course it was! I wouldn't purposely choose to almost faint in front of the Pope. I felt… awful."

"Hm. But you feel much better now? You look better." Michelle passed Meric the wine who held it for Gwyn to sip. She took the goblet from him and rested it on the arm of her chair.

"Don't fuss, Meric. Yes, I feel fine now. It was…" She hesitated. "It was like when history changed before I went to Ancient Rome. Only that was a wave that came and went—this was like being churned in the surf."

Michelle pondered this. "Perhaps because you are playing such an active part in changing history it affected you. You seem to have a heightened sense for the currents of time."

"I'm a history barometer, you mean," Gwyn commented sourly.

"A what?" Meric and Michelle asked simultaneously.

Gwyn sighed. "A weather-detector thingy that sailors use. It doesn't matter. What you're saying is I'm sensitive to turning points and whatnot. Makes sense, I guess. Maybe that's why I can do this visualisation trick."

"It would seem so," Michelle agreed. "I'd love to get you in a lab."

The horrified look on Gwyn's face almost made her laugh. "It'd be with your consent, you know. We're very ethical in our time."

"Uh huh." Michelle could tell Gwyn wasn't convinced.

"So what's the plan?" Meric poured himself a wine and sat with an "oof" on a velvet cushioned settee.

"Send for our things from the boarding house," Michelle replied, strolling to the window and considering the heavy drapes. "Wait for the Pope to receive Cesare's letter. Ride for Naples."

"How are we going to rescue him?" Gwyn asked.

Michelle tapped her lips with her finger. "I'm hoping his letter will tell us something about where and how he is kept, otherwise we'll have to wait until we're closer and you can use your timepiece to locate him."

"Like I did with Meric in Florence."

"Correct. We'll need to be in range but since you've met him, you should be able to do it. We'll scout out the grounds from there and work out how to release him. If the Pope supplies us with a fast ship we can sail straight to Genoa, and then ride for Milan before the French reach there."

"We'll be cutting it close," Gwyn muttered.

Michelle walked over to her and lifted the girl's chin. "I'll need your help to make sure we succeed, then."

As she walked away she heard Gwyn whisper, "No pressure."

\* \* \*

The Pope stared at the letter in his hand then dropped it on his desk with a heavy sigh and rubbed his knuckles. The January frosts had arrived and his arthritis made itself known every morning. He glanced at the scrawled lettering on the parchment—Cesare must have written in haste; his usual handwriting was elegant and refined.

"Father, I sent a message to you three hours ago, why have you not replied?" Juan burst through the door to the Pope's private rooms, Vatican guards trailing behind. "Get back out there and guard his holiness against some real enemies, you blockheads—I'm his son!" he snarled. "Father, Rome is under attack!"

"Yes, I received your message, Juan," the Pope replied, his voice terse. "I think you'll find they are preparing to lay siege to Rome."

"Well... yes. Those cowardly Sforzas and Orsinis and—"

"Yes, I know! And what do you expect me to do about it? Are you not the Gonfaloniere? You are responsible for our military welfare, not I! Cesare is imprisoned by those wretched whoresons in Naples, and you cannot even perform the simple duty of overseeing the defence of our city?"

Juan stared at him, baffled. Then he looked at the letter in the Pope's hand and strode over to snatch it. Reading aloud, "Father, my hosts betray us. I am kept against my will—I shall try to escape. C." He frowned. "Cesare is being kept in Naples? Does that mean they will not be coming to our aid?"

"Isn't that what I just said?" the Pope yelled.

Juan paled. "But, who will come to break the siege? My army can defend the city, but they are too many for me to ride out against. I mean, I can try, I'm not a coward after all. I shall assemble my forces!"

"You shall not! You said in your message they outnumbered us greatly. Most of your army has disbanded for the winter, we do not have the men."

Juan's voice took on a whiny note. "I did not expect those treacherous lords to march against us in winter, mild though it is! How dare they?"

Rodrigo Borgia poured himself a glass of wine and drank it in several gulps. "They know the north is busy preparing for the French. They think their lands are safe with us penned in like pigs in Rome, and they know Naples is not a threat."

"So what are we to do?" Again the whine. Rodrigo hated it. Cesare would not whine, but Cesare had been foolish enough to be captured by the Neapolitans. He growled.

"Must I think of everything? See that we are prepared to defend against a siege. I shall remove myself to Castel Sant'Angelo and wait for terms. We must bluff and delay, and pray to God for rescue."

"Rescue? By whom? The Spanish?" Juan's confusion played all over his face.

"Worse." The Pope grimaced. "The French."

* * *

Slipping out through enemy lines was a challenge. With hooves muffled by rags and tack bound tightly to prevent it clinking, they led their horses in the dark up a winding goat track that led away from the city. There were two unwelcome additions; the Pope had sent two of his servants with them—Giovanni and Bruno—men he trusted to accompany and spy on the trio. They carried the gold and letters of passage required for the rescue mission, but Michelle noticed weaponry and deduced that they weren't ordinary servants.

"Be wary of those two," she said in Turkish to Meric and Gwyn. Meric gave her a sardonic look and Gwyn just huffed and rolled her eyes.

"We're not stupid, you know," she said.

Michelle bit her tongue. Perhaps she had been hard on Gwyn to begin with, but this attitude was immature. *If we ever did work as a team, she'd have to learn to take orders without being a smart-arse.*

They rested at sunrise—Meric kindled a small fire. They stamped warmth into their legs and wrapped their cloaks tightly around themselves. Michelle decided to lay down the law. "Bruno and Giovanni, will you join us for a moment?" The two Italians looked at her in surprise, but complied, joining Michelle, Meric and Gwyn where they were eating. Michelle nodded to Meric to hand them a stuffed pastry roll each. He raised his eyebrow at being made to play servant but she ignored it. He was easy-going enough for her not to worry. "Thank you," she said. "I want to get a few things straight. You two," she nodded at the Italians, "have been sent to assist with the rescue of Cesare and keep an eye on us."

"Keep... an eye on you?" Giovanni widened his eyes in the appearance of innocence.

Michelle zeroed in on him with her gaze. "I don't have time for playing games—let the nobles do that. His holiness knows we seek to help, but he didn't get to be Pope by not including a little extra insurance. You're here to make sure we don't run off with Cardinal Borgia, or with the gold and letters of safe passage. That's fine—I respect that. Since we don't intend to do that, it won't be an issue."

Giovanni looked at Bruno, who shrugged. "Very well."

Michelle acknowledged his comment with a brief smile. "Good. Since we all have the same goal I want it clear that I am in charge of this mission. You may seek clarification when I tell you things, but I need you all to follow my orders."

This drew a less favourable response. "You're a woman," Giovanni protested.

"Well observed." She stared him down.

He grinned but stopped when no one joined him. Bruno frowned, looking at Meric, who munched nonchalantly on his pastry. "She's the boss." He took another bite and gazed at the Italians. "We can settle it with fists if you want."

Bruno and Giovanni exchanged glances. "No, no," Bruno said. "We're not here to fight."

"His holiness sent us to assist you," Giovanni added. "We'll do as you say."

"Good. Gwyn?"

"Huh? What?" The girl started.

Michelle repressed a sigh. "You'll follow my orders."

"Yeah, sure, you're in charge." Gwyn didn't meet her eyes.

Michelle considered pushing the issue, but didn't want the men to see defiance of her authority coming from a teenage girl. *Lucky in this society lack of eye contact is considered respectful.* "Good. It's for all our safeties."

That sorted, they finished their breakfast and checked their gear. Meric had his sword and a crossbow, Michelle a crossbow and several knives. Bruno and Giovanni carried short swords, and Gwyn was permitted a crossbow with the strict instruction not to shoot herself or anyone else unless she was told. Michelle waited for the mutinous glare but Gwyn just mumbled, "Yeah, I know."

*Let's deal with this.* Michelle waited until they were riding again then fell in beside Gwyn. "Is there a problem, Gwyn?"

She read confusion in Gwyn's eyes. "With what? The timeline?"

"No, with you following my orders."

"Oh." Confusion gave way to melancholy. "No, I'm just... Never mind."

"Tell me."

Gwyn eyed Michelle dubiously. "I'm nervous about meeting Cesare again, if you really must know. I told you he's not a nice guy."

*Oh!* She remembered what Gwyn had said about Cesare threatening her, about Vlad attacking during her time in Wallachia. Anger surged in Michelle. "I will not let him touch you, I promise, Gwyn."

"Thanks," Gwyn mumbled. "Just wish I could protect myself."

Before Michelle could reply Gwyn kicked her horse and trotted ahead to ride with Meric. Michelle rubbed her chin, frowning. *She should just be grateful I'm around to protect her.*

She shrugged off the thought and concentrated on riding instead.

\* \* \*

Seven days riding took them far from the armies milling around Rome. They followed the coast road—fishing villages clung precariously to the steep cliffs that fell away to their right. The afternoon before they were due to reach Naples, the weather changed. What had been a pleasant and sunny winter's day turned into roiling grey clouds and gusts of wind. Birds flew to roost and insects went quiet. Michelle pulled her cloak tightly around her.

"Let us find a place to camp." Meric sat forward on his horse, examining the sky. "Looks like rain or even a storm."

The others nodded and the group kicked their mounts into a trot. "There are hills to our left," Bruno shouted above the rising wind. "We will be less exposed there."

They left the road and made for the low, tree-covered hills. They were part-way there when a crack of thunder split the air. Horses whinnied and reared, and Michelle's feet slipped from the stirrups. Unable to restrain her horse, she yelped as the gelding took off and bolted towards the trees.

Trying to regain her stirrups was useless—the metal bounced about as if possessed. Rather than be jolted off backwards Michelle dove forward and wrapped her arms around the horse's neck. Her breath came hot as her face pressed into the animal's mane and the scent of horse sweat filled her nostrils; the pommel dug into her belly. Peeking forward revealed trees leaping up at a terrifying rate. If the horse stumbled and she was thrown she would break her neck.

"Woah!" A shout came from her left. A hand appeared and grabbed the reins, pulling hard. "Woah!" The rider used their weight to slow her mount and together they dropped from a gallop to a trot, to a jolting walk.

"Whew!" Michelle's rescuer said. "Holy shit, that was insane." It was Gwyn, sweating and looking terrified and exhilarated. She blew loose strands of hair from her face. "Are you okay?"

Michelle pushed herself upright carefully and held on tightly to the pommel. Hoof beats sounded as the men caught up to them.

"Michelle, are you alright?" Meric called, looking anxious.

"I'm fine." She sounded braver than she felt. "Let's get under cover." A fat raindrop spattered on her face. She wiped it away quickly, not wanting it to be mistaken for a tear, and scuffled for her stirrups.

Meric led the way and found an overhang big enough for the five of them. He and Gwyn picketed the horses under the shelter of several large trees, while Michelle and the Italians grabbed the saddlebags and got under cover.

The storm passed but the night remained blustery. Gwyn rolled herself up next to Meric and the old soldier smiled as he dragged a blanket over them both. The Italians sat next to the fire, feeding it wood even as the wind tried to blow it out, and Michelle lay quietly, thinking.

Family was something she'd never had. She has always been self-sufficient, worked hard and any patronage she'd received in the Time-Space Agency had been earnt on merit. She worked solo, and liked it that way.

But Gwyn and Meric had been useful in the last few weeks, both as travel companions and in the mission to right history. Yes, Gwyn had botched it in the first place but Michelle had to credit what the girl had achieved with no guidance, no training, and no support. Multiple missions in a row were not recommended even for experienced Agents, and Gwyn had gone from Masada to Transylvania, to Ancient Rome, to this time, and not done too badly. Yes, she was immature, but her talent at seeing timelines was unique, and she had successfully handled the Pope—a cynical, ruthless man—with quiet confidence. And to gallop after her like that took courage, perhaps the same kind of courage that had helped her succeed in those other times.

"Stop snoring, Meric," Michelle heard Gwyn mutter. She looked at the pair, companionable as siblings, and tried to ignore the hollowness that lay heavy on her heart.

# *Twenty*

**1493 AD**

Cesare lay on his bed, seemingly asleep. He had once been told that he possessed the rare skill of utter stillness when he chose to be inactive. It made up for the energy he displayed when he moved about, the observer had chuckled. Cesare couldn't remember who had said it—a tutor at university, perhaps, or a friend. Not that it mattered. He felt that stillness imbue his body while his mind remained wide awake.

*Whoresons! Bastards!* The slurs were unsatisfying. He couldn't insult the breeding of King Ferrante, nor his son Alfonso—their lineage was older and more royal than a Borgia ever would be. But breeding was of no import—what mattered was that he, Cesare, had been outwitted by a senile old man and his loud-mouthed son.

*How to escape?* His father would be so disappointed at Cesare's stupidity. What stung even more was that Cardinal Sforza had been right. Naples cared not for Borgia interests—Alfonso had laughed in Cesare's face when he aired a veiled threat of harm to the Lady Sancha. *He brays like a donkey,* Cesare thought bitterly. And when he floated the prospect of marriage to Lucretia by one of Alfonso's sons, the Prince shouted to his deaf father, "He wants to exchange one soiled bastard for the other, Father!" and the whole court had laughed.

Cesare fumed. His fingers twitched, the only movement aside from the rise and fall of his chest. When he'd arrived in Naples over a month ago he had been confident. Now—while he refused to give in to despair—he railed helplessly. Had his letter even reached Rome? Would his father send help, demand Cesare's release? Or would he be so furious and disappointed with his son's failure he would leave him to rot, just as Lucretia wasted away in Giovanni Sforza's clutches?

*Tap. Tap. Tap.* A stupid bird at the window. Cesare kept the shutters closed. He preferred the darkness to suit his mood.

*Tap. Tap. Tap.* His eyes flicked open. The noise came not from the window, but the door. His guard never tapped politely, instead he hammered on the door with the delicacy of a battering ram. Cesare lifted himself from his repose and crept over to the door. It rattled. There was a bolt on either side and he kept the inner one drawn so they couldn't sneak in and stab him in his sleep.

"Cardinal Borgia? Are you in there?" The whisper was female and somehow familiar.

"He had bloody better be. I don't fancy searching every bloody tower." Another voice sounded—also female but irate.

"Who's there?" he demanded.

"Shh! We've been sent by your father to rescue you." It was the first voice again. "The door seems to be stuck."

Cesare hesitated. If it was a ruse to murder him it was rather elaborate. Poison in his food would be simpler, and he couldn't guard against that. What danger could two women pose? He slid back the bolt and stepped back. "It's open now."

The door swung in. His eyes widened. It was the girl, Gwynia, the one who had foretold the future for him. "You!" He lunged forward to snatch her wrist.

The second woman stepped in front and blocked his hand, grabbing his arm and forcing him backwards into the room and away from Gwynia, who looked frightened. "You don't touch her," the woman said. She shared features with the girl; the same nose, tilt of the chin, dark eyes. But her skin was as dark as a peasant's and her expression was fierce.

"Take your hand off me!"

She released him. "I'm Michelle, Gwyn you know. We're here to rescue you—your father sent us."

"Don't be ridiculous." Cesare sneered. "Why would my father send a pair of whores to free me? This is a poor joke of Alfonso's."

Gwynia pulled a squashed scroll from her bodice and handed it to Cesare. "He wrote this to you. We have some men arranging a ship but we must go quickly before your guard returns."

Cesare took the scroll with a frown, examining the seal—it looked real—before breaking it and scanning the contents.

*My son,*

*A seer has come to me with visions of the future. Your mother vouches for her identity and says she warned you of the poisoning attempt by the Cardinals. She and her companions brought me word of your imprisonment three days before I received your letter. I am thus convinced they speak the truth and I have sent them to ensure your release by whatever means necessary.*

*But do not hasten back to Rome directly. We are under siege and your presence here will serve no good purpose. Instead, you must go to Charles of France and negotiate passage for him through Milan and Florence. In return for this diplomacy and my blessing on his campaign against Naples I wish you to bring about his assistance in quelling our enemies in the Campagna. The seer and her companions will assist you, as will two servants of mine I have ordered to accompany them to ensure their trustworthiness.*

*This mission will take all your diplomatic skill and intelligence. Do not fail me as you have in Naples.*

*God's blessings on you, my son.*

Rodrigo Borgia had signed his name with a flourish and marked the date. Cesare knew his father's hand, but even if a scribe had taken dictation the tone WAS unmistakable. Direct and lacking in affection, with none of the charm reserved for political allies and opponents. *Am I such a failure, Father?* After all he had achieved in the north, he was to undo his good work because of treachery in the south.

Cesare had never been one to shirk a challenge. He gripped the parchment until it scrunched in his fist. "I shall get my cloak," he said. "We will discuss this on the road." How these women had gained entrance and tricked the guard away he did not know, but a Borgia took every opportunity presented him.

"Actually, wear this cloak." The woman called Michelle handed him a beautiful black cloak, complete with hood threaded with gold and fastened with an ivory brooch. It was something a prince would wear. Cesare looked at it and began to chuckle.

"So I'm to be Alfonso?"

"Yep. And Gwyn and I are your lady companions joining you for a seedy night out. But I warn you," Michelle looked Cesare straight in the eye, the way no lady should look at a Cardinal, "don't try anything inappropriate, or I'll break your fingers."

He was appalled. "You know who I am!"

Michelle smiled. "I do. That's why you're being rescued. But you follow my lead, and you don't touch Gwyn."

Cesare clenched his jaw and gave a stiff nod. He swiftly gathered his purse, knife and several other items into a bundle, swung Alfonso's cloak onto his shoulders and raised the hood. "Let us go."

\* \* \*

"I know this thing helps," Gwyn said, waving her left hand with the timepiece in it, "but why do guards always fall for the 'this woman is a prostitute, therefore can't possibly be any danger'?"

Michelle eyed her as they picked up the pace through the streets and laneways down to the docks. "You sound as if you've done this before?"

Gwyn felt her face grow warm. "Once," she muttered. Between them, Cesare looked sidelong at her and she blushed even more.

"Well, men throughout most of human history tend to underestimate women, and the moment you add sex into the mix their thinking goes south. Look, there's Meric."

Cesare halted. "This has gone far enough. You were sent by my father, that I accept, but I shall dictate the terms of our escape from here on."

Gwyn looked at Michelle in panic. "Umm."

Michelle cocked her head. "Your eminence," she drawled, "your father sent us not just to extract you, but to escort you to Genoa. I'll advise you of the rest of his plan on the ship."

"Ship?"

"You are a valuable hostage to Naples. Escape by horseback is unfeasible. We need to leave before they discover you are gone, and we are leaving by ship." Michelle bowed slightly and gestured with one hand. "After you."

Gwyn expected Cesare to blow up in a temper but he appraised Michelle as if weighing up an opponent, gave a cold half-smile and offered his arm. "I would offer you my other arm, signorita," he told Gwyn, "but I like my fingers unbroken."

She frowned and reddened again, choosing not to answer. "Meric!" she called.

Her friend looked relieved and hastened towards her. "Hurry, the captain won't wait. Tide has already turned. Your eminence." He nodded at Cesare, who nodded back regally, Michelle smirked beside him as she rested her hand lightly on the inside of his elbow.

They strode down the dock to a gangplank manned by two weathered-looking sailors. "Last on? Lift it up, lads!" The captain stood by the rail, accepting a heavy purse from Bruno who hovered nearby.

"We haven't told him who you are," Michelle murmured to Cesare, who nodded.

*Does she always gravitate to ruthless bastards?* Gwyn eyed the pair, relieved that Michelle was here to handle Cesare but ashamed that she was so jittery around him. *I've got to be wary. I'm not as good at this whole business as I thought I was.*

"Here, our fare gets us two cabins, but they are tiny so me and the Italian lads will bunk down with the crew." Meric took Gwyn's elbow. "I'll show you where you're to sleep."

It was later that night, as the ship creaked in the dark and the waves knocked against the hull, that Gwyn tossed restlessly her bunk. The cabin was barely more than a large cupboard, but she was grateful it was night so she could lie down and better fight the mild nausea that plagued her.

"Can't sleep?" Michelle's voice came out of the darkness above Gwyn.

"Sorry. I get a bit seasick." Gwyn cringed. Why had she said that? Just another weakness for Michelle to mock or criticise.

"Yeah, I get a bit that way myself sometimes. Can time-travel or space-travel no problem, but put me on a boat and bleh. Here, have one of these." A hand appeared over the edge of the top bunk with a tiny pill. Gwyn reached for it dubiously.

"What is it?"

"Anti-nausea medication. Good for a week so you should be alright until we reach Genoa."

Gwyn put the tablet in her mouth. It instantly dissolved on her tongue and within a minute she felt better. "Thanks," she said into the gloom.

"No problem. Now, if you're worried about Cesare, rest assured that I sleep lightly enough to hear anyone come through that door. I won't let him hurt you."

Gwyn chewed her lip. "I did tell him not to bother me. You don't need to worry about it."

She heard the surprise in Michelle's voice. "Gwyn, you told me he threatened you, and history records him as a ruthless prick, so I don't trust him in the slightest. Not to mention your previous experiences with men assaulting you—I'm not going to let that happen to you."

"Why are you being nice?"

"I'm sorry?"

"Look, I know you think I'm a liability, that I'm useless and I've stuffed up this time more than you would have believed possible. You asked Meric to look out for me so you wouldn't have to. Why are you suddenly being all protective and sounding nice about it?"

Silence. The ship rocked and groaned and Gwyn shivered at the thought of all that water underneath them. "Well?" she demanded.

Michelle spoke slowly. "I... am not the easiest person to get along with. I pretend all the time when I'm on a mission, but it's work, so when I'm around people who know what I am—I tend not to make the effort."

"It's more than not making an effort." Gwyn's voice grew heated. "You're nice to Meric. You don't like me—you've made that clear. I get it—I'm not the great time-traveller you are, I've just blundered my way through several turning points. I can't fight, I can't shoot, my plans are rubbish and I know you wish I never picked up your stupid timepiece in the first place!"

The ship caught a cross-wave and jolted Gwyn. Cursing quietly, she adjusted her position in the bunk and burrowed into her blankets. After a minute she decided that Michelle wasn't going to reply so she shut her eyes. Then Michelle spoke. "Has it ever occurred to you, Gwyn, that… that I might be… stars, this is hard to say, that I might envy you?"

Gwyn opened her eyes again. Confusion bubbled in her brain. "What?" she said eventually.

Michelle sighed. "Look, I thought you survived Masada by fluke, and you did well in my time. You have a natural aptitude for time travel. But then you fixed the Transylvanian turning point, albeit in a roundabout way. You identified and fixed Roman turning points in two different times before you came unstuck. You couldn't have done that by fluke."

"But… you said…"

"Do you know how much training I've had? Historical research, psychology, combat skills, not to mention how to use the chronokinetor itself. I've spent years doing this and in you walk and work it out with no help! Not to mention you're brave! I can fight my way out of dangerous situations if need be, but you've had to talk your way out—that's much harder."

"But I get scared! You saw how I was with Cesare. He reminds me of Vlad."

"Yes, but it doesn't stop you from doing what has to be done. How you were with the Pope was excellent. I'm starting to realise that two of us can achieve a lot more than just me alone. That's been hard for me to come to terms with. I'm used to operating solo."

"Aren't you scared I'm just going to mess things up even more?"

Another sigh. "No. I think together we'll fix things faster than I could alone. What you can do with seeing timelines is unique—I'd have a much harder job trying to fix things without you because the history I have recorded on my computer doesn't change as we act. I know what to aim for, but you need to steer us."

Gwyn tried to think of what to say.

"And you're a better horse rider than me," Michelle added.

"Okay, now you're just making fun of me!" It was cruel. A tear leaked out of the corner of Gwyn's eye. She was glad Michelle couldn't see.

The bunk creaked and Michelle's head appeared over the side. Gwyn couldn't see her expression in the gloom but the woman's tone was hushed. "I'm not, Gwyn. I noticed it on the way from Florence. Then you saved me when my horse bolted—that was brave and quite skilful. I never thanked you for that. I'm sorry."

Gwyn struggled not to gape. "I didn't even think," she mumbled. "I just did. I could have been thrown myself."

"Perhaps. But you weren't and you saved me from breaking my neck. Thank you."

Michelle withdrew to the top bunk and neither woman spoke for several minutes. Then Gwyn said, "I am a liability though. We'd never be in this mess if I hadn't interfered with Lorenzo de Medici. You can't guarantee that kind of mistake won't happen again. What if I mix up the timelines?"

"Gwyn." Michelle's voice was emphatic. "You made a mistake. It happened to me once too. You didn't have all the facts but that wasn't your fault. You did what you thought was right. We will fix this, and any other turning point we come across. I can't do this without you."

"Really?" Gwyn's voice was small.

"Really. Now go to sleep. Unless you need something for that too, but I recommend meditation over a sedative."

"No. I'll be fine. Um, thank you."

One final sigh. "Thank you. You're doing well."

Gwyn rolled over. She thought sleep would be slow to overcome her, given all she had just been given to think about, but she closed her eyes and was asleep within seconds.

# Twenty-One

**1493 AD**

"We should put in at Ostia at least, so I can send word to my father," Cesare said.

"No," Michelle replied. "I've paid the captain to take us to Genoa as fast as possible. The longer we delay the more chance we have of being caught in another winter storm." She examined the map spread on the small table. Gwyn had watched her copy it from a holographic projection earlier that day.

"How do I know you aren't kidnapping me for your own gain?"

"Because Bruno and Giovanni are loyal to your father, not to me, and they have orders from him."

"Hmph." Cesare paced—an impressive feat given the size of the cabin. It was bigger than Gwyn and Michelle's but still cramped when occupied by more than one person.

"We will see you back to Rome, your eminence, never fear. But Ostia will be watched and if word of your presence gets out your enemies will try to kill or kidnap you."

"I am not a helpless babe!"

"No, but we can't risk it. Between us you have a seer and four bodyguards to get you to Milan and undo the work you did several months ago."

"You? A bodyguard?" He looked Michelle up and down. "I suppose the appearance is deceiving." Gwyn held her breath. Was Cesare trying to force Michelle to carry out her threat of breaking his fingers?

Michelle gave him a level look. "Don't try me," she warned, then returned to the map. "Right, the French will likely cross through these passes. You need to convince the Duke and Duchess that Charles will be satisfied fighting the lords of the Campagna. If they think Charles won't make it to Naples, they will hopefully expedite the French army through the Duchy of Milan. The best route would be here and here." She pointed. "Then we talk to Florence."

Cesare glanced at the map. "And how do we convince Charles to stop in the Campagna? We're trading one devil for another. Unless..." He eyed Michelle.

She smiled. "Our bargain with Charles is to relieve the siege on Rome as part of his march to Naples. You arrange easier passage, he frees Rome."

"What's to stop him from occupying the Campagna anyway?" Cesare's face soured.

Gwyn cleared her throat. Both Michelle and Cesare looked at her. "Smallpox," Gwyn told him softly. "His army will be stricken in Naples and they'll limp back to France. I have seen it."

Cesare smiled broadly. "Thus all of our enemies will be laid low! God smiles upon us!"

Gwyn looked down. The French army would be as dangerous as a wounded beast; they would wreak havoc on the old-fashioned Italian forces. If they got to that point history would be back on track, or so she hoped.

"I need some air," she announced, and stepped out, heading for the bow. On deck, sailors scrubbed surfaces, spliced ropes, and occupied themselves with the innumerable tasks that filled a life at sea. Meric and the Italians were playing dice so Gwyn amused herself practising the knots she'd learnt from the Ancient Roman sailors.

"Can you teach me that one?" Meric's shadow fell over her.

She smiled. "Did you win?"

He chuckled and seated himself cross-legged beside her. "Just enough so they don't hate me. The only men who dice better than soldiers are sailors—I'm not fool enough to gamble against them." The sailor scrubbing the rail near them laughed, showing chipped black teeth.

Gwyn showed Meric the knot she was practising. "I know we can't here, but once we're back on land can you train me again? To fight, I mean? I know we did the crossbow practice but if we're going to start a war I need to be able to defend myself better. Even peacetime here is far more dangerous than where I'm from."

"Aye, we can train. I'm getting too old to fight but I can still teach you a few tricks. Maybe you'll end up protecting me." He laughed and she elbowed him.

"I'd be happy to be a sparring partner, if you like." Michelle stood over them. Gwyn hesitated. Sparring against Michelle would highlight Gwyn's uncertainty and clumsiness. Michelle offered a crooked smile. "Between Meric and I, we'll make sure that if Cesare or anyone else bothers you, you can break their fingers if you want."

Gwyn nodded, flashing a small smile in return. "Thanks. That'd be great."

"You're handy at knots." Michelle seemed to want to continue the spirit of goodwill they'd established.

"Yeah, I learnt them when I disguised myself as a ship's boy to sail to Pandateria." She told them about the voyage to find Flavia Domitilla and how she convinced the Emperor's niece into blackmailing her nasty steward into assassinating Domitian. Meric shook his head in admiration of her nerve—even Michelle dished out a little praise.

"You showed good initiative. Still incredibly lucky, but…" She gave a rueful smile. "You did well."

Michelle's words should have warmed Gwyn, but a heavy weight pressed on her heart instead. What good was changing history if she only brought bloodshed and warfare wherever she went?

* * *

They put in at Corsica for supplies and to wait out a week of bad weather. When the skies had cleared to the captain's approval they set sail again. On the third day out, the weather turned foul as a mistral wind blew cold out of France from the north-west. Heavy clouds, the likes of which they'd fled from on their ride to Naples, scudded across the sky and the wind blew stronger.

"Storm coming," Meric observed, holding onto the rail.

Gwyn stood beside him. "I thought you were a soldier, not a sailor."

"Any idiot can see those clouds aren't bringing just a light shower of rain. You learn to read the weather for battles—mud bogs horses and men alike, rain dulls bowstrings."

"I'm just glad Michelle gave me something for seasickness." Gwyn watched the roll of the waves—a deep grey-green with white caps.

"It's well you two are getting along. You're both determined women. She's a fierce one, but lonely."

"Lonely?" Gwyn's next words were cut off by a rumble of thunder.

"Get below!" The captain hurried past, bellowing orders. Sailors reefed sails and fastened the sheets, then took their places on the oar benches. Meric followed Gwyn down the ladder. Cesare's cabin door was ajar. As Meric and Gwyn approached, Michelle stepped out.

"Have you seen Cesare?" she demanded.

Both Meric and Gwyn shook their heads. "Maybe he's on the head?" Meric offered.

"Can you check?" Michelle asked.

He shrugged and followed the passageway to the other end of the ship.

"We were just up on deck and I didn't see him," Gwyn said, clutching the door frame as the ship gave a particularly large roll. "It's getting rough, so the captain sent us below."

"Shit, we can't afford to lose him."

"It's not a large ship—he has to be somewhere," Gwyn pointed out. They locked eyes as a thought crossed her mind. "Hang on." She lurched into their cabin and lay on the bed, closing her eyes. She took deep breaths and tried to block out the shouts of sailors and the increasing roar of the sea. She connected to the timepiece and searched for Cesare.

"He's at the stern!" She launched herself upright. "He's going to go over!"

"What?" Michelle was out of the cabin in a second, yelling, "Stay there!"

Gwyn ignored her and followed. If Cesare went over only she would be able to locate him in the rough sea. If he didn't simply drown. If they could convince the captain to put about and try to save him. The vision she had showed the future only minutes from the moment they were in.

The tempest had intensified in the brief time she'd been below. Sea and sky blurred angrily on the horizon and rain swept the deck in a raging pelt.

"Michelle!" Gwyn yelled, grabbing hold of the rail as the ship bucked under her feet. She half-ran, half-stumbled up the stairs to the rear deck and spotted two figures at the stern.

"Get below, ye daft wench!" the captain yelled, gripping the shoulder of his helmsman, legs braced wide against the ship's roll. Gwyn ignored him and sprinted after Michelle, who grabbed a retching Cesare by his collar. He flopped against her, almost sending them both toppling into the ocean. Gwyn threw her arms around Michelle and braced her.

"I told you to stay put!" Michelle yelled over the roaring wind.

"You're welcome!" Gwyn hollered back. Together they dragged Cesare back across the deck, losing their footing and tumbling in a heap.

"Come on!" Michelle took the lead again, heaving the man up. He was a peculiar shade of green; vomit and rain speckled his face and tunic.

They closed the gap between them and the hatch. Michelle fumbled, trying to lift it.

"Wave!"

Gwyn registered the sailor's shout just before the wall of seawater hit, slamming into them and lifting all three off their feet. Gwyn struck something hard with her legs and she flipped end over end into the sea.

Raising her head, she gasped. Another wave plunged her down and she kicked hard against her heavy skirts. She held something in her hand and almost let go before she realised it was Cesare. *Up! I need air!* They broke the surface. Gwyn fought to raise Cesare's head, almost losing him as he slipped. They went under again. Their clothes dragged but there was no way she could lose layers without losing Cesare. *Let him go.* She ignored the whisper and gripped harder, flailing legs and spare arm against the freezing, relentless sea. Another gasp at air. The panic was foremost now. She was going to drown. She couldn't swim with this dead weight—pulling herself up was almost more than she could bear.

One more kick and she thrust her head free from the grip of the waves. Oxygen flowed into her lungs. *Come on!* Gwyn heaved Cesare up before the swell fell away and the surface of the sea became choppy. Gwyn glimpsed a great circle of clouds spiralling above her.

The wind dropped. "Gwyn!"

Was someone shouting her name? She cast about and a shadow eclipsed her view. It was the ship! It loomed over them. If she went under again she would strike the hull when she came up. If she came up.

"Gwyn!"

Something splashed in front of her. A thick, sodden rope. She lunged for it and dragged it under her elbow, looping it for a better grip. Her other arm was still wrapped around Cesare, though the temptation to let go burnt as strongly as the ache in her muscles. She felt the wind rise again and knew the eye of the storm was almost past. She prayed whoever was on the other end of the rope was strong.

*Whack!* They struck the ship. Gwyn screamed in pain as they thumped against the wood. Slowly they rose from the angry waves and juddered their way up the side until hands reached and pulled them back to safety. It was Michelle, Meric, Bruno and Giovanni. They dragged Gwyn and Cesare over the rail and onto the deck. As one they stumbled to the hatch and thrust themselves below just as the rain came down again in earnest.

"What were you doing?" Meric yelled.

"She saved Cesare and me," Michelle admonished him. "Don't yell, get them into the cabin and find some blankets."

The Italians took charge of Cesare, who spewed seawater all over them. Michelle and Meric manoeuvred Gwyn into the smaller cabin and the two women collapsed on the floor.

"Silly git was hurling his guts up over the stern." Michelle coughed. "Gwyn used the timepiece to find him, and stopped us from going over when he made me lose my balance. Freak wave caught us just as we got to the hatch."

Meric grunted. "You're lucky. I found the lads and they said they hadn't seen the Cardinal either, so we were in the passage just as you opened the hatch and a gush of seawater came in. I heard you yell so we rushed up and saw you with the rope."

"Thanks. I couldn't have got them both up by myself."

Gwyn closed her eyes. "Shit, I almost died. You guys saved me."

Michelle smiled wryly. "Luck. I was crouched down when the wave hit, so it didn't sweep me overboard. I grabbed a rope, then managed to spot you. It all happened in seconds—could have easily gone the other way."

"I'm just glad it didn't." Gwyn sagged in relief.

"Strip off and get dry." Meric fished their blankets off the tiny bunks and thrust them at the women. "I'll give you some privacy." He left the cabin.

"Eh," Michelle grunted, obviously not caring. Gwyn was more circumspect and felt embarrassed when she was unable to disentangle herself from her saturated dress without Michelle's help. Meric returned in a dry shirt and breeches, and the three of them huddled together in an effort to keep warm.

Day drifted into night and they dozed uncomfortably, jerked awake by loud thuds and the incessant battering of the waves. The morning brought no respite even though the direction of the wind had changed completely. Michelle went to check on Cesare and reported back that the Cardinal was horribly seasick and she had to dose him with an anti-nausea pill. "Idiot should have said something—then he never would have been at the stern feeding the fish when the storm struck!"

"He wasn't to know you had medicine," Meric grunted.

Gwyn was grateful she had said something early on. The confines of the cabin were awful enough without adding nausea to it. "Will this storm ever end?"

As if her words were prophetic, the wind dropped. Meric braved a look out the hatch and reported that the captain was shouting renewed vigour into exhausted-looking sailors and oarsmen.

"It's not raining anymore. They've still got most of the sails reefed but I think the worst is over," he said when he returned to the cabin. "Where's Michelle?"

"Checking on Cesare." Gwyn continued straightening the cabin.

"Gwyn!" She heard Michelle demand.

"I'd better go see what she wants." Meric followed Gwyn in.

"Gwyn—oh, Meric, you're here too, good—can you two help me clean him up please? It will take a bit for the medication to kick in. I sent the Italians to find him some broth. Meric, if I give you his clothes can you dump them in a bucket? They're disgusting."

The cabin stank of vomit, much of which was on Cesare's tunic and shirt. Gwyn pulled a face but assisted in steadying the man as Michelle stripped him down to his breeches. She handed the soiled items to Meric, who disappeared above.

Cesare groaned while Michelle forced him to sip water. "You'll feel better soon, stop moaning," she said.

He looked pitiful; dark circles under his eyes and pallid skin. "It's alright," Gwyn comforted him, squeezing his shoulder. "Michelle's medicine is excellent; you really will feel better soon."

He looked blearily at her, a contrast from the immaculate and intimidating man she'd first met. "We should have gone overland," he wheezed.

"Yes, so Naples could recapture you or become trapped in Rome like your father and brother. Very useful." Michelle's tone was brusque and her hands not as gentle as they might be. Gwyn frowned at her and took the cloth Michelle was using, wiping the bile from Cesare's face. Michelle raised a disdainful eyebrow at her, which Gwyn repaid with a defiant look.

"I know he's not a nice guy but you don't need to be so rough. The man almost died," she said in Turkish.

Michelle retorted in the same language. "Be careful. Men like him take kindness for weakness."

"Yeah, yeah. Make sure you two look up Machiavelli if we swing by Florence again," Gwyn snapped.

Michelle looked taken aback, then laughed. Gwyn blinked with astonishment and Cesare glared at them both. "If you ladies are quite done laughing at my misfortune you may locate a fresh shirt for me since my escape from Naples permitted only the clothes on my back." He spoke peevishly but his eyes were brighter—the medication was working.

"Forgive us for not packing your trunk," Michelle snapped back. "I'm not your maidservant."

He threw his gaze to the ceiling. "Why did God curse me with such ill-mannered wenches to save my family's future?"

"Stop your whinging and just be grateful Gwyn leapt overboard after you."

Cesare regarded Gwyn with astonishment. "You?"

Michelle winked at Gwyn over Cesare's head. She blushed and scuffed her foot on the planks. "I'm a good swimmer," she shrugged. "Michelle and the others pulled us in."

He bowed his head. "I am indebted to you."

*You were indebted to me when I first rocked up and warned you about the poisoning attempt!* She turned to freshen the cloth in a bowl of water, hiding her anger.

"Well then, we'll see if Bruno or Giovanni have a shirt you can borrow. We can sort out a new wardrobe once we reach Genoa." Michelle took the cloth back from Gwyn and made a shooing motion. "Go chase them up, Gwyn—how hard is it to rustle up some broth?"

"The cook has them straightening the galley," Meric said from the doorway. "I have some bad news, though."

"No broth," Cesare commented dryly.

"Worse than that." Meric ignored his sarcasm. "We won't be making port in Genoa."

Michelle frowned. "Where then? Were we blown off course?"

Meric grunted affirmation. "Aye. Too far west. The crew said something about the Marin wind. We'll put in at Marseilles."

Michelle swore in a language Gwyn didn't recognise, but she didn't need the timepiece to translate the sentiment. "We'll just have to make the captain take us to Genoa."

"No." Cesare rose, managing to look imperious despite his lack of shirt. "We will ride, and we will go to Charles first. We have more chance negotiating passage through Milan if we can convince the French king to appear non-threatening. My man Michelotto is at the court at Milan and he has the ear of the Duchess. I will send a message for him to prepare the way for us."

Michelle looked ready to argue, but then she shrugged. "Very well. Paris it is."

# Twenty-Two

**1493 AD**

"We'll dress as men," Michelle stated. "It'll be simpler, and we need to travel fast."

"That's immoral!" Cesare spat in disgust.

"That's a bit rich coming from a Borgia," Michelle heard Gwyn mutter in Turkish to Meric. She couldn't fault the girl's observation.

"It's practical. Bruno, Giovanni and I will be your guards; Meric our captain. Gwyn can be your page or something—she'll pass as a lad."

"Hmph, you're both coarse enough."

Michelle pursed her lips. They were on deck with their packs, waiting for the ship to dock. Many of the sailors spat and crossed themselves as they passed the group—everyone knew women were bad luck on a ship, and the storm hadn't helped convince them otherwise.

"Here we go," Meric said. The gangplank was down. While still maintaining his dignity, Cesare disembarked with impressive speed. The others followed him onto the wharf, bracing themselves against the cold February wind.

"Gwyn, you and Meric sort out horses and supplies, Bruno and Giovanni—lodgings for tonight. His eminence and I will source him a suitable wardrobe. One fit to meet a king." Michelle started down the dock, then paused when she realised Cesare wasn't following. The others had already disappeared into the crowd on their designated errands, so she raised an eyebrow. "Unless you have somewhere better to be, your eminence?"

He strode up to her. "Who put you in charge, Mistress Michelle?"

She eyeballed him. "Your father."

He narrowed his eyes. "My father is not here. And I will give the orders from now on."

She smiled blithely. "Of course you will. And what would you like to do now, your eminence?"

He clearly wasn't fooled by her polite tone. "A tailor, yes, but then a drink."

She shrugged and fell into step behind him. "As you say." He would be an effort, but she had plenty of practice manipulating arrogant people. She would have to be more subtle now they were back on land and the power dynamic had shifted back to him.

A fresh wardrobe appeared to cheer Cesare up, so it was with a more tolerant air he deigned to consult her on matters political over a glass of fine red wine. They were in a private parlour of the tavern where the Italians had arranged lodgings. A warm fire had them shucking their heavy winter cloaks. Cesare leaned back on his chair and sipped his wine. "So, mistress, do you have a plan for how to approach the French King?"

"I always have a plan," she assured him with a smile. "Approach the French court, send Gwyn in with a message that a Papal envoy has arrived to see the King and voila, you flatter and impress upon Charles that you will negotiate passage without fighting through Milan and Florence in return for relieving the siege on Rome. Your name and position will gain you access."

Cesare sipped his wine. "You make it sound so simple. Maybe I don't need you then."

Michelle propped her chin on her fist. "Simple doesn't mean easy. Gwyn is still having visions. That will be useful for your family's future."

Cesare locked dark eyes on hers. "Indeed it will," he murmured. She wondered what ambitions were rising in his mind. She felt confident that she had convinced him she and Gwyn wanted to attach themselves to the rising star of the Borgias. Wealth and prestige would follow loyalty. It was a common enough tale in all times.

She raised her glass and said quietly, "To God and the Borgias."

Cesare smiled. "To God and the Borgias."

\* \* \*

They rode north and Gwyn was happy to be travelling on horseback again despite snow and rain slowing them. Cesare pestered her for visions for weeks until Michelle ordered him to stop one evening as they huddled around their campfire. "She's not a trained monkey; leave her be."

At the mention of monkeys Cesare narrowed his eyes.

"I'm sorry, your eminence, the only vision I've had lately is of the French king. His cooperation is critical," Gwyn said.

"Charles had better be grateful for our assistance," Cesare muttered, sulking by the campfire.

"It's your job to convince him of that," Michelle reminded. "You're the diplomat."

"I'll need a cardinal's robe when we reach Paris."

"Yes, of course."

"He really becomes a great general?" Meric asked Gwyn in Turkish. "He acts like a petulant child."

"He's got a ruthless streak, don't forget. His name will become infamous in Italy in ten years. And you know how you got that lawyer Machiavelli to bail us out in Florence? He writes a book called *The Prince* about how a ruler should be feared rather than loved. Greatly inspired by our friend here, though historians can't agree if it's actually satire or not."

"Aye, if you say so."

Giovanni entered the circle of light cast by the fire, a bow in one hand, a dead rabbit in the other. "There're gypsies o'er that way, camped on the other side of the road."

"Ugh." Cesare's face told his opinion. Even Meric didn't look thrilled. But Gwyn felt her heart lift.

"They might have news—can I go and talk with them?" she asked Michelle.

"You speak with gypsies?" Cesare asked disdainfully.

She faced him. "Is there a problem with that?"

"They might try to rob us," Meric warned.

Gwyn was angry. "They're not thieves. No more than any other people I've met in my travels."

Michelle was hesitant. "I'd rather you stayed with us, Gwyn."

"Fine!" she huffed.

But in the morning, before the sun rose, Gwyn stole away from her sleeping companions and sought out the gypsy camp, tiptoeing across the frosty ground. She was in sight of the horses and covered wagons when a hand fell on her shoulder. "What are you doing, gadje, sneaking around our camp?" The owner of the hand was a large, unfriendly looking man dressed in a leather tunic and coarse breeches with a thick scarf and cloak to fend off the chilly dawn air.

"I just wanted to say hello." Gwyn tried to smile, hoping that speaking the Roma language would alleviate the man's suspicions of her. "I have travelled with Secani in the past and always like to exchange news." Her breath appeared in puffs of moisture before evaporating.

"Hmph." He didn't appear to be impressed, but did drop his hand. "You are travelling alone, lad?"

"No, I have companions." She almost pointed in the direction she had come then realised it might not be the smartest thing to do. "It's just, they don't particularly like Secani, which is rather unfair, so I thought I'd come by myself."

The man's mouth twisted as if he had tasted something sour. "You are a strange lad. But you speak our tongue. I would offer you food and a place at the fire but we are packing to leave."

Gwyn wondered if it grated on him to broach the rules of hospitality. "It's alright," she assured him. "I can't stay long. I just wondered if you had word of the French army being on the move. You see, we heard a rumour that the king wishes to invade Italy to conquer Naples. Being the travellers you are, wouldn't you hear of such things?"

He stared at her in puzzlement. "It is no rumour lad. King Charles passed this way over a week ago. I suppose he wishes to be in position for when the passes clear this spring."

Gwyn's jawed dropped. "Damn!" she said. "Um, thank you! Um, I can't repay you in any way. Wait—where are you headed?"

"Why?"

"Um, no matter. Just don't go to Spain. The Inquisition is going to make things very nasty there soon. Secani won't fare well there!" She bolted back through the trees and arrived at their burnt out campfire to face the ire of Meric.

"Where did you go? How can I look after you if you keep disappearing?"

"We have to ride east now!" she gasped. "Charles has already left Paris to prepare for invasion. We must catch him before he reaches Italy!"

"How do you know?" Cesare approached. The Italians looked up, mildly interested.

Gwyn squared her shoulders. "I went and talked to the gypsies. Well, a gypsy."

"Gypsies are liars and thieves," Meric growled. "Don't you remember what they did to us in Transylvania?"

Gwyn huffed in exasperation. "That was a long time ago—even longer for you than me. Yes, they weren't particularly friendly, but as I see it, most outsiders aren't friendly to them. I've met some who are decent, just like I meet gadje who are decent or awful."

"It was still foolish." Michelle frowned. "We didn't know where you were, and they might not have been so friendly."

"Look, you said I've managed well-enough with no training, so why don't you trust me a little? I could have jumped out of trouble!"

"To when?" Michelle raised her voice. "I can't locate you geographically if you're not in the same time and vicinity! We could waste a day looking for you and we can't afford that! Do I have to remind you that the Shift has arrived and we can't go back in time? Not to mention you might end up in a different timeline altogether. If we're not physically in contact with you, we can't guarantee that we stay together!"

"And don't you remember when you couldn't do your magic trick?" Meric said. "It might be thirty years ago, but I recall how you said we were stuck after you did a lot of it in a row."

Michelle looked incensed. "You burnt out? Stars, girl, you're lucky you didn't fry your brain! Why didn't you tell me you suffered burn out?"

"I didn't know it was a thing!"

"I warned you about it!"

"No, you—oh. Actually, I think you did." This recollection stopped Gwyn briefly, but she remained adamant. "Look, you said we could fix this timeline faster if we worked together, so let me do more than just spout prophecies and run errands."

Michelle took a deep breath. "That's fine, but you must consult me first."

"I did last night, and you said no!"

"Would anyone mind explaining to me what is going on?" Cesare shouted, silencing them all. Gwyn bit her lip, realising they'd been arguing in Italian, and that he'd understood every word.

Michelle glared but seemed just as chagrined at herself. "Your eminence," she began.

He held up a hand. "No. When you speak I find myself with a peculiar lack of curiosity about this strange situation. Nothing about this makes sense. That she is a seer, I accept, she has proven that. Are you also a witch? You have convinced me that you serve my family's interests but I am uneasy with witchcraft. You speak of magic and of going back in time—is this a spell?"

"Thanks a lot, Meric," Gwyn muttered. "You could have left the word magic out of it."

Meric had the grace to look embarrassed. "It's magic to me."

Michelle cut in. "It's not magic, your eminence, but it is a power you don't understand."

He stroked his chin—his goatee had grown into a beard in the last few weeks. "There is God's power, or the Devil's. From which does this magic spring forth?"

"Neither!" Michelle ground her teeth. "And it is irrelevant. Our mission is to ensure the rise of Borgia power in Italy over the next few years. Whether you think that is God's work or the Devil's probably depends on where you stand politically."

Cesare fell silent. Gwyn noticed that Michelle had not mentioned the fate of the Borgias beyond a few years. *Smart.* They should be long gone by then. She also noticed Bruno and Giovanni were listening closely now. They looked uneasy at the talk of magic and the Devil, exchanging glances and crossing themselves.

Gwyn got everyone's attention. "We are wasting time." She turned to Michelle. "I promise I'll consult you but you have to promise to listen to me." Next she spoke to Meric. "Stop babying me and get over your prejudice against gypsies." Finally she addressed Cesare. "And haven't we established that we're helping you? If you have that much of an issue with the means, we can leave you to it and you can sort out the siege of Rome all by yourself." She crossed her arms and set her jaw mulishly. "Well?"

A small smile played on the corner of Michelle's mouth, while Meric huffed and headed for the horses. Cesare looked as nonplussed as when Gwyn had first spoken non-deferentially to him, then he made a small noise of acquiescence. "East, you say? Charles has already left Paris?"

She rolled her eyes. "That's what I said. As quickly as possible. We have to hurry or he will invade Italy and we won't have any leverage."

He looked at Michelle and she nodded. "Very well. Let us make haste."

# Twenty-Three

**1493 AD**

"Make way! Make way for His Eminence Cardinal Borgia, special envoy of Rome!" Meric's parade ground voice would have woken the doziest guard, but there was no need. The sentries at the edge of the camp were alert and at the ready, eyeing Cesare and his party with unconcealed suspicion. They were respectful enough when Gwyn—dressed as a page—trotted up and presented an elaborately sealed and beribboned scroll. Cesare eyed her critically. *Her bow needs work.* But the guard accepted the scroll without a blink.

"We... were not told to expect a Papal envoy, your eminence," he drawled.

"That is why you may send me ahead to announce the good Cardinal," Gwyn replied in perfect French. "So his grace may have time to prepare the courteous reception he will no doubt wish to give. His Eminence Cardinal Borgia is a great admirer of King Charles and very much looks forward to their meeting, but he understands that correct decorum must be followed."

The sentry beckoned to the other guard. "Corporal, take the Cardinal's herald to find the king as quickly as possible so his eminence is not kept waiting." He handed back the scroll with a short bow. "Your Eminence, if you and your men would take your ease here. I'm sure it will not be long."

Cesare nodded regally and dismounted, his red robe dragging in the mud. They had stopped in Lyon to have it made—a cardinal must look like a cardinal however much he hated the robe and the colour. *Black suits me better.*

"Let us hope my herald does not take long." He eyed Michelle, disguised as one of his guards. She had smudged a dusting of ash on her face to give the impression of stubble. *Unnatural woman. Do not think for a second you have power over me, wench. When we get back to Rome...* She returned his look and swung herself off her horse. Meric and the Italians followed suit.

"I'm sure the king will see us soon," Meric replied. His rough voice couldn't hide his concern.

*Worried for your precious little girl-boy? Are you bedding them both, or just the younger one?*

Half an hour later, Gwyn returned with the corporal. She flashed a smile at Michelle and bowed to Cesare. "My lord, the king requests we refresh ourselves at a tent he has ordered set aside. He will see us this evening and begs our forgiveness that he is inspecting the troops and cannot receive us just yet."

Cesare nodded. No ruler liked to be surprised. Charles would have his advisers scrambling to discern the purpose of Cesare's visit. They would have to guard their words. *Let us hope these fools can play the part.* He trusted Bruno and Giovanni more than the others, knowing them from his father's household, but even they might be bought. He had to hope that the promise of Borgia gold would keep them faithful.

"Please, lead us there," he said to the corporal, waving his hand graciously. "The sun is bright but the wind is cool off the mountains; we would welcome a brief rest." *Don't keep me waiting too long. A king may outrank a cardinal but the Pope has the ear of God.*

The corporal led them to a large tent near the centre of the camp. Cesare sat with relief on a carved wooden chair. Playing the captain, Meric ordered Bruno and Giovanni to stand guard outside while he and Michelle followed Cesare in. Gwyn accepted the wine brought by a servant and poured. Cesare nodded thanks and noted with amusement the girl eyeing the dried fruit and cheese on the table. He deliberately nibbled his way through the entire plate, not offering her any.

Conversation was impossible—anyone could be listening. Several hours passed in silence and Cesare glared at Gwyn when she fidgeted.

Michelle and Meric stood at watchful ease. Cesare flicked his eyes over them. *What a strange woman. But perhaps it could be useful to have her as a fighter—she could guard Lucretia, and go where a man could not.*

He toyed with the thought, watching Michelle surreptitiously. *You could never trust a witch like her.* She was cannier than Gwyn, that much was clear, and not intimidated by Cesare. He didn't like that. Money might buy her for a time, but fear was better. He was surprised she hadn't tried to seduce him—bitches like her usually sought to lead a man by his cock. Perhaps she knew he would never be attracted to her mannish ways. She was brash, coarse and behaved as if she had the right to order him around—something he tolerated from few men and certainly no women. She also thought she was cleverer than him. *Let her. I can have her staked and burnt any time I like, but until I understand her witch's powers I will tolerate her manner.*

And what were those powers? A spell to go back in time, it would seem. Was that what had happened when Gwyn had disappeared— taking a horse with her, no less—in a cloud of blue smoke?

He needed to find out more. His tutors at the university had called his mind brilliant—he would draw out the answers. Meric would be no good—that soldier had been tight-lipped when Cesare had sought to engage him in conversation, joking about the world being topsy-turvy with a woman in charge, and what did *he* think their powers were?

*Humourless old bastard. And my father's men know nothing.* He'd questioned Bruno and Giovanni to no avail—they were capable servants; could fight and guard, be trusted with Borgia business—but they had not realised that Gwyn and Michelle had powers beyond Gwyn's visions of the future.

Gwyn was the key. She was the seer, the witch who could travel through time. Could she travel into the future too, or just see into it? Either way, she was invaluable. But she was wary of him—unsurprising given his treatment of her. She had a soft heart though—as evidenced by her kindness on board the ship. She was simple too—a bit of nice food and kindness and she would be his.

*Not just yet though.* He snaffled the last piece of cheese and consumed it with pleasure. A sudden change of behaviour on his part would be suspicious, but with her acting as his page he would have ample opportunity to pretend to notice her value, extend small courtesies, trickle words of praise into her ear. The challenge of doing it in front of the arrogant Michelle and the taciturn Meric made him smile to himself. It would take time... but he had time.

\* \* \*

A French soldier entered and announced, "The King will see you now." Cesare rose and brushed crumbs from his robes. Gwyn passed him his hat and he donned it.

"Please, take us to his grace."

Charles was not what he expected. He knew from reports the French king was short and ugly, but he expected more dignity than this energetic man who looked like a well-dressed soldier.

"Your eminence! Bienvenue! When my men told me a cardinal had arrived, I scarcely believed them. But to hear the cardinal was yourself, well—let us say I was eager to learn of your purpose here."

Cesare bowed. "Forgive me that no notice was sent of our arrival, your grace. We came by ship, eager to catch you before you crossed the Alps."

"Eager to dissuade me from crossing the Alps, oui?"

The directness caught Cesare off-guard. He was used to the circuitous scheming of the Italian aristocracy. He hid his confusion beneath a practised courtier's smile and reassessed what he might say. Gwyn had told the sentries that Cesare was a great admirer of Charles, and perhaps there was something to admire about someone who spoke their mind, but he doubted it. It left one vulnerable, so it was likely that the French king was doing it to disconcert Cesare. That kind of ploy he admired, and would rise to the challenge.

"Actually, I'd rather hoped to convey our Holy Father's blessings on your venture, your grace, and offer my services in facilitating passage through the Italian states." *There—make of that what you will, ugly little man.*

Charles' beetle-black eyes glittered with intelligence, and he conveyed astonishment. "You come here in support of my invasion? Mon Dieu! How incredible!" He looked around at the generals and other officers standing behind him. "Is this not incredible, my friends?" They murmured assent.

"An invasion?" Cesare warmed to his task. "How can it be an invasion when you are simply asserting your right to the throne of Naples? You are reclaiming what is yours, and I'm sure you do not intend any disturbance to the rest of Italy except to pass peacefully through."

Charles locked eyes with Cesare. "Why would you think that, monsieur? I have an army; armies are made to fight."

Cesare shrugged a shoulder. *The arrogance of the bully.* "Of course, but to have to fight your way through Italy only to arrive exhausted at your goal... such a thing would be a pity. Milan, Venice and Florence make up the backbone of a northern alliance. Do you truly wish to expend your energy on them?"

Tension twanged between them. Charles smiled, and exclaimed, "But how rude of me—please dine with me, and you can tell me what you propose instead."

\* \* \*

As Cesare's page, Gwyn was permitted to stay in the king's tent but did not have to wait on him. She focussed on the conversation between the two men.

"I am not sure my army should interfere in a matter between Italians." Charles shrugged.

"Riding to the aid of the Pope is scarcely just a 'matter between Italians'," Cesare pointed out. "It is a matter that should concern all of Christendom."

"Mhm. When you put it like that, it certainly casts a different light." The king gestured for more wine. The remains of a huge roast boar graced the table, and Gwyn could barely keep from salivating. *I hate being a servant who gets fed last!*

Cesare speared the last piece of meat from his plate. "It is akin to a crusade." He chewed thoughtfully, letting his words sink in. "You would receive his blessing on your campaign for Naples, that is for certain. Perhaps even a coronation there in Rome."

Charles' nostrils flared and his stubby fingers twitched. He tapped a knuckle on his lips and smiled, his wide mouth stretched in a way that reminded Gwyn of a thick-lipped toad. "For a cardinal you certainly know a lot about temptation, monsieur."

Cesare laughed. "A cardinal should be an *expert* in temptation, your grace, so he knows how to resist it. We live in the world, not a hermit's cave. In order to carry out God's work, we must deal in the affairs of men."

"Mhm."

"Of course, the lords of the Campagna will likely flee when they hear you are coming, but even if they do not, they should prove little challenge to your soldiers' prowess. Practise, as it were, for Naples."

"Mhm. And all this in exchange for allowing you to negotiate passage for my army through Milan and Florence."

*Allowing you? Cesare's doing you a favour!* But Gwyn knew that kings were the ones who issued favours, as did Cesare, who gave a diplomatic bow of his head. "It would be my honour, your grace."

"That's settled then!" Charles thumped the table with his fist. "My scouts tell me the passes shall be clear enough for my army to pass through in two days. Tomorrow you shall inspect the troops with me, and the next day we shall ride for Italy!"

Gwyn breathed out slowly. After months of travel it was all coming together. She looked forward to telling Michelle.

\* \* \*

The crossing of the Alps took time; Charles was careful not to rush his army through terrain that was vulnerable in the spring thaw. Avalanches and mudslides were possible, and the icy breeze still gripped the mountain air.

Gwyn and her companions sat by their campfire one evening, the peaks looming in the darkness above them. Cesare was inside the tent making himself ready to dine with the king again; Bruno passed around a skin of wine he had liberated from a nearby village.

"Don't drink too much," Michelle warned Gwyn.

Gwyn lowered the skin with a glare. "What are you, my mother? I can handle a little drink."

"I'm sure you can, just remember if you do ever have to jump out of trouble, alcohol will severely impair your ability."

Defiantly, Gwyn took another swig and passed the skin to Meric. "You said we aren't to do that anyway."

"Only if we're not in contact. If we're touching we'll go together."

Cesare stepped out from the tent. He paused when Gwyn jumped up. "No, stay here, I don't need you this evening. You only sulk and stare at my plate over my shoulder." He snapped his fingers at Giovanni. "You can accompany me."

Gwyn sighed with relief as the two left. "Good. I hate watching them eat when I'm hungry."

"Aye, help me with the fire, then—we'll get this rabbit cooking." Meric brandished the carcass he'd just finished gutting. Gwyn sharpened a long stick to skewer it with.

A couple of Swiss mercenaries passed near their fire, talking loudly. "These French are soft. We should sack Milan and Florence too. Imagine the booty!"

"There are easier pickings further south, they say. We'll get paid, don't worry."

The first mercenary noticed their group. "Look, here are some Italians! Even softer cocks than the French—traitors to their own kind!"

Bruno growled, but Michelle put out a warning hand.

"Just ignore them," Meric ordered.

"Too soft to even defend their honour." One mercenary spat on the fire.

"Mercenary scum like you shouldn't speak of honour," Bruno snarled.

"I've got honour… and balls!" The first mercenary cupped his crotch and grinned. "Why don't you show me yours?"

"Fuck off," snapped Michelle, rising to her feet. "You want a fight, I'll give you one, but if all you're going to do is start a pissing contest, take it somewhere else."

Gwyn choked on her rabbit. She spat out the mouthful and clutched the stick the meat was on. There was no way she wanted to get into a fight with a couple of soldiers. Her hand-to-hand combat training with Meric and Michelle had ceased once they joined Charles' army—they didn't want to attract attention.

Michelle's challenge worked. The Swiss grumbled several incoherent insults then decided two against four weren't the odds they wanted and stomped away.

"Idiots." Michelle sat back down on her log.

"We could have taken them," Bruno muttered.

"I'm sure you could have," Meric said. "But whoresons like them aren't worth the broken wrist or cracked skull you might get for your trouble. I'm sure we'll see our share of fighting soon, despite negotiations."

They would, Gwyn realised, heart sinking. They might save Milan and Florence from the carnage of war, but the rest of Italy was about to get ugly.

# Twenty-Four

**1493 AD**

"You told me to fight the French!" The Duchess of Milan's voice was strident. Her attractive face was scrunched in fury, and Cesare didn't blame her.

"That was then, this is now," he commented dryly, unmoved by her outburst. "I'm here to negotiate the best possible arrangement for Milan, which is to permit free passage of Charles' army through your lands. In exchange, no violence will be committed on your people."

"Yet he expects us to feed and supply his army!" Isabella snapped.

Cesare shrugged. "Armies are expensive. Think of this as an investment, rather than expenditure." He looked around the chamber, redecorated since Il Moro's death, and had to admit that power suited Isabella well. Her dress was red and gold, glinting in the sunlight that splashed through the high glass windows. The subtle tones of the wall tapestries accentuated her colour choices—Cesare suspected it was deliberate and silently applauded her taste.

"I'm curious, Cardinal Borgia, what caused this change of political position." She appeared to be calming down, but the flush on her creamy skin showed that anger still simmered.

He bowed. "The politics of necessity, my lady."

"And what of your friendship and familial ties with Naples?"

Cesare gave her a smile. "Never fear, your grace, I have not forgotten Naples. By gaining the ear of King Charles, I am in the best position to influence him. In return for negotiating passage through Milan and

Florence, his army will lift the siege of Rome, thus wearing themselves out fighting, from which point I will dissuade him from advancing further south. It is a simple plan."

She rose from her chair—the Duke's chair, Cesare noted—and paced, tapping her hand in agitation. "And what happens when the French wish to return north? Am I to pay for the privilege of hosting them again?"

Cesare leant forward. "They will be weakened by that time. Milan may do as it pleases, then."

"We must be grateful for that."

"Your grace—where is your husband the Duke, by the way? You seem to think I am acting against your interests. Let us not forget that it was I that restored you to your rightful position of honour and, it would seem, power."

Isabella looked at him sharply. "I think you act in your own interests, Cardinal Borgia."

*She is a quick student.* He bowed rather than answer.

"My husband the Duke is… out inspecting our soldiers. Michelotto is with him."

*Ah.* Cesare had wondered. He wanted a report from his servant. "It is pleasing to see you are handling things in the Duke's absence." *I imagine she encourages that absence.*

"He will see you upon his return. But no doubt you wish to return to Charles quickly, so let us discuss the terms of his army's presence in my Duchy."

Cesare bowed again. "Let us indeed."

\* \* \*

"So you used to run this joint, Meric?" Michelle lounged in the courtyard, tapping a knife against the stone walls. She watched the main doorway where Cesare had disappeared. Bruno and Giovanni accompanied him as guards, Gwyn once again his page.

"Ssh." Meric glared at her. "I'm hoping no one will recognise me. It'll raise questions."

"You've got a helmet on. Besides, who looks at the guards?"

"Other guards," Meric muttered, "if they're doing their job correctly. Things have obviously slackened in the months since I've been gone."

Michelle tossed the knife in the air and caught it. "I'm sure we'll be out of here soon. Charles is impatient and Cesare knows that. He'll want to work fast or the king might decide to invade rather than wait for an invitation."

Hoofbeats clattered on stone and several riders entered the courtyard. A garishly dressed young man dismounted and swept back his cloak with a flourish. "Nothing like a springtime hunt, eh, Michelotto?"

His companion, a short, wiry man, answered, "Aye, your grace," and followed the Duke into the castle. The other riders collected the reins of the now riderless horses and turned to go. Their captain spotted Meric and Michelle. He hesitated.

"And who are you, signors?"

Meric didn't reply. Michelle shot him a puzzled glance then answered, "Guards for his eminence, Cardinal Borgia, signor."

The captain stared hard at her, then Meric. "By the Virgin's cloak, it's the captain! And... and you are that—"

"Filippo!" Meric's voice rang out. "As you were!"

The captain, Filippo, paused, then his lip curled. "You're not captain here anymore, Meric, I am. And I have some questions for you."

Michelle was on her feet. "You have more important duties, captain, such as seeing to the Duke's horses and men. You'd best get to them right away." She loaded her tone with authority and conviction, hoping the power of the timepiece was enough to dissuade Filippo.

The hatred in his glare told her it wasn't. Perhaps he was one of those people naturally resistant to the subtle influence of the chronokinetor. "Seize that... that monstrosity!" he yelled, pointing at her. His men looked at each other, evidently puzzled by the description, but two of them dismounted and advanced towards her all the same.

Michelle drew her second knife. "We are the personal guards of His Eminence Cardinal Cesare Borgia, son of His Holiness Pope Alexander VI, emissary of King Charles VIII of France."

This gave the guards pause. Filippo, focused as he was on Meric, had no such compunction about attacking a servant of a Cardinal.

"Disgusting sodomite!" he hissed, spurring his horse towards Meric and drawing his sword.

It was a large courtyard, but even so, it was not enough space for Filippo's mount to gain much speed before he was upon Meric. Michelle watched as Meric side-stepped the attack, unclipping his cloak and whirling it around his forearm.

Filippo wheeled his horse, but Meric rushed him, thumping into the side of the animal and hauling Filippo off. They fell in an ungainly heap and the sword clattered onto the paving stones.

"Pull your head in, Filippo!" Meric landed a solid punch on the other man's jaw.

"Traitor! You'll burn in hell for your sins!"

The other two guards grabbed Michelle. She kicked one in the kneecap and the other in the groin. The first staggered while the second grunted and sank to his knees, clutching himself.

The remaining guards rode forward to intervene, and Michelle didn't like their chances when two voices rang out.

"What the devil?"

"Cease this violence at once!" An imperious young woman stood beside Cesare, richly dressed and furious. Everyone froze except for Filippo, who lunged for his sword and swung it high. Meric fumbled at his sword belt, too slow to draw.

Michelle dived, rolled and swept her leg around in a powerful kick that knocked Filippo's feet from under him and sent him crashing to the ground. She was up in a flash and stomped hard on his wrist, which crunched. Filippo released the sword with an agonised scream.

"My apologies, my lady, my lord," Michelle bowed. "This man attacked us unprovoked and we were forced to defend ourselves."

"You mangy b—"

"Silence!" the woman yelled. Michelle saw Gwyn hovering anxiously behind Cesare.

"Forgive me, your grace," Cesare intervened. "I will get to the bottom of this and punish them for brawling. It is most unbecoming behaviour for a cardinal's guard." His eyebrows knit together and his dark eyes were cold.

"You should dismiss such ruffians from your service," the Duchess spat. Cesare's lips tightened.

"I shall deal with them, I said. Now I do not wish to monopolise your time, especially as I see the Duke has just returned. Perhaps you would allow me to speak with my servant, Michelotto?"

The Duchess didn't appear to like being told what to do either, but either she was less practised at getting her way, or she was wary of pushing Cesare too far. "I cannot spare him," she said sulkily.

Cesare bowed. "I'm glad to hear he is of such service to you. Please excuse me—I must return to Charles."

Their horses entered the courtyard, led by grooms. Michelle grabbed the reins of Cesare's mount and led it to him, keeping an eye on the silent but furious Filippo, clutching his wrist. When they were all ahorse Michelle glanced back at the Duchess, who regarded Cesare through narrowed eyes before turning and sweeping back into the castle. As they rode out, a servant pressed a letter into Gwyn's hand. Michelle nudged her horse up beside her.

"What's that?"

"No idea," Gwyn replied. She peered at it. "It's addressed to him." She nodded at Cesare, who rode up front with Bruno and Giovanni. She kicked her horse into a trot and caught up to him.

"Are you alright?" Meric asked Michelle.

She looked at him, surprised. "Me? I'm fine, are you?"

He grimaced. "Damn fool almost had me."

"He sure has a problem. Ironic that he got your position."

Meric growled. "Hot-headed fool would have bought it. Family connections."

They increased the pace as they exited the streets of Milan and cantered along the road into the countryside. After half an hour Cesare called a halt, ordering Bruno and Giovanni to water the horses. "I have a problem," he announced to the rest.

Michelle sighed. *Don't we all?* She noticed Gwyn's face was still apprehensive and wished the girl wouldn't telegraph her feelings so.

Cesare approached Meric and Michelle. "You two could have cost me the agreement with Milan. You almost ruined everything!"

"But we didn't. So calm down." Michelle replied.

"Don't tell me what to do! I am a cardinal! You are a witch—I could have you tried and burnt."

"Your eminence, they did attack us. Completely unprovoked." Meric looked as though he would have preferred to stay silent.

"Why the devil would the Duke's guards attack you unprovoked?"

Meric shifted uneasily. "Their captain, Filippo, recognised me."

"He thought he recognised you," Gwyn interrupted. Cesare spun and glared at her. She quailed but continued all the same. "Meric, your cousin used to be a guard in the Duke's service, before he went missing all those months ago? You told me people often mistook you for him because you looked so similar. Likely this Captain Filippo had a grudge against your cousin, and didn't let you explain."

Cesare pinched his lips and looked from Meric to Michelle to Gwyn and back again. Meric hesitated, then nodded.

"It was a misunderstanding," Michelle said quietly. "It won't happen again."

Cesare narrowed his eyes. "It had better not." He stalked into the trees, leaving the three alone.

Meric heaved a great sigh. "The closer we get to Rome, the trickier he will be to handle."

Michelle snorted. "I know. Good work, Gwyn."

The girl rolled her shoulders back. "You haven't seen him really angry. If he thinks we're a risk or he doesn't need us…"

"Mmph." Michelle rummaged through her saddlebag to find something to eat. "He needs us to save Rome—we'll be fine until then."

She heard Gwyn mutter, "If you say so."

# *Twenty-Five*

**1493 AD**

With the success of Milan behind them, Gwyn allowed herself to relax somewhat as they rode into Florence. However, their reception there was not nearly as cordial.

"No. My father, Lorenzo the Magnificent, worked to unite northern Italy against the imminent threat of King Charles. You yourself, Cardinal, spoke to us of that very same goal when you were here last. Now you come preaching conciliation and say we should suffer to let the French pass unmolested? Nay, to *pay* them to pass unmolested?" Piero de Medici's nasal voice contradicted his fleshy appearance. The broad doublet and richly embroidered collar he wore may have sat well on his father, Lorenzo, who by all accounts had been a dignified man, but Piero resembled a pig that had tangled itself in a tailor's stall.

"Your esteemed father, God rest his soul, was a diplomat, signor. He would have understood that his responsibility to his people would be to avoid bloodshed, and with Milan no longer participating in the northern alliance—"

"Because of you!" Piero cried. "No doubt you convinced the Duke to let the French pass. What a betrayal of all your fine words from before. Never trust a Borgia!"

Cesare's face remained implacable. "I am sorry you feel the need to insult our Holy Father. Perhaps Florence no longer wishes to remain under Rome's guidance."

Piero's face paled.

"You cannot threaten Florence with excommunication, Cardinal Borgia!" A sonorous voice echoed through the great audience chamber of the Medici. The speaker, a bald, ugly Dominican friar with a large mole on his face entered, his black robes swirling around him. Gwyn shot a puzzled glance at Michelle.

"Savonarola," Michelle whispered, a small frown on her face.

Cesare appeared to have reached the same conclusion. "Does Florence not have a bishop to advise it on ecclesiastical matters, Lord Piero? A friar has no place in this discussion."

"God has a place in every discussion!" Savonarola bellowed.

Piero looked a trifle embarrassed. Gwyn didn't blame him. Specks of spittle arced through the air when Savonarola spoke—he had the look of the deranged.

Cesare tapped the scroll he held against his leg then passed it to Gwyn, motioning her to give it to Piero de Medici. She paced forward cautiously, keeping an eye on the glowering Dominican friar as she passed him, bowing and presenting the scroll. Piero didn't accept it himself, he beckoned a man forward to take it.

"Here are Charles' terms, as I have outlined," Cesare announced. "You have three days to consider them, after which the king of France will advance into Tuscany and demand billeting for his soldiers, food and other supplies. If you choose to provide them, no Florentine shall be harmed. If you do not... I cannot be answerable for what the French king does."

"Let the armies of France come!" replied Savonarola. "The impure and ungodly will be burnt out and a new Church shall arise. Yea! The end of days is nigh. Prepare thyself!"

Piero sagged. Cesare cocked an unimpressed eyebrow at him. "Choose your counsel wisely, my lord." With that he turned and strode from the hall, Gwyn hurrying to keep up, Meric and Michelle in their wake.

"He's caught betwixt and between," Michelle observed as they rode through the streets. The people of Florence looked fearful—fewer colours were in sight as sombre dresses and black robes became the order of the day.

"What do you mean?" Gwyn asked.

"She means Piero isn't half the leader or diplomat his father was," Cesare told her. "Lorenzo kept Savonarola in check—that mad friar has been stirring up trouble in villages around here for years. Now he's set his sights on the city, worming his way into the hearts of the people, frightening them with talk of the apocalypse and Judgement Day. I don't think he cares whether Florence resists the French or not—either way it will upset the balance of power there, the power of the Medicis."

"Well, that sucks for Florence," Gwyn observed. "Coz the end of days isn't coming."

Cesare shot her a sharp look. "That is well. There are things I wish to accomplish before that time."

Gwyn shut up and sidled her horse closer to Michelle. "Is Florence meant to resist? Are we correcting the timeline?"

Michelle frowned. "Initially, yes, but Piero surrenders quickly. I think we're alright."

Gwyn sighed. She used the timepiece to look forward every night, but couldn't tell if they were nearing their goal of restoring history. "Haven't things already changed? Like the Duke of Milan—wasn't he supposed to die and Il Moro be in charge?"

Michelle glanced ahead at Cesare. His horse had slowed to a walk as they negotiated the crowds near the gate. "It depends. Historical timelines are like rivers. They submit to social and economic pressures and aren't easily shifted. But the turning points are where the Shift has provided an easy alternative—like a rock that diverts the stream. Usually, these are political events, because only a few people decide them. If the Duke and Duchess of Milan play a similar enough role to Il Moro history will sweep onwards. So many rulers are interchangeable."

Gwyn frowned. "If rulers are interchangeable, why did saving the Pope matter? Or killing Domitian?"

"I said many, not all. After Domitian came a number of Senate-approved emperors, who were prevented from becoming despots. And while the current Pope is no more corrupt than many of the others of this time, his family represents some of the worst excesses of the Church, helping to spark the Reformation." She flicked her fingers towards Cesare. Gwyn followed her look.

"He's the key. Not the Pope."

"Uh huh. And as long as the Pope is in power, Cesare Borgia will continue to carve out a new Italian state, one that is subordinate to Rome."

A thought struck Gwyn. "What happens when...?"

"Well, you were right about withdrawing my money from the Medici bank!" Meric joined them. "The war is almost here. I'm glad I'm not inside those walls!"

Gwyn shivered. It grew warmer as they moved south and spring drew on, so she could not blame the breeze for her shudder. She didn't want to see another siege. She wanted to finish with this Italian War, but they had a long way to go yet.

* * *

Florence did not agree to Charles' terms. The French king gave the order to advance, satisfied that he could finally use his soldiers and artillery. "Have you seen cannon at work before, Cardinal?"

Cesare confessed he had not.

"Mhm, then you are in for a treat. It is an impressive sight!"

Cesare stroked the edge of his robe. "Will it not be a shame to batter the walls of such a beautiful city, your grace?"

Charles squinted at him, then snorted. "Pah, you Italians. So obsessed with beauty and style. The battery of cannon has its own beauty—like watching God's fist smite the unworthy. It is the beauty of power, not of pictures and statues and the like."

Cesare fidgeted. Michelle and Gwyn had told him that after the French attacked, he must convince Charles to give Florence a second chance, with far less generous terms. But the bloodlust he sensed made him wonder if he could persuade the French king to stop once he started. And did he want him to stop? Cesare was curious to see cannon in action. There would be little opportunity on the field outside Rome— cannon being ineffective against charging infantry or cavalry.

He mused on this as the troops drew into lines and marched towards Florence. The assembly was grand. Banners snapped in the stiff wind and the *thrump, thrump* of soldiers in step create a sense of great momentum. What would it feel like to ride at the head of his own army?

He was far better suited to general than his brother. If he were Gonfalonier there would have been no need for sneaking and pretending. Not that he was ill-suited to diplomacy, but an army lent weight to any arguments he might need to make.

He looked around. "Gwyn," he summoned. The girl, still dressed as a page, rode chatting with Meric. She frowned at the interruption, then kicked her horse to catch up to Cesare.

"Yes, your eminence."

He looked her over. *Still makes a better boy than woman.* "What will happen if Florence does not submit to Charles?"

She blanched. "I don't know, my lord."

He tapped gloved fingers on his leg. "I wish you to look."

"You know it doesn't work like that." There was reproof in her voice, but her face remained apprehensive.

He thought for a few moments. "Well, if a vision should come to you, I wish to know immediately. Perhaps a defeated Florence would be well for Rome."

Something flashed in her eyes, then she shrugged. "I'll tell you if I see anything. Will that be all, my lord?"

He nodded, still lost in thought. She slipped back into line and he continued planning his imaginary campaign. A weakened Florentine republic. The lords of the Campagna smashed to bits by Charles' army. Disease and battle wearing the French down in Naples and as Charles limped back north, Milan would strike the final blow.

It left Milan and Venice as his two most dangerous enemies, but Rome would mop up the rest of the Peninsula with ease. Especially with Cesare in charge. He would convince his father to let him renounce his office of cardinal, and with the witch-girl at his heel the advantage was all his. Lucretia would be retrieved, most likely as a widow, and his father would be grateful to avoid the effort of procuring an annulment.

There was still the problem of getting Juan to relinquish his position, but Cesare was confident he could solve that problem. He was far more intelligent than his brother, and more determined too.

Power beckoned to Cesare, and he rode towards it with a smile.

\* \* \*

Gwyn fell back to talk to Michelle. She spoke quietly in Ancient Hebrew, dredging a few words she remembered to the forefront of her brain to trigger the language. "Michelle, are you sure you can control Cesare? I'm worried he's going to get a little, well, enthusiastic about attacking Florence."

"Don't worry about it, Gwyn. He'll do as I say."

Gwyn frowned. Michelle was probably right. She shook her shoulders and tried to enjoy the springtime ride.

Her uneasiness returned as they approached Florence and Charles' army fanned out to take up positions all around the city. "It's like Masada all over again," she muttered.

Meric overheard and cocked his head in question.

"When I was in Israel—the Holy Land—the Romans were attacking the Jews." She tried to speak dispassionately, but a small hiccup of emotion clouded her voice. She blinked furiously, trying to dispel tears she thought she had finished shedding for the place. After all, her friends had survived, gone on to live full lives, though they were dust in the ground now.

"We will be safe, Gwyn—we're far back in the field."

She stared at him. "Oh! It's not that." She tried to describe to him the sick feeling she had at the thought of people trapped inside the walls, at the carnage that would ensue. Meric nodded sympathetically.

"Aye, best not to think about it. Just be glad we're on the outside!"

She nodded unhappily. She'd been using the timepiece the night before, and while her visions centred mostly on Cesare and Charles, snippets of the attack itself appeared and made their way into her dreams.

"We're getting there!" Michelle clapped her on the shoulder. "After Florence and Rome this timeline should be back on track!"

"Yeah." Gwyn opened her saddlebags and concentrated on setting up camp.

When the assault began the next morning, she tried to block out the noise of the cannon but it was impossible. Each boom made her jolt, every crash of masonry caused a shudder. Bruno and Giovanni elbowed each other and imitated her. Their mockery grated. When had they ever seen mass death and destruction? Even Meric seemed excited by the tactical aspects. "They're not as accurate as the Sultan's cannon, but they have power."

"Try not to let it get to you," Michelle said, coming to stand beside Gwyn as she watched the bombardment.

"Easy for you to say," Gwyn muttered.

"Do you think I'd be doing any of this if it wasn't for a purpose?" Michelle asked.

Gwyn's brow furrowed. "What, the greater good and all that? When has that excuse ever worked?"

Michelle sighed. "I know it must seem like that to you. You haven't seen all the projected timelines, all the ebbs and flows of history. Humans spend most of their existence being awful to each other, so in my time, when some of them are being decent, I think they actually deserve a chance at a future. Plus they are critical in the war to come, and the other species of the Allied Planets don't deserve to get shot down because humans weren't around to pull their weight."

Gwyn stared at her. "You sound like you care more about the other species than the humans."

Michelle shrugged. "As I said, humans spent most of their existence being horrible. Maybe they don't deserve redemption, but they're getting it. Or they will if we succeed."

"You talk like humanity is a person, not billions of individuals. You can't say that individuals deserve something just because their ancestors were shitty."

Michelle spread her hands wide. "Like I said, I'm doing my best to give them a chance at a future."

Gwyn shook her head. Michelle's convoluted logic didn't help her detach herself from the carnage right in front of her. Sections of the wall were already crumbling, and it was only noon.

"Come on." Michelle tapped Gwyn on the elbow. "They'll be at this all day. Let's go and find somewhere quieter."

# Twenty-Six

**1493 AD**

As the last rays of sunlight relinquished their hold on the trees and hills, silence reigned as the cannons ceased their barrage.

Giovanni came up behind Gwyn and clapped her on the shoulder. "Hopefully you won't be so twitchy tomorrow!" She jumped and he bellowed with laughter. She glared.

"Shut up." She collected a torch, lighting it from the campfire and stalked away to look for Cesare.

He was deep in discussion with an artillery officer, who seemed pleased to have such an interested audience. Gwyn heard them refer to angles and distances and thought about how much mathematical knowledge had lain dormant for over a millennia. She wondered what the Romans could have achieved with such firepower and shuddered.

"Gwyn. I'm glad you're here." Cesare noticed her and turned with a friendly smile. She paused, confused. Was this the same man who ordered her about and ate in front of her? Then she remembered how he'd been when she first stood up to him—conciliatory, generous—and narrowed her eyes.

"May I speak with you, your eminence?" She eyed the artillery officer. He looked crestfallen at the interruption. "If you are not busy."

"We'll speak more on the morrow, signor." Cesare nodded to the officer. "It is truly fascinating, and I look forward to seeing the other aspect in action."

The officer bowed and Gwyn wanted to know what this other aspect was, but it would have been improper for a page to ask. Cesare put an arm around her shoulders and steered her back through the camp, past tents and fires and the general activity of an army camp. Gwyn grew tense at the contact. *Why so buddy-buddy all of a sudden?* "I don't want to detain you, my lord, I just want to confirm you will speak to King Charles this night about ceasing the attack?"

"Ah, yes. About that. I think maybe it is not such a bad thing if Charles does continue to assault Florence. Not to mention the use of cannon is quite impressive to watch."

Gwyn tugged away and stopped. This was exactly what she feared. "It cannot be, my lord." She stared meaningfully at him. There were too many people around for her to speak plainly, so she couched her warning in respectful tones. "It would be better for Rome if we press on."

A small frown crossed Cesare's face, then he smoothed it and replied blandly. "You truly think so?"

Gwyn huffed. "I know so." She didn't. Florence felt like a turning point but the timelines became vague after that. She didn't think it would affect breaking the siege on Rome, but from what Michelle had said it would likely affect the development of the Renaissance. Cesare didn't need to know that.

He took her elbow and guided her under the trees. There at the edge of the camp it was quieter, and he pushed her gently to sit on a big tree root that scooped its way from the trunk into the earth and out again. He took the torch from her hand and thrust it into the ground, then perched next to her, leaning close. "You've had a vision," he said understandingly. "What did you see?"

She bit her lip and inched away a fraction, fighting the urge to run. She couldn't deny seeing the future—she needed him to believe it to make him act as she wanted. And she had said she would tell him if she saw anything. "I have, but how about I get Michelle? She can–"

"I don't want to talk to Michelle, Gwyn, I want to talk to you. You're the one gifted with the visions. You are the special one, not her." His dark eyes bored into her, and while she knew it to be false flattery, a tiny part of her preened.

*Don't trust him!* She scolded herself—she wasn't stupid. She knew how cunning he could be. "Michelle will tell you the same as me," she retorted primly. "Florence cannot be destroyed—it would delay the march on Rome and the possibility of your father being deposed as Pope is too great."

Cesare shrugged. "Then we reinstate him. With a French army at my back, how can they say no?"

"Not if they kill him, you can't."

For a second Cesare looked wild. "What have you seen?" he demanded.

"N-nothing!" *Shit.* She was getting in too deep. She needed Michelle to make him back off.

He cocked his head and smiled. "Then you can't possibly know. I say we stay and sack Florence. I shall find Charles right now and encourage him to intensify his attack at dawn." He rose and looked down at her, his countenance smug.

Her fingers twitched, wanting to smack the smile from his face. "Fine! I'll look!" He was goading her, but how else to stop him? Meric and Michelle weren't close enough to help.

The flash of victory in his eyes told her she'd blundered, and she realised what she had said. Cesare sat back down beside her and grasped her chin very gently, bringing his face close to hers. "Look, then," he commanded. Gwyn couldn't turn away—he was hypnotic. She gulped and closed her eyes, seeking the timepiece.

It was hard—she was so unsettled—but her practice was paying off. She slipped into the trance-like state and fell hard against the turning point that was upon them.

Cesare and Charles—just as she'd seen before. Florence under attack; Florence opening its gates. Swiss mercenaries smashing up precious artwork; the Florentine council handing over bags of silver and gold. Nothing of what she wanted Cesare to hear, so she would have to bluff.

"I see two futures," she rasped. That was true. "You encourage Charles to attack, and the walls of Florence fall. But his army is greedy. They grab all the booty they can—they are reluctant to proceed south. Charles sees no hurry—he needs to keep the mercenaries happy, and he wants to send some of the treasure back to France. In the meantime Rome falls. Your father hides out in Castel d'Angelo." As she invented she was struck by inspiration. "They bring your sister!" She felt Cesare tense. "If the Pope does not step down they will ravage her before the walls. They call her a whore, and tear her clothes. Your father refuses. He does not believe they will do it." Gwyn clutched Cesare's arm and let her eyes fly open to stare at him. "It's so much worse than I imagined!" she gasped, throwing her other hand over her face and taking short, sharp breaths as though she was fighting off tears. She waited for his response.

"Lucretia," he breathed. "No! I will not let anything happen to her!"

"You must convince Charles to proceed with all haste to Rome!" Gwyn clutched both his hands. "Please—she is such a sweet girl, she was so kind to me." That was true—even though the humiliation of Cesare's sister was Gwyn's invention, the thought of it actually happening turned her stomach. Her fingers tightened involuntarily, and Cesare stared back at her.

"I will do anything to protect my sister." He was adamant. "Thank you for this warning, Gwyn. I will go to Charles at once." He kissed her cheeks and lips rapidly and stood, leaving Gwyn no time to recoil. "I will not forget this." He seized the torch and was gone, leaving Gwyn sitting in the dark, astonished at her success.

*Not bad.* A slow smile crept across her face. *Didn't need Michelle after all!* She would tell her, of course.

Or would she? A nagging thought reminded her that she had looked into the future in front of Cesare, after all this time of telling him the visions came unbidden. Gwyn didn't fancy confessing that she'd slipped up.

*Maybe just leave it. After all, you got the result you wanted. It's up to Cesare now.* Her stomach did an unpleasant flip. *I just hope he doesn't have any problems with Charles.*

\* \* \*

"Why should I offer them terms?" Charles looked distinctly unimpressed by Cesare's proposal. "Another few days and I will have smashed their walls into rubble, emptied their coffers into my war chest, and I will listen to the wails of their women as my soldiers ravage them."

He lolled on his chair, wine cup in one hand, and belched.

Cesare thought about how best to manipulate the situation. "Your grace, you know me for a diplomat, but I am a man of the Church first. I cannot condone the rape and pillage of one of Italy's finest cities. Your goal is Naples, and we agreed that you would relieve the siege on Rome, not burn your way through Tuscany."

"Pah. Are you so squeamish, Cardinal?"

Cesare maintained his calm. "I do what is necessary, your grace, and you well know I intend to reach Rome. I do not hide that from you. But I have a duty to protect the innocent. There will be plenty of time for spoils further south. In the meantime I suggest the terms you offer are far less *generous* than your original pledge. After all, they have now seen the might of your army unleashed, and will hasten to reach into those coffers rather than bury their gold." He gave an elegant shrug.

Charles tipped his cup towards Cesare, sloshing wine. "They have not truly seen my might. My men want a fight. My mercenaries want spoils."

"And they shall have them." Cesare spoke with dark conviction. "On the fields outside Rome, and in Naples. But surely you do not wish them distracted from your true purpose?"

Charles drummed his fingers on the arm of the chair. He belched again and sat up. "Very well. You may offer them terms. But if they refuse..."

Cesare bowed. "You shall raze their city to the ground." He bowed again and backed out of the tent. He would go before dawn broke; ride into Florence before Charles changed his mind.

As for the other thing—Cesare smiled, like the wolf who had sighted the lamb grazing there defenceless. It would take several days but what he had learnt about Gwyn's powers cemented his desire to keep her by his side. A seer was useful. A seer that could deliberately summon visions even more so. Armed with knowledge of the future, nothing would stop his rise to power.

# *Twenty-Seven*

**1493 AD**

Several days after the attack on Florence, Cesare's skills of persuasion combined with the prospect of more cannon fire rapidly changed the minds of the Florentines. Piero de Medici protested that they should resist but he was shouted down and the council threw him out, forbidding him and his family from remaining in Florence.

"See, Gwyn? Nothing to worry about." Michelle elbowed Gwyn in the ribs as they rode south again. Her horse danced back as Gwyn's mare swung its head around to bite, irritated by the invasion to its personal space.

Gwyn hauled her mount's head back around. "Stop that!" she ordered. "Yeah, I guess not," she replied to Michelle.

"Gwyn, ride with me!" It was Cesare. They rode in a place of honour, near the front of the column, but not with Charles himself, and Cesare kept his own company. Gwyn tapped her heels into her horse's side and trotted up to him.

"Yes, your eminence?"

He smiled at her. "Is it not a beautiful day? I have been in such a dark mood of late, I had quite forgotten to enjoy God's sunshine and the flowers of spring." He began reciting poetry in Latin. It was prosy and he wouldn't expect her to understand so Gwyn gave a blank smile.

"That's Petrarch," he finished. "A little-known ode to the coming of spring."

"Wonderful," Gwyn lied, baffled.

"It's the thought of my sister that lifts my spirits," he confided.

*Ahh. That makes sense.* She relaxed and they rode along in silence. Gwyn wondered if she might drop back and re-join Meric and Michelle when Cesare asked suddenly, "Do you think she misses me?"

He sounded so anxious, so unlike his normal, confident self that she pitied him. "I'm sure she does. She looks up to you so much!"

Cesare sighed. "But now she is a married woman. Barely more than a girl—my father was wrong to marry her so young. Especially to Giovanni Sforza." He scowled. "He may be scarce older than me, but he has the sour demeanour of a crusty old man. Would that I could ride to his lands and free her from his clutches."

Gwyn raised her eyebrows. Maybe he wasn't so ruthless—at least when it came to his sister. She remembered seeing them together at the house of their mother and blushed. Whether their affection was innocent or whether the rumours of incest were justified, it was clear that Cesare loved his sister deeply.

"You blush, Gwyn. Have I embarrassed you with talk of marriage?" He lowered his voice and glanced around conspiratorially. "Are you but a maid yourself?"

Gwyn's cheeks felt as though they were on fire and hastily changed the subject. "I just hope Lucretia is safe and as happy as can be expected."

He winked at her and she nudged her horse to the side of the road, dismounting and checking its shoes. As Meric and Michelle passed they looked at her enquiringly. "Thought I caught a stone," she lied. She regained her composure and caught up to them.

"What did his lordship want?" Meric handed over saddle rations— dried meat that took forever to chew.

"Talking about his sister." Gwyn concentrated on tearing small strips and chewing them in between sips of water.

"His sister?" Michelle enquired.

"Yeah, he's worried about her." *Chew, chew.* "Pope married her off to an older bloke and he's worried she's unhappy."

"Oh yes, I remember reading about that on my computer. Lucretia's first marriage is to Giovanni Sforza except the Pope annuls it in a few years." Michelle nodded sagely. "Got any bread, Meric?"

Meric passed it over. "Computer. That's that thing you showed me, the one you wear on your wrist? Different from the time-jumpy thing?"

Michelle nodded, mouth full. She swallowed and said, "I've been re-reading the recorded history of this time. I think once the siege on Rome is lifted, and Charles marches on to Naples, we'll be back on track. Gwyn should be able to see ahead to the next turning point. By taking this alternate timeline we seem to have skipped a number of turning points that we would have otherwise had to correct."

Gwyn perked up at that. "Really? That's great!"

Michelle waved a finger at her. "There are still more, but not in Italy. Once we have finished here we'll have to hurry to Spain. After we drop Meric off somewhere peaceful, of course."

"Oh." Gwyn remembered the deal. Meric also looked uncomfortable at the reminder. She wondered if he would miss her as much as she would miss him. With that, she subsided into her thoughts and rode alone for the rest of the day.

Three days later they neared Rome. Scouts reported forces encircling the city and while Cesare was not privy to all the discussions, he advised Gwyn and the others that Charles was deciding on the best terrain from which to mount an attack. The hills offered many options for high ground, but a battle required flat land to make a charge and having had warning of Charles' advance, the armies of the Campagna had already selected the best position from which to defend.

"He is quite keen to employ his cannon," Cesare said. "That will even up the field."

"What good is cannon in the field?" Meric looked sceptical. "The Sultan never used artillery against infantry—it's only useful in a siege."

Cesare looked down his nose and replied with a smug smile. "You'll see."

Gwyn rolled her eyes. She walked away, trying to find somewhere to sit alone—a difficult thing in an army of thousands. A nearby hill provided some respite—she nodded to the sentries and climbed to the top, panting a little by the time she reached the summit. The vista below took in the armies of the Campagna dotted around the sprawling city that was Rome.

"Peace and quiet," she muttered, sitting on the grass with relief.

"Oh, I'm sorry—I didn't realise you wanted to be alone."

Gwyn started—it was Cesare. "Did you follow me, my lord?" The habit of address was so ingrained she kept it up even though there was no one to hear them.

He smiled apologetically. "I did. I called out but you didn't hear me."

"Oh." Had he? Surely she would have heard. Maybe she'd been too wrapped up in her thoughts. She was sad about the prospect of losing Meric and apprehensive about going to Spain to fix yet another turning point. She was tired of it all. "I'm sorry, I'm a little preoccupied."

He nodded. "As am I. I'm trying to persuade Charles to lend me a small company of mercenaries to ride to Pesaro to free my sister. She has been much in my mind of late."

"Is that so?" Gwyn responded politely. She didn't feel like talking to Cesare. Why had she suddenly become his confidant?

As if he read her mind, his sharp eyes locked with hers and he knelt beside her. She twitched uncomfortably. "I owe you thanks for warning me about what could have been her fate, Gwyn. I know now not to dally and suffer no delay in seeing her safe. As soon as my father's position is secure I shall leave for Pesaro. Will you come with me?"

"Excuse me?"

He took her hands. She squirmed and tried to tug them free. "Gwyn, Gwynia, stay with me. Twice you have saved me from death—you have served me well and I would see you rewarded for it. The power of the Borgias will rise, but with you by my side we will conquer all of Italy!" He spoke passionately. Gwyn tried not to freak out.

"No! Wait–" She couldn't afford to antagonise him. She tried to smile and failed. "Let us just get to Rome first, then we can make plans."

He leant close and whispered, "I need you, Gwyn. Be mine, and you shall have whatever your heart desires. Even if you do not wish to be my mistress, I will treat you well. Your own palace, servants, dresses of silk, jewels and gold. A respectable marriage—name it, and it is yours. Just serve me, and me alone."

The panic must have shown in her eyes because he clutched her close and kissed her. She froze momentarily then flailed and shoved him back. He was much stronger and only broke the kiss to declare, "Do not fear me—only fear if you should betray me. I will keep you well."

"Someone will see!" she hissed, revolted and trembling. "I'm dressed as a man!"

Cesare looked around. "No one can see us here." But he desisted, and settled for holding her hands.

She refrained from yanking free. *Keep it together. Not the first time some jerk has put the moves on you.* "As I said, my lord, let us get to Rome, then make plans from there. I won't be leaving you before then."

He sat back on his heels, still kneeling. With a mournful look in his eye he raised one of her hands to his lips. "I will hold you to that, Gwyn." He rose and with a lingering look, gently dragged his fingers from hers and walked away, leaving her sitting in shock and bafflement.

*Ew. Just ew. How do I tell Meric and Michelle about this?* Meric would want to punch Cesare, cardinal or not. Michelle was just as likely to inflict physical harm on him—Gwyn remembered with a flush all the times Michelle had stepped in on her behalf and ordered Cesare to back off. *What would they think of me now?* Gwyn threw her face in her hands, humiliated. After all their efforts, wandering off alone and letting him get that close to her! How could she explain Cesare's fixation with his sister without confessing that she had looked into the future in front of him?

No. Best to keep quiet and push for a rapid departure as soon as Charles' army lifted the siege on Rome. It would only be another day or so.

Gwyn stayed on the hill until the sun went down, then ate dinner in silence and rolled herself into a blanket to sleep. It would all be over soon.

This part, anyway.

\* \* \*

From his vantage point on the hill, Cesare admired the colourful uniforms of the soldiers and their banners rippling in the breeze. The French in their white and blue ranged on the north and eastern sides of Rome. The Italian forces of the Campagna under their various generals camped between them and the walls.

"They don't seem especially concerned," Charles commented to

Cesare, seated on his horse beside him. They observed the parley parties make their way back into their own lines.

"Italian warfare consists of parading, skirmishing and taking hostages," Cesare explained. "I don't think they expect anything different from you."

"Hmph. They will be in for a rude shock."

Cesare agreed. The chained cannonball would certainly frighten them. He looked forward to seeing Lords Orsini, Gaetani, Savelli and Colonna wave their white flags frantically. He frowned. Caterina Sforza's forces were nowhere in sight—typical of that harlot to barricade herself in her fortress and let the men do all the dirty work, though it proved her to be more intelligent than the rest.

Trumpets sounded. The last of the Italian forces shuffled into line. Charles stared across the battlefield, so neat and pretty, and seemed to be savouring the moment. He turned to his general. "Begin the attack."

More trumpets, this time on the French side. Officers signalled and shouted, sergeants relayed orders. Cannon crew pushed artillery into place, wound barrels up and readied them to fire. It was like the scurrying of ants and Cesare watched it all with keen interest. It was a chess game, only chess was never this deadly, and that offered a thrill that made him tug subtly on his breeches.

*Boom!* The first cannon fired several seconds before the rest, which exploded in a volley like the thundering of giants. Swathes of men were cut down on the Italian side even as the cavalry began its charge. A faint thrumming marked galloping hoofbeats, accompanied by war cries and screams of pain as soldiers bled and died.

*Boom! Boom! Boom!* Now the cannon spoke continuously, spitting death and destruction in a manner never before seen by Italians. Even knowing about the chained cannonball in advance, Cesare was astounded at how quickly they pounded holes in the enemy's lines. *Probably not as astounded as they are,* he thought dispassionately as the men changed direction and tried to flee.

He glanced sideways at Gwyn, sitting on her mare beside him. Her lips parted attractively and he recalled their softness. *What was she thinking, pushing me off her? She must be a maid.* He remembered the first time she had pushed him away. It irked that she couldn't see the advantage of obeying him completely, but he would overcome that squeamishness.

She was certainly too squeamish for battle. A grey pallor crept up her face and Cesare turned back to the battlefield to see what she was observing. The French soldiers were advancing now, meeting what was left of the Italian side. It was a slaughter.

"Are you not going to give the order for a halt? It is clear you have won the day." he enquired of Charles, who watched avidly. The king cocked an eyebrow and frowned.

"And cut short the enjoyment of my men as we did in Florence? Certainly not!"

Cesare felt his cheek twitch but otherwise managed to keep his face impassive. Still, the French king noticed, his thick lips twisting into a smile. "I did say your Italian friends would be in for a rude shock. We take warfare seriously in France—none of this, as you say, parading and taking of hostages. We fight to win, and the best enemy is a dead enemy." He grinned wider. Cesare bowed to hide his face while he schooled his expression. When he rose, a little smile played on his own lips.

"It is a good lesson, your grace. I thank you for it."

Charles made a disparaging noise and returned his attention to the carnage below. Hacked bodies littered the field. French cavalry chased fleeing infantry, whooping with delight. The screams and shrieks floated up and intertwined in an unholy chorus, punctuated by a choking noise from much closer. Cesare glanced around again and saw Gwyn swaying in the saddle, and sighed. "I beg your leave, your grace, since it is clear you have garnered such a decisive victory. I shall prepare a letter to his holiness to advise him to prepare a grand welcome for the saviour of Rome. Also," he leant closer and whispered, "my page appears to have the stomach of a woman, so I would prefer to remove myself and him before he disgraces us both."

"Mmph." Charles flicked his fingers in dismissal. Cesare bowed again and backed his horse enough to turn, gripping Gwyn on the forearm as he passed.

"Let us go." Her eyes flashed wariness, but he saw a spark of gratitude too, and that gave him an idea. Instead of leading her straight back to camp, he halted partway down the hill, out of earshot of Charles' party at the top, and too far for Meric and Michelle to hear, waiting as they were at the bottom.

Gwyn took several deep breaths, then let out a shuddering sigh.

"Are you alright, Gwynia?" Cesare painted concern on his face.

The wariness was back. "Yes, my lord." She gripped the reins, clearly ready to ride away if he tried anything untoward.

Cesare gestured sorrowfully. "I'm sorry you had to witness that. The French truly are bloodthirsty. Will you have a sip of wine to restore your nerves?" He lifted the small wineskin from his saddlebag and offered it to her.

Gwyn's nostrils flared and she shook her head. "No thank you, my lord. I'm quite alright."

"Please." Cesare sounded mournful. "It is dreadful to see you look so unwell, and I feel quite guilty for upsetting you yesterday evening. It was most ungentlemanly of me, and I beg your forgiveness."

She looked at him, startled. He pressed on. "I fear that living amongst the Italians for so long has made me passionate, not that the Spanish are dispassionate to begin with, and I let my feelings overcome me. It has been tormenting me ever since, and when I saw you look so ill up there it crushed my heart, and I contrived some excuse to bring you away."

Gwyn's normal colour returned from the grey it had been—two spots of rosiness bloomed in her cheeks. "Thank you, my lord." Her body was rigid and her mare, sensing the tension, shifted under her. Cesare had the thrilling sense of drawing a snare closer around a fluttering bird.

"Please," he implored. "Call me Cesare."

Her mouth twitched. He hadn't meant to be humorous, but obviously something he said amused her. *Hmm, perhaps humour is the key. One is scarcely frightened of something that makes one laugh.* While he preferred to be feared, he had tried that with her and failed, so another tactic would have to be employed. He tried a hesitant smile and received one in reply. "Lord Cesare," she said.

"You are my only connection to my sister at this time," he said, recalling that mention of Lucretia also warmed her temperament. "I have felt so alone." He mustered the most genuine voice he possessed. "I would very much like us to be friends, Gwynia. I am sorry I have scared you in the past—you must think me a fool."

"No, no," she assured him. "It's just… it's complicated."

"Then let our friendship be uncomplicated, driven by trust and respect." He raised the wineskin again and toasted her silently, then took a sip and offered it. This time she accepted, and he crafted a grateful smile on his face.

"Your eminence." It was Meric, with Michelle riding close behind. "Is everything alright?"

Cesare nodded. "Quite so, captain. Charles has won the day and I must write to my father. Well done, everyone. We shall be in Rome by nightfall." He nudged his horse into a walk and headed towards the camp.

"What did he want?" he heard Michelle ask Gwyn as they followed. He listened carefully while pretending to be unconcerned.

"Just talking about his sister again," came the reply, and Cesare let his lip curl. The snare was drawn—the bird just didn't know it yet.

# Twenty-Eight

**1493 AD**

They entered Rome. Michelle continued her disguise as a man, but Gwyn reappeared in a dress the second morning. Her breeches had been taken away for laundering and not returned to her.

"Cesare said he wants a companion for his sister when she returns," Gwyn said. "I didn't want him to find out we were going, so I kept quiet."

"Hmm." Michelle had exchanged glances with Meric, but said nothing. Cesare was up at the Vatican most of the time anyway, so she supposed there was no harm. He'd been well-mannered towards all of them since Charles' victory. They were treated as guests in the Borgia household, with new outfits and comfortable rooms. Michelle had no problem accepting these luxuries—regular baths and decent food meant he was trying to win their loyalty, but she smirked at the thought it would make her trust him. She wasn't stupid.

"So we're almost there," she declared. It had been two weeks— Michelle had asked Gwyn to examine timelines every day and that morning Gwyn declared that after tonight the future *felt* right. From what Michelle could crosscheck from her computer data, it would seem that history was back on track.

Meric tapped his whetstone thoughtfully, then continued to sharpen his sword. Gwyn, perched on a barrel, straightened her shoulders and smiled.

Michelle continued, "We seem to have circumvented a number of turning points in this historical detour. My data shows the next one in Spain some years from now, so we should be fine." Relief showed on Gwyn's face, sadness on Meric's. "Still want to be dropped off somewhere peaceful?" Michelle asked him.

His eyes had brightened and a slow grin spread across his face. "Surely you still have need of a mercenary in Spain? Mayhap I come with you?"

Gwyn took a sharp breath and looked hopeful. Michelle returned Meric's grin. "Alright, then—if you don't think you're too old for it."

He laughed. "I think we all know retirement won't really suit me. I'll be a soldier and adventurer till I die."

"Hooray!" Gwyn hopped off her barrel and kissed him on the cheek, her skirts flouncing. "I have an errand to run—I'll see you both later."

Meric stayed and Michelle joined him in checking weapons. Then he left the stable for sword practice with several of the household guards and she conducted her own set of exercises and stretches, finishing with meditation.

Now she paced. The stables of the Borgia household provided ample room for pacing, though whinnies from the horses told her that her restlessness was infectious. Meric had disappeared to practise sword fighting with the household guards, and Gwyn had been summoned to run an errand for Cesare. Knowing that the French king's coronation and the subsequent celebration tonight was the culmination of Charles' feting and feasting did not ease her sense of forced stillness.

Should they travel overland or by ship to Spain? Ship would be faster, though more fraught with peril—she thought of the storm they'd experienced and grimaced. She didn't want to waste the anti-nausea medication either; one of the last turning points would be at sea. Overland would be best.

It would be good to escape Rome and Cesare's attempts to woo them.

A church bell tolled the noon hour and was echoed by others nearby. Michelle started—she hadn't realised the morning had slipped away. Gwyn should have returned from her errand by now. Michelle strode from the stables and entered the house. Gwyn wasn't in her room. Michelle huffed.

"Something for you, signor?" A maid carrying a pile of linen batted her eyelashes at Michelle.

"I'm looking for Signorita Gwynia, have you seen her?"

"Ooh, the signorita isn't here, signor. Went out in that fine dress of hers."

Michelle frowned. In a household where the mistress wore silks and damasks, she'd hardly call Gwyn's outfit 'fine'. "Where did she go? I know she had an errand to run, but that was hours ago."

"Aye, she returned, with the dress the master sent her to fetch. Had to dress her myself, signor, and put pearls in her hair and jewels on her fingers." She waggled her own fingers in a suggestive manner and Michelle sighed. The chit was flirting with her.

"What on earth was she so dressed up for?" This was getting painful.

The maid sauntered closer. "For the coronation, signor. The master bid her accompany him."

"Why would he do that?" Cardinals surely didn't bring plus-ones.

She shrugged. "Perhaps as a companion for his mother, seeing as his sister is still in Pesaro. But why do you want to know about her, when she's in his bed for sure? If you're lonely, I'm sure there's some around here as would keep you company." Eyelashes batted again; the maid leant in and pouted prettily.

*Oh bloody hell.* Michelle had slept with women when she was younger, but these days preferred males in her bed. This maid would be in for a shock if she discovered Michelle was not the dashing Spanish guardsman she pretended to be. She smiled at the maid and touched her cheek lightly. "I have a message to deliver, but perhaps I'll come and find you later?"

This time the pout was real. Michelle sighed, kissed the maid fiercely and walked her backwards into Gwyn's room. Then she stepped back and shut the door. A gasp of indignation followed her as she escaped down the stairs.

"Meric!"

He was cleaning his sword in the entrance courtyard, finished with his swordplay. "Aye, Michelle?"

"Have you seen Gwyn?" she demanded.

He shook his head. "Not since we met this morning. What's amiss?"

Michelle paced. "Apparently she's gone to the coronation with Cesare. Why wouldn't she tell us? There's no need for her to be there!"

Meric stood and sheathed his sword. "I don't like this. She shouldn't be alone with him."

"I know." Michelle tapped her fingers. "We'll have to go after them and fetch her."

"How are we going to get in? Surely—"

The clip-clop of hooves interrupted and both of their heads snapped up in anticipation. Vannozza entered the courtyard through the tunnelled arch that led to the street. She slid from her side-saddle, a disgruntled look on her normally beatific face.

"Excuse me, Signora." Michelle planted herself in the way as the groom took charge of Vannozza's horse.

"Sí?"

Michelle bowed. "Forgive me, but shouldn't you be at the coronation, signora?"

"Ha! It seems our dear friend King Charles, while being bloodthirsty on the battlefield, is a prude when it comes to appearances at his crowning. None of the Pope's family are permitted to attend. Even Juan is only allowed to come to the feast afterwards." She sniffed and continued her progress into the house, then halted. "Shouldn't you two be with Cesare?"

Michelle exchanged a glance with Meric. "We were not ordered to attend on him. Surely a cardinal doesn't need guards for the coronation?"

Vannozza was not so inelegant as to show complete exasperation, but her expression hinted it. "I just told you—the Pope's family is not permitted to attend. Cesare has gone to fetch Lucretia. I'm surprised at him not taking you, considering he borrowed twenty Swiss mercenaries from Charles."

Meric's eyes widened; Michelle felt her stomach drop. "When did they leave?"

Vannozza looked down her nose at this continued questioning. "Several hours ago, I believe." She turned and swept into the house.

"Shit."

"Aye, you have that right." Meric's brows drew together and his hand groped for his sword hilt. "Has he taken her, you think?"

Michelle considered. "Shit! Here I was thinking he was trying to woo all of us to stay—he was really just after Gwyn."

"He thinks she's a seer."

"Yes." She weighed up their options. More than feeling responsible for Gwyn's welfare, she needed the girl in Spain. Leaving her in Cesare's clutches was not feasible. "We have to go after them."

Meric stared at her. "Of course we do! But I'm not up to fighting twenty mercenaries, even with you by my side. We can catch up to them easily enough if we know where they're going. We have to find out where the sister is."

Michelle tapped her chin. "Pesaro. That's where she is—the maid told me. And I have a better idea than trying to storm in and snatch Gwyn—that will just get us both killed. But we must ride fast."

# Twenty-Nine

**1493 AD**

Gwyn found it easy to smile at Cesare's chatter—a sense of euphoria imbued her, and after all the death, deceit and dirt of the last few months, this glittering, fairy-tale day was like riding a rainbow. She was dressed like a princess, riding side-saddle next to a handsome prince. She had no romantic or sexual interest in Cesare, but he was charming and gallant on this triumphant occasion, dressed as finely as her in his slashed silk doublet and feathered hat.

*Please, call me Cesare.* Such a clichéd attempt to flirt with her—she'd had to laugh. He had been a perfect gentleman since that day, and Gwyn now found it easy to relax as he gave amusing commentary on the crowds, particularly other guests making their way towards the Vatican for this momentous event.

"It is quite a coup for Charles," Cesare explained. "To be crowned by the Pope, to have his claim to Naples ratified by the Holy Mother Church. Shows the world that he's not just an ugly little butcher, and will make Spain think twice about intervening once he invades."

"Everyone certainly seems to think it's a big deal," Gwyn replied cheerfully. She admired her dress again—silver and blue panelled skirts bordered by silver brocade. A sapphire adorned her neck on a silver chain, matched by a ring; pearls and tiny sapphires clustered across her hair net. The maid had braided Gwyn's normally dull brown hair in a pattern so intricate she would never be able to recapture it—when she had glanced in the mirror it had taken a moment to recognise herself. She had never felt so beautiful in all her life.

Cesare noticed Gwyn smooth her skirts. "You look radiant." He reached across and lifted her hand to his lips with a meaningful smile.

Gwyn felt heat rise in her face. *Don't get carried away, Gwyn! He's dangerous if he doesn't get what he wants.* She and the others would be long gone before he pushed the issue, she thought, but it was safer to play along in the meantime.

"Why aren't you in your cardinal's robe?" she asked to change the subject.

"I'll throw it on for the ceremony," he replied. "I'd prefer not to wear that hideous smock for the feast. Other men may believe you to be alone if I do not compliment your beauty with my own efforts. Come, let us ride this way to avoid the crowds."

*Okay, the flirting is getting a bit too heavy. Maybe I'd better skive off early from the feast if he's planning on making his move tonight. Probably thinks to get me drunk and take a romantic ride home by moonlight. No way, buddy—I'm wise to you!* She smiled demurely and tried to change the topic again. "Your sister is far more beautiful than I, Lord Cesare. Have you heard how she is? Was her husband part of the battle?"

Cesare's lips twisted downwards. "The coward fled before Charles' army could capture him. Would that he had been killed and she freed as a widow. Still, not to fear—we will see her soon."

"Oh, yes?" Gwyn looked at him with interest. He nodded and returned her gaze intently.

"Indeed. We shall ride to Pesaro with all haste and rescue her from his clutches. I have borrowed twenty Swiss mercenaries from Charles with his agreement—a little thank you from him."

Gwyn became aware they were on a quieter street. A dozen guardsmen trotted towards them. All were heavily armed. She recognised two—the same Swiss who'd attempted to pick a fight one night on the Alps. Her eyes widened. Cesare leant over and gripped her arm. "I'm so glad you're coming with us, my dear. Lucretia will be so pleased to see you again."

"What? No!" Gwyn tried to wrench free from his grasp. The mercenaries closed around them and halted.

Cesare hauled her from her horse onto his saddle in front of him. "I'll not have you disappear on me again. You are mine and I shall bind you to me." One of his men put a lead rope on Gwyn's horse and they began to ride.

"No!" Gwyn squirmed, tried to fight, but Cesare's arm was around her with the strength of iron. If she jumped in time she would bring him with her. And... *If I jump in time this close to a turning point I might end up in the wrong timeline.* How would that work? Would Meric and Michelle still exist in the new time? It was too big of a chance. "Let me go!" she screamed.

They thundered out of the city. *It's okay, stay calm. You'll just have to wait until he lets go of you and make a small jump. Just enough for them to quit searching and move on, then you can ride back to Rome. The turning point is only hours away—just let that pass and then make a jump.* That decision dealt with, she threw all her concentration into rolling with the motion of the galloping horse.

They rode for hours. Gwyn felt the turning point come and go with dizzying relief. When they stopped at nightfall, she declared the need to visit the latrine.

"Of course, my dear. But drink this first—you must be parched." Cesare waved a flask under her nose.

Gwyn couldn't twist around to see his expression. "Can I get down first?" All around them the Swiss pitched tents and cared for horses.

"No." Cesare's voice was hard. "Drink."

Gwyn subdued the temptation to knock the flask from his hand. *Just play it cool and jump as soon as there's a bit of space between us.* She lifted the flask to her lips.

Alcohol—was it brandy? Something far stronger than wine. She spat and Cesare snarled. He gripped her jaw with one hand and the flask with the other, pouring it into her mouth. He forced her mouth shut and pinched her nose. Gwyn had to swallow or choke.

"Ugh! What the fuck? Stop!" She threw force into the order. He ignored it.

"Drink!" He did it again, and again. Nausea rose. "If you vomit I shall simply give you more."

Gwyn blinked burning tears away. "What? Why? You're a f-fucking maniac!" She felt Cesare dismount and slid sideways into his arms, flailing.

"Something I heard your witch friend say, about alcohol preventing you from doing your magic trick. I'll not have you vanish." He held her tightly. She fought him. "Stop struggling. Look at me." He twisted her head to face him. Gwyn blinked and groaned. He smirked and beckoned to a soldier. "Escort Signorita Gwynia to a suitably private location for the latrine. Do not touch her unless she tries to escape. If she does run, break some of her fingers and bring her back to me. She is mine, understand?"

"Yes, milord." The soldier leered at Gwyn. She vowed to give him no reason to touch her.

Upon returning from the latrine, Cesare ordered her to sit by the fire and eat. How long would it take for the alcohol to wear off? She'd never drunk so much before. Her vision swam and she knew she was incapable of running, let alone saddling a horse in the dark.

*Wait until the middle of the night.* Would she wake? A yawn cracked her jaw and drowsiness settled on her like a cloak.

"Come, then." Cesare loomed over her. She stared up, apathetic, too tired to even think insults at him. He pulled her to her feet, more gently than she expected, and led her to a tent in the dark. Gwyn thought idly that it was a shame her pretty dress would be ruined, then scolded herself for caring. Cesare's arm around her firm but not rough. *Must have decided... I'm no risk now...* Another yawn.

"There you are, lie down." Inside the tent a saddlebag acted as a pillow and a blanket spread on the ground. Nicer than what the mercenaries had—from what she'd seen they rolled themselves in cloaks, nothing more. Gwyn couldn't help but relax.

Cesare let the tent flap close behind him.

# *Thirty*

**1493 AD**

"You're not to leave." A Borgia house guard stood squarely in front of Meric and Michelle, blocking them from exiting the tunnel onto the street. Two guards stood behind him holding spears, and a noise to their rear alerted Meric to the presence of more guards.

"Let us pass," Michelle ordered. "His eminence sent for us."

"His eminence was the one who told us to prevent you from leaving," the guard told them, drawing his sword. "Now you can return to your quarters, or we have orders to cut you down where you stand."

Meric gripped the reins of his horse. They were not mounted yet—they'd thrown their gear into saddlebags and were trying to leave quietly. *Aye, well—that ain't about to happen.*

Michelle turned to look at him. It was too dark to see her expression, but she asked in Turkish, "Can you reach your sword?"

"Aye, but I don't fancy our odds." The confined space would work in their favour, but six against two with only a sword and a knife... He didn't like it. Spears would skewer their mounts if they tried to ride out, and there was no time to reach and cock their crossbows.

"Mm, me neither. I'm going to jump us out of here, to the early hours of the morning. I need you to be touching your horse and me. Be ready to cut down any guards standing watch."

"Stop your heathen gibbering!" The guards advanced, menace in their movements.

"Now, Meric!"

He lunged for her and grabbed a fistful of horse mane. Blue haze rose up around him and a horrible lurch took place. It was a sensation he'd never forgotten—it made him retch and stagger. The blue faded— the tunnel was dark as pitch.

"Meric!" Michelle hissed from somewhere nearby. He groaned, leaning on his horse. "For fuck's sake."

Exclamations, a scuffle and a sickening meaty thud followed by a horrible gurgle sounded at the street end of the arch. Meric fought the nausea and fumbled for his sword—he knew the sounds of someone being stabbed and having their throat cut. He grunted and drew the blade.

"It's alright, I took care of them." Michelle's silhouette bent over two shapes on the ground. A second gurgle followed the first. "Come on, let's go. Didn't realise you'd get sick from time travel—you should have said."

"You didn't give me the chance," Meric croaked.

They led their horses quietly through the streets, looking out for city soldiers who might arrest them for breaking curfew. They wasted precious hours waiting for the dawn when they could leave through one of Rome's many gates. By that time Meric recovered and they rode hard, taking the road north.

* * *

"Will we overtake them? Word in the last village was that they're still ahead." Meric kicked his horse into a canter and Michelle grimaced as she followed suit.

"Stars, I hope so." Her riding skills were being put to the test—they pushed as hard as Meric judged the horses could go, trotting and walking intermittently, travelling long days in order to make up time.

She dreaded the next question when it came. He asked it every day. "Do you think she's alright?" he asked.

"I really hope so." Guilt crept in—if Cesare mistreated Gwyn, it would be Michelle's fault. She had intended to look after the girl—she should have kept her close. Lulled by Gwyn's growing confidence and the tantalising prospect of escaping Borgia clutches, Michelle had become lazy.

"I blame myself." Meric's comment caught Michelle by surprise.

"What?" They had been forced to slow as the road ascended the Apennines. The mountain range extended north and south as the veritable backbone of Italy. Michelle cursed every ridge and every pass they had to surmount because it slowed them down.

"I said, I blame myself. I know how she was with Vlad—that monster terrified her, as well he should! May he rot in hell." He spat. "I should have kept her away from Cesare. She's like a candle to a moth— her innocence attracts them."

"Wait just a second. No one is to blame if he harms her except him. He chooses," she stated. Except it was Michelle's fault for letting him get too close. She had seen Gwyn's wariness of Cesare and approved, promising herself not to baby the girl. It was only in the last two weeks when they'd been more separated. "Dammit!"

"What?" She had startled Meric from his melancholy.

"He singled her out, he was grooming her. Shit—I should have seen it." Michelle twisted the reins in her hands, eliciting a snort from her gelding. "He knew he couldn't get around you or me, so he made sure he got her alone."

Meric grunted. "We both failed."

They didn't speak for some time, halting by unspoken agreement on the other side of the pass to rest the horses and water them in a stream that trickled down by the road. Michelle dug in her pack for the bunch of spinach she'd picked that morning from a farm they'd passed. "Here, wash this, we can have it with the bread and sausage." She tossed the greenery to Meric, who knelt by the stream and turned back to her saddlebag.

"Hand over your goods and horses and nobody gets hurt." The cracked voice of a filthy bandit got their attention. Meric's hand went to his sword hilt and Michelle gripped the loaded crossbow that hung from her saddle. She scanned the area—four other bandits backed up the speaker.

"Have you seen a company of soldiers pass?" she asked, sounding unconcerned. "Swiss mercenaries, with a nobleman and a girl." The bandits frowned and blinked. Michelle seized the silence and continued. "You can have the horses, and our gold, I'll even sleep with you if you want, just tell us if you saw anyone answering that description."

She had them floored. Initial confusion gave way to greed, and licking his lips one said. "Aye, thems rode this way this morning."

"Rich pickings, but sharp teeth," muttered another, eyeing Michelle. "You is a woman?"

She flashed a smile and batted her eyelashes. "How far ahead are they?"

The bandits looked at one another and shrugged. "Mebbe three, four hours. We came up the shepherd's track rather than cross them on the road."

The leader got angry. "Nuff chatter! Give us the goods!"

Michelle lifted the crossbow and shot him in the throat. She hurled a knife in the shoulder of another bandit before the first had hit the ground. A roar from Meric signalled his charge against two more of their assailants. A man screamed wildly and brandished a rusted sword. Michelle coolly retrieved the second crossbow, cocked it and fired at him. The bolt hit his chest and he died gurgling.

Several solid grunts and thwacks snapped Michelle's attention to Meric. He stood over his fallen foes, chest heaving. "Don't think... they expected us... to fight..." he panted.

"Yes, I was going for that effect," Michelle replied, scanning the rocks and bushes around. The man she had knifed groaned. She walked to him, leaving Meric to calm the horses. "Will this shepherd's track you spoke of let us overtake the Swiss?"

"Fuck you," he spat, clutching the blade.

She sighed and squatted next to him, tapping the knife hilt. He screamed.

"If you help us, I'll see that you live." She held his bloodshot gaze.

He grimaced and spat. "Fine. Patch me up and I'll show you the way."

* * *

Gwyn woke cold, despite the warm body beside her. She inched away, preferring the chill over the unbearable shame the heat procured in her. *Dirty*. And it wasn't just the dirt of the road—that grime would wash away. Through all her time travels Gwyn had missed hot showers, but even one of those would be useless against the bone-deep grubbiness that imbued every aspect of her being now.

Her movement disturbed Cesare—he opened one eye and frowned, tugging the rope that bound her wrist to his. "Be still," he muttered.

Gwyn couldn't sleep. She heard the sentry wake his relief; heard an owl hoot in the darkness. They were half a day from Pesaro—escape would become much harder then, even if Cesare ceased drugging her through the day and tying her to him at night. It was only in these wee hours of the morning that her head felt clear, but then utter wretchedness overtook her spirit and silent tears tracked their way down her face in salute to her misery.

Cesare grunted. "Crying again?"

Gwyn stiffened. He hadn't gone back to sleep. She sniffed and stared at the tent wall.

"Be quiet or I shall gag you."

She believed him. She bit her lip and forced her mind to think of nothing. Sleep must have overcome her because when she opened her eyes again it was daylight and the camp was stirring.

"Up, my dear. Time for your morning drink." Cesare sounded perky. *Probably because we'll see his precious sister today. Maybe he'll leave me alone then.* She could only hope. Rousing herself to escape would require distraction on her captor's part.

She still fought when he drugged her with the brandy. The last time he'd slapped her so hard it broke the skin at the corner of her mouth. She could still taste the blood—metallic on the tip of her tongue.

She didn't fight when he came to her at night though. She froze and closed her eyes and tried to pretend it wasn't happening. Pain reminded her, but at the end of every day she was so exhausted and sore, she couldn't bring herself to struggle. The tiny voice at the back of her mind screamed at her to fight, to escape. The other part of her cowered, shutting the voice out, scared of more pain.

Perpetual inebriation dulled the pain sometimes but added to her misery.

They saddled up and rode. The Adriatic glimmered in the distance, sunlight sparkling on the water. A fresh breeze carried the aroma of brine and the faint shrieks of seagulls. It soothed Gwyn, and she steeled herself. She would get out of this situation. *I'm just so tired.*

The road took them through the gates of Pesaro. Townspeople moved quickly out of their way, wariness very much the prevalent expression. Foreign soldiers were never a good sign. They approached the castle of Rocco Constanza—a squat, square fortress with thick round towers at each corner.

As they clattered over the moat on the stone bridge Gwyn felt Cesare tense.

"Gate's open, milord," one mercenary said.

"I see that," Cesare snapped. "Advance and be ready for anything. It might be a trap."

Even in her lethargic state Gwyn understood that to set a trap, Giovanni Sforza would have had to know they were coming. She stared blankly at the stone courtyard as they trotted in—it was empty. The carved wooden door at the top of three wide steps stood open.

"Sforza!" Cesare rose in the stirrups and roared. "Sforza, show yourself!" Gwyn winced.

"Lord Sforza is indisposed, I'm afraid." Meric stepped out, a loaded crossbow in each hand. "You are welcome to enter and find him, but you must hand over my young friend first."

Gwyn blinked. Looking exhausted, grey hair mussed and askew, Meric's tone nevertheless held steel. Hope and fear clawed at Gwyn's throat as a short sob escaped her. Cesare gave a short, ugly laugh. "I think not. Put those down before I order my men to kill you. In fact—"

"Let Gwyn go," Meric interrupted. "Now."

"She is mine!" Cesare snarled.

"Cesare Borgia!" Michelle stepped out into the light. "Meric asked nicely, but I'm not as nice as him." She had an arm around a terrified Lucretia Borgia, a knife to the young woman's throat.

# Thirty-One

**1493 AD**

Fury rippled through Cesare and the temptation to scream 'kill them' bubbled to his lips. But he sat down hard in the saddle and gripped Gwyn's shoulder, digging his nails in. She cried out and squirmed.

"Do not hurt her!" Michelle ordered. "I have no hesitation in harming your sister!"

To his horror, Cesare watched Michelle jab her blade into Lucretia's precious skin. His sister gave a shriek and a drop of blood rolled down her neck.

Cesare forced his fingers to release, making a show of lifting his hand from Gwyn. "If you harm Lucretia, you will die, Gwyn will die."

"Ah but Lucretia will be dead first." Michelle showed her teeth. "And if you harm Gwyn, Meric will shoot you—he's an excellent shot with a crossbow. So tell your men to stand down and we'll discuss this like civilised people, though I doubt you recognise the concept."

Cesare ground his teeth. He felt the excitement thrumming through Gwyn and his rage increased. *Little bitch thinks she's being rescued!* That would not happen. She belonged to him. *But... Lucretia...* His sister's skin was chalk-white, her eyes wide and frantic. He dragged his eyes from her distressed visage and shot hatred at Michelle. *You'll pay for this.*

"Let my sister go—she is innocent." He injected a note of reasonableness into his tone.

"Tell your men to stand down now!" Michelle's command hit him with the force of a hammer. He found himself stuttering the order for the mercenaries to leave, ignoring their sideways looks and grunts of disapproval. No doubt they thought him weak for giving in over a woman, even if she was his sister. He clenched his fists.

"Now, let Gwyn down, and she will walk to us, and I will walk to you with your sister." Michelle returned to a normal speaking voice, though her face remained hard.

Cesare worked his jaw. "Go," he muttered, pushing Gwyn. She slid off the horse, landing with a thud and stumbling to her feet. She half staggered, half ran towards Meric and Michelle. The latter advanced, passing Gwyn with a nod and a question Cesare couldn't quite make out. Gwyn paused, shook her head and carried on.

Cesare tore his gaze from her and refocussed on his sister. "Release her," he croaked.

"Here you go." Michelle dropped her arm and gave Lucretia a shove. She gasped and stumbled—Cesare was off his horse in a moment and running towards her. He heard a yell but could only concentrate on reaching his sister. She fell and he skidded onto his knees, throwing his arms around her.

"My precious Lucretia, are you alright?" He breathed in the scent of her hair, holding her tight, glaring up at Michelle and Meric and Gwyn.

Or at the space where they had been. The steps to Pesaro Castle stood empty.

* * *

The blue cloud faded. It was dark, and the stars shone above. The night was still. Michelle felt Meric tear himself loose from her grip and heard retching. She sighed. "Gwyn, are you alright?"

"When are we?" Gwyn sounded wary.

"A week ahead. Enough time for Cesare to have scuttled off back to Rome with his precious sister. Don't know what chaos he might have left so we need to be careful."

"Can we leave?"

"Ugh—don't know how you ladies stand that." Meric straightened and groaned. His outline was visible—Michelle could see him looking around.

"Let's get to the stables and see if our horses are still here," Michelle said.

She didn't let go of Gwyn's arm as they made their way down the steps and across the courtyard. A light shone out of the gatehouse window—they avoided it. Michelle used the torch function on her computer to shine the way to the stables. They crept in, wary of grooms that might be sleeping there.

"It's not long till dawn," Michelle whispered. "We'll just hole up here and leave at first light." She guided Gwyn into an empty stall packed with sweet smelling hay. The girl lay down without a word. Meric eased onto the hay with a grunt, then sighed.

"I'll just rest my eyes, Michelle. Kick me if anyone comes."

She nodded. The ride from Rome had been intense, but she suspected—better horseman or not—that she would recover faster than Meric. The time travel didn't help either—he wasn't immune to the nausea like she and Gwyn were.

They snuck out at daybreak, Michelle ordering the guard to open the gate. He was too befuddled by the chronokinetor and ready to finish his watch to argue, so they left without a fuss. They took the road north, winding their way through the hills as the sun lit the sea below like a golden mirror.

"To where are we riding?" Meric asked. "We can take the road to Bologna, and thus west to France, or if you want to take ship, Venice would be ideal."

"Whatever takes us out of Italy as fast as possible," Gwyn stated flatly.

Michelle glanced at her. Gwyn kept wincing—unusual for someone who was a good horse rider. What had Cesare done to her? She kept her tone nonchalant as she answered. "I'd hoped to avoid another sea voyage, but it would be faster to reach Spain that way. Many merchant ships will sail out of Venice—we'll buy passage on one. In the meantime, we'll make for Rimini. It's an easy day's ride, and large enough to have an inn. I think we all deserve a decent night's rest." She didn't add that Meric looked haggard, not wanting to insult him.

"And a bath," Gwyn interjected in that same flat tone. "I don't care how much it costs, I want a hot bath. And soap—lots of soap." She kicked her horse and rode ahead, leaving Michelle to exchange a worried look with Meric.

Michelle paid for the bath, and the room at the inn, then sent Meric out so the girl could have some privacy. When the kitchen maid hauled up the last kettle of hot water and poured it into the linen-lined tub Michelle tipped her a coin and shut the door. Gwyn stood staring at the bath, seemingly mesmerised by the wisps of steam.

"Go on, get in," Michelle encouraged. "It'll get cold."

Gwyn didn't reply.

"Do you want me to leave the room?" Michelle asked gently. It wasn't an issue of modesty—travelling together for the last few months meant she and Gwyn had seen each other bathing or swimming.

Gwyn shook her head and gritted her teeth. She unlaced her dress and stepped out of her skirts. As she pulled her shift over her head, Michelle's worst fears were confirmed. Bruises ran up and down Gwyn's body—black, purplish, yellow. Gwyn stepped into the wooden tub, shuddering at the heat. She reached for the soap and attacked her skin with it, scrubbing viciously.

"Here." Michelle lifted up the bowl of olive oil she'd requested from the kitchen. "Do you want me to wash your hair?"

Gwyn nodded. Michelle used her foot to drag a stool over and seated herself beside the bath. She worked carefully, touching Gwyn no more than necessary as she worked the oil through and rinsed with a jug of clean warm water. When she finished she tidied around the bath and unfolded the towels provided. Gwyn sat in the bath. Soap congealed on the now lukewarm water.

"Come on," said Michelle. "Stand up and I'll rinse you."

Gwyn eyes rotated up from their stare into nothingness and focussed on Michelle.

"Soaking yourself in water won't help you feel truly clean again." Michelle tried to keep the pity from her voice and failed. Gwyn complied, hugging herself as Michelle poured rinse water over her. She stepped out and Michelle wrapped a towel around the girl's shoulders. "I'm so sorry." Michelle's voice cracked. "I let you down."

"What?" Gwyn looked bewildered. "How did you let me down?"

"I..." Michelle swallowed and got her voice under control. "I promised I would protect you from him and I failed."

Gwyn shook her head and towelled her hair half-heartedly. "I was the stupid one. I knew he was dangerous. I should have kept away from him." She tossed the towel on the stool and dragged on breeches and a shirt.

"No," Michelle growled. "Gwyn, Cesare Borgia goes down in history as one of the most ruthless, nasty, manipulative arseholes ever to have walked the earth, and I've got an extra six hundred years of history on you. Far wiser people than you will be duped by him—I have no doubt he planned your kidnap in detail. He fooled me, he fooled Meric—we should have looked after you better."

"I should be able to look after myself!" Gwyn yelled. "I don't want you to have to protect me! I don't want to be babysat and looked after and be a liability to everyone. I never should have picked up this stupid timepiece in the first place!" Tears finally leaked from her eyes; her voice cracked in fury. She picked up the towel and scrubbed her face with it.

"Gwyn," Michelle tried.

"Leave me alone!" the girl sobbed. She seized her boots and tugged them on without stockings. A cloak went around her shoulders and she stormed from the room, still crying.

Michelle sat abruptly on one of the narrow beds, surveying the detritus of the bath and rapidly cooling water. "Well, shit," she sighed.

# Thirty-Two

**1493 AD**

Gwyn barrelled past Meric as he opened the taproom door, back from a stroll around the small town of Rimini. He blinked after her as she ran down the street.

"Gwyn? Gwyn!" he yelled. No reply—she disappeared amongst the late-afternoon traffic. He turned back to the inn door only to narrowly avoid being run over by Michelle, who exited at a similar pace. "Michelle! Where's Gwyn going?"

"Oh! Meric—she got upset and ran off." Michelle's face was contorted by worry. She shifted her weight from foot to foot. "I need to go after her."

"Wait a moment, I'll help you." He let the door swing shut and started in the direction Gwyn had gone. "Why is she upset? Do you want me to talk to her?"

"Ohh." Michelle sounded uncertain—a most unusual occurrence for her. "Maybe. I tried—I thought because I was a woman—but I'm no good at talking to people!"

"Just stop." He halted and put his hands on her shoulders. "Is this about what Cesare did to her?"

In that moment Michelle looked more like Gwyn when she bit her lip. "He raped her, Meric. She's got bruises all over her body."

Meric hands tightened involuntarily and he forced them to relax. "I was afeared of that," he said in a low voice.

"But the worst part is she thinks it's her fault! I tried to say I'm sorry, that I should have protected her, but she got all upset and screamed at me then ran out. I have to find her before something happens to her," Michelle babbled.

Meric considered. "She can't go far—it's a small town. And she's dressed as a boy, I saw—no one should harass her. You go back inside in case she comes back—get yourself cleaned up and order us all some dinner. I'll search the streets nearby."

"But I can use the chronokinetor to find her!"

"Michelle," he kept his tone firm, "I'll find her. She might need a little time to herself."

He could sense the conflict in her. He suspected she wanted to go after Gwyn, to assuage her guilt, but she dreaded it too, knowing she was ill-equipped for the discussion.

"Go." He gave her a little push. She stepped back reluctantly.

"Come back if you don't find her soon."

"I will. Shoo." He sighed as Michelle retraced her steps to the inn. *Where would I go, if I were an abused young woman who didn't belong in this time?* He continued down the street. *A headlong dash, tears in my eyes? Aye, this street leads straight along the river to the quay.*

The waterfront was busy—this close to Venice, merchants traded a variety of goods. Oared ships docked at the wharves that extended from the opposite side of the quay. On Meric's side the river emptied straight into the ocean, with a long breakwater extending from the shore. Fishermen brought the day's catch in; gulls and pelicans vied for their dinner as men flung fish scraps overboard. Meric side-stepped buckets and nets, striding along. The late sun was to his left—he squinted at the silhouette at the end of the breakwater. It might be a tall rock, or it might be a person.

A fat pelican honked as Meric disturbed it. It flapped awkwardly and landed with a splash; beady eyes fixed on him as it bobbed on the waves. The air was fresh out here—no stench of rotting fish guts and sweating men—and the tall rock became a hunched figure, standing and staring out to sea.

Meric coughed and scuffed his feet. She half turned, saw that it was him, then returned to gazing at the Adriatic. Meric reached her, tapped his fingers on his leg, then sat down. Gwyn looked at him, irritated.

"Did Michelle send you to talk to me?" she demanded. Her eyes were red and puffy.

"No." He grunted and stretched out his legs, resting his feet on the rock below.

Several breaths passed. "How did you know to find me then?" The accusatory tone remained at the fore, but it was fading.

"Aye, you almost knocked me flat when you left the inn. I could see you were upset."

"Oh. I didn't see you."

"Aye, I figured."

Another short period of silence. "So you didn't see Michelle?"

"Aye, I saw her. She was set to come after you, but I sent her back in."

Gwyn's face twitched. She clenched and unclenched her fists, then sat down with a sharp sigh. "What did she say?"

Meric had thought carefully about this moment on his long walk. He settled on honesty. "She said Cesare raped you. That you had bruises all over and you thought it was your fault."

There was no sound save for the waves striking the rocks and the screech of gulls overhead. Gwyn replied in a tight voice. "And?"

"Many men rape, Gwyn. It's what they do."

She didn't look at him. "Do you think it was my fault?" Her voice rose in pitch.

"Gwyn." He looked at her then. After a moment she glanced sideways then resolutely looked back out to sea. He waited.

"What?" She faced him, hurt warring with uncertainty.

"Gwyn, I've been in many a war, seen men do terrible things. Rape, pillage, burn families in their homes. It's never the fault of them that suffer it."

"I know." Her voice was meek, helpless.

"But folk seem to blame them. Oh, they're charitable at first, but then whispers get about. They make signs to avert evil, particularly if the mark of the sin is visible on a victim." He shrugged helplessly. "Do people still do this in your time?"

Gwyn shook her head, then nodded, then put her face in her hands. "I *know* it's not my fault, but I *feel* it is. I should have been smarter, or faster, or fiercer. I should have fought him off, jumped away, even if he came with me, then used the disorientation to get free and jump again. I should have... done something."

A black shag dived into the water, surfacing several yards away. It cocked its head then dived again, coming up with a silvery fish, which it gulped.

"Tell me," Meric said.

Impassive as he tried to be, Meric couldn't help but growl when she spoke of how Cesare had drugged her, tied her and threatened her. He waited patiently every time she stopped. She fought to speak the words without choking on them. The sun had almost set when she finished. She looked deflated, like a wineskin bereft of its contents. "Come on, now," he murmured, reaching for her hand and squeezing it.

They walked back along the breakwater. "When I was a lad in the Empire," Meric said, "I thought myself in love with Radu."

"Radu? You mean Vlad's brother?"

"Aye, the same. A boy's infatuation, though I carried it for years. Thing is, Vlad found us together one day, and he was furious. Called it a heinous sin, said that the Empire had corrupted Radu. He struck his brother and then set upon me."

Gwyn's eyes were wide. She had feared Vlad terribly; she knew what he was capable of.

"I won't say all that he did to me, but cutting off half my ear wasn't the worst. Thing is, for years after I felt responsible—like I should have fought back, stopped him. I never blamed Radu, even though he just sat there, too frightened to do anything. We were both younger than Vlad, not as strong, but together we could have overpowered him." He stared into the past, then shook his head. "I've gone over that day a thousand times in my head. It wasn't until you were taken prisoner by that crazy countess bitch that I realised I had to let go, and forgive myself. Saving you was more important than my vengeance."

Gwyn paused. He looked at her, golden sunlight on her face, shining on the tears that streaked down it.

"It might take time," he said, "but I hope you can forgive yourself. Because it was never your fault."

Wordless she reached out and hugged him around his middle, squeezing hard.

"Aye." He kissed her hair. "Saving you t'was worth it."

* * *

"He planned well, the maggot-eating whoreson. The devil was his teacher and a she-demon whelped him," Meric remarked bitterly, downing the last of his ale.

"If he wasn't essential to history…" Michelle tapped her fingers on the table, looking about the taproom. Back from the waterfront it wasn't as rowdy as some inns, but there was plenty of noise to cover their conversation.

"Aye, but you told me he was. Pity. S'always bastards like him and Vlad that get ahead in this life. Seems the only way to get the better of them is to be a bigger bastard."

"Indeed." Michelle sighed glumly. "I'd better go up and check on Gwyn."

"She was fast asleep when I left her. Locked the door from the outside too."

"Still." Michelle rose. "Maybe we take our time getting to Venice. This part of the coast is nice—we could travel on slowly, give ourselves a chance to recoup."

"Aye, I won't say no to the chance to amble on a bit." Meric stretched and cracked his knuckles. "There's no danger, you think?"

"I doubt it." Michelle shook her head. "I suspect Cesare would be keen to get his sister back to Rome, but how would he find us anyway? We'll travel as men—father and brothers perhaps."

"Aye, that we shall then."

Amble they did—riding slowly up the coast, taking scenic detours and buying food from farmers. Gwyn was quiet for the most part, and Meric and Michelle didn't push her. The weather stayed fine, with occasional spring showers. They stopped for several days in the town of Ravenna. Meric had been there before, so he took it upon himself to play tour guide around the city. Michelle chipped in with knowledge from her computer—history of the Ostrogoths and the Byzantines. She pointed out the mosaics and architecture of the basilicas. Gwyn appeared politely interested but every night she retreated into herself and went to bed early.

The room they had taken was upstairs in a quiet street away from the great canal that led to the sea. As usual there was one large bed, a small hearth and a table with several chairs. It was far enough from the clamour of the taverns and brothels to have a sense of respectability. Meric decided to venture out one evening to try his hand at cards.

"Don't get beaten up and robbed," Michelle warned.

He laughed. "I can look after myself."

"Hmph." Michelle didn't like the way Gwyn became more anxious when Meric wasn't around. She accepted that she didn't have the same relationship but it hurt that the girl couldn't relax with only Michelle as a companion.

"Come on, tell me about your time?" she prompted in an effort to draw Gwyn out. Silence would have suited Michelle just fine but guilt gnawed at her, making her want to restore Gwyn to her old self.

"What do you mean? Haven't you been there?" Gwyn didn't look at Michelle. She sat by the open, western-facing window to catch the last of the light, preparing to sew a large tear in her shirt.

"I've passed through, but none of my missions have been in the early twenty-first century. Did a few in the twentieth-century, but mostly they sent me back further coz I could handle more jumps."

"Oh. I forgot this one is more advanced than your timepiece." Gwyn gestured vaguely then returned to threading a needle.

"They upgraded mine just before I came to this time." Michelle smiled. "Can do up to fifty year jumps now. That's quite decent."

"Mmm." Gwyn began sewing.

"So, yes—what's your time like? What did you do there? I remember you said you studied history. Lucky, hey?" Michelle tried to inject a note of humour.

Gwyn looked at her, then back to her shirt. "Yeah. Lucky."

Michelle persisted doggedly. "Are you going to be a historian? Or a teacher? Maybe you could write?"

"I don't know what I want to do. My parents wanted me to study science. I…" She broke off. "I wanted to defer my studies for a bit, stay in Europe, do some travel. Live a little. I think now maybe I just want to go home, back to Brisbane. Maybe I should switch to science. Forget the history."

"No!" Michelle was astonished at how dismayed she felt. "Not if it's what you love doing." Why did she care what Gwyn studied? *Because whose fault is it she's been damaged by history? That's right—yours.*

Gwyn shrugged. "Not many jobs for a history degree."

Michelle sensed the real reason was that Gwyn wanted to forget. She railed against it. "Gwyn, you're a smart, capable young woman—you learn so fast and you're adaptable. You wouldn't have trouble finding work in the field you love."

"How would you know?" Gwyn challenged, finally looking squarely at Michelle. "You just said you don't know anything about my time? Ow!" She had stabbed her finger with the needle.

"Are you alright?" Michelle rushed over.

"I'm fine! Stop fussing! You can't–" She took a deep breath, closing her eyes then reopening them. "You can't change what happened—I just have to deal with it. Don't tell me I have to talk about it 'cause I don't want to."

Michelle swallowed and nodded. She backed off. "You don't. I'm sorry. I just... if you do want to talk—I know you'd rather talk to Meric!" she added hurriedly. "But if you do want someone else to talk to, I'd like you to know you can talk to me. I understand we're not exactly friends, but I do respect you, even more for surviving what you have."

Several moments went by, then Gwyn nodded. She glanced out the window. "Oh! Meric's back."

Puzzled, Michelle joined her, looking down onto the street. "Forgot my money!" Meric shouted in Turkish upon seeing them.

"Wait there!" Gwyn called. She rummaged in Meric's packs and retrieved the non-descript leather purse stashed there. She tossed it out the window for him to catch. "You're losing your memory, old man!" she teased. He grinned and saluted, then returned the way he had come.

Gwyn returned to her sewing while Michelle watched Meric a moment longer. A large blonde man with the bearing of a warrior was also watching their friend, then his head swung around to spy Michelle at the window. She withdrew, uncomfortable. "Gwyn, come away from the window."

Gwyn looked up, surprised. "Why? I'm almost done."

"Just…" Michelle looked back out. The blonde man was gone. She scanned the street but couldn't see him. "Never mind. Shall we see if the landlady has dinner ready?

# Thirty-Three

**1493 AD**

Meric returned later that night, unharmed and in possession of his winnings. "My contribution to the cause," he yawned, shucking his boots before tossing his purse to Michelle who sat up waiting.

She caught it with a clink. "I've enough for our purposes," she said dryly, "but I appreciate the effort."

He grinned. "Our girl asleep?"

"As you see." Michelle gestured at the form on the bed. "Toss you for the middle?"

"You can have it. Makes it easier for you to boot me out if I snore."

"Ha." Michelle rose. "Blow out the candle, will you?"

"Aye." He stretched, cracking his back and neck.

"Meric?"

"Hmm?" He paused in removing his tunic. His stockings were already bundled neatly in his boots to stop any mice or spiders from creeping in during the night. A soldier's habit, one he couldn't shake no matter how clean the lodgings seemed.

"Did you... notice anyone following you earlier? When you came back for your purse?"

Meric frowned. "I don't believe so. Why?"

Michelle tapped her fingers on her leg. "I thought I saw someone watching you. Maybe it was because you called out in Turkish and it attracted his attention. He made me nervous."

Meric finished folding his clothes. He didn't like hearing that—

Michelle had a good instinct for danger. "What did he look like?"

"Blonde. A soldier, I thought. It was hard to see because the sun was shining straight in at us and he was down in the shadow."

"Hmm. Perhaps we ride on tomorrow." When he'd been gambling in the tavern, the talk of war focussed on Rome and Florence and Naples, but that didn't mean this side of Italy was immune. It had only been in autumn that Cesare's brother Juan had tried to conquer the Campagna. Meric knew that Cesare would succeed where Juan had failed, but they would be sailing for Spain by the time that happened.

"I think that's a good idea." Michelle climbed into bed, sliding under the blankets beside Gwyn.

"Aye." Meric checked the fire and blew out the last candle. *Surely I would have noticed if someone was following me—it must have been a coincidence.* But his instincts clamoured. They'd tarried long enough. Time to get to Venice, and sail away from this country.

\* \* \*

Cesare considered the sleeping form of Caterina Sforza as he rose from her bed, the late morning sun peeking through the shutters. Older than him by a decade, the Countess of Forli and Lady of Imola was sensual and experienced compared to that frigid bitch Gwyn. Thinking of Gwyn, he scowled. He had waited in Pesaro the best part of a week, expecting her to reappear with Meric and Michelle. When she hadn't, even his joy at reuniting with his sister had been overtaken by rage and frustration.

His mood hadn't improved when Giovanni Sforza insisted Lucretia should stay in Pesaro, safe from ravaging French armies. Cesare had argued, but Lucretia astonishingly remained under the sway of her husband.

Instead of riding for Rome, Cesare paid a visit to the Countess of Forli. Instrumental in foiling his brother's attempt to invade the Campagna, Cesare knew he had to handle her with care. *Bitch,* Juan had called her. *Harlot* was the word Cesare was more inclined to use, and it suited him in this instance.

She had welcomed him courteously, and he had used all his charm and wit to draw out her intelligence and warmth. Enjoying the political banter, she'd no doubt thought it to her advantage to permit him into her bed to set him against his brother and thus divide Borgia loyalty.

*Foolish whore.* He startled a servant entering through the outer door of Caterina's apartments. Cesare moved to pass him while belting his doublet, but the servant bowed and said, "Your Eminence? A man has come with a message for you."

"What man? From where?"

"I know not, my lord. He appears to know your soldiers—he is Swiss, like them."

*Ah!* Cesare had sent pairs of mercenaries west, south and north to watch for Gwyn and her companions, taking the remainder with him as a retinue to Forli. "Where can I receive him?" he demanded.

"The lesser hall, my lord. This way." The servant led Cesare down from Caterina's apartments to where one of his Swiss mercenaries waited.

"Milord." The man bowed. "I found 'em."

"Where?"

"Ravenna. I left Henri there to follow them and left before dawn to ride here."

Ravenna! Less than a day's ride. Cesare smiled like a shark. "Gather the men!"

"Leaving so soon?" Caterina Sforza swanned into the hall, dressed but hair unbound. She appeared unhurried but Cesare would have bet the entire contents of his purse the Countess launched herself out of bed to chase him down.

"Something urgent has come up, my lady, you'll have to forgive me." Cesare turned on his most charming smile, quelling the urge to tell her to shut up and leave him alone. He didn't want to lose what diplomatic advantage he had achieved during his stay.

Caterina pouted. It didn't suit her. *An old ewe prancing like a lamb,* he thought uncharitably. Too large a nose, sallow skin—he'd been grateful for the dim light the night before when he'd bedded her. But he forced himself to walk over and kiss her hand, glancing up seductively. "Nothing short of the most serious matter could tear me from you, dear Countess. I shall return in a few days, if I am still welcome?" He let his tone hold a tentative note, as if he craved her permission.

She smiled coquettishly. "How can I say no to you?"

\* \* \*

A sense of uneasiness remained with Michelle though it lifted as they left Ravenna and rode north. "Let's pick up the pace," she said. "We have some time before the next turning point in Spain, but lots of things could delay us between now and then."

Gwyn accepted that explanation—perhaps she thought Michelle and Meric had given up on trying to cheer her. Michelle couldn't worry about that. She urged them on at a trot and over the course of two days they crossed innumerable rivers, including the Po, as they made their way towards Venice.

On the third day they reached a crossroads and Meric called a halt to the gruelling pace. "The land to the west of here is swampy and the road is narrow. I've heard of travellers forced to camp on the road itself because of the bogs to either side. I know you two prefer to ride, but perhaps now is the time to sell the horses and take a boat from Chioggia."

Gwyn slapped a mosquito on her arm. "Sure. Guess it won't be too rough inside the lagoon."

"Shouldn't be," Meric assured her. "The islands of Pellestrina and Lido protect the lagoon from the ocean—it should be fairly calm."

"I have seasickness medication for when we sail from Venice," Michelle said, waving away a cloud of biting insects. "Come on then, let's go."

They sold the horses in a hamlet just south of Chioggia. Michelle left Meric in charge of the haggling—she was impatient and would have ruined the sale by dropping the price too low.

"It really is the most painful thing about these times," she confided in Gwyn, shifting from foot to foot. They listened to Meric extoll the horses' virtues to the potential buyer—an innkeeper who agreed that he could resell the mounts to travellers coming south from the lagoon.

"What's that?"

"Prices aren't fixed. And if you don't know the value of things, you stand out. I don't like to stand out." Michelle tapped her leg. Their packs were piled neatly—ready to be grabbed and carried to the nearby jetty where a sleepy ferryman had agreed to row them to Chioggia.

"This 'ere bloke won't 'aggle," Gwyn commented enigmatically.

"Huh?"

"Oh." Gwyn blinked and looked at Michelle. "Just a quote from… from a movie. Never mind."

"Oh, good, he's done." Michelle flung her bags onto her back as Meric approached, beaming.

"Less than we could have got but not too shabby," he said, patting his belt purse.

"Wonderful, let's go." The sense of unease returned, and Michelle's agitation infected Gwyn. They hustled the ferryman from his nap and loaded their gear. The man rowed them through the canals to the northern end where larger boats docked.

"Ask any of them, my friend." The ferryman pointed to several sailing boats. "They do the run to Venezia every few days."

They split up. Gwyn guarded the bags while Michelle and Meric worked their way up and down the docks, querying captains. "Nothing for a few days," Michelle huffed, returning to Gwyn. "Let's hope Meric has better luck."

"Is Cesare following us?" The question startled Michelle. She floundered for an answer as Gwyn went on. "You were so cruisy before, now you're itching to get away."

Michelle gave up. "I don't know. Maybe. It seemed like someone was watching us in Ravenna but it's probably just coincidence."

Gwyn gave her an even look. It was the most alert Michelle had seen her since they rescued her. Perhaps the slow pace had been a mistake. But they had all needed the break.

Michelle shrugged, tight-lipped. "I trust my instincts. And they're telling me we ought to move it. I can't just jump myself out of trouble if something goes wrong." She looked at Gwyn. "I won't risk losing you again. I need you to fix these turning points, then I'm going to take you home." She realised she meant this promise with all her heart—a surge of protectiveness overwhelmed her and she looked away, blinking fiercely.

"Found one!" Meric strode up the dock, puffing. "Doesn't leave until tomorrow though—we'll have to find somewhere to stay the night."

"Argh!" Michelle kicked a bollard then took a deep breath. "That's fine. Thank you, Meric." She rubbed her temples. "One more night won't make a difference."

# Thirty-Four

**1493 AD**

"What do you mean, gone?" Cesare demanded of Henri, the mercenary waiting in Ravenna.

"Packed up and left this morning, milord. Landlady said they was riding for Venice."

Cesare kept his fury in check. *So close!* "We will go after them."

Henri exchanged glances with the other men. "Milord…"

"You are getting paid, are you not?" Cesare snapped.

"Yes, milord," they chorused.

"And you're not risking your necks fighting Neapolitan soldiers."

"No, milord."

"And as long as you keep your cocks out of dirty whores you won't catch the pox like the rest of the French army!"

"Milord?"

Cesare paused. "Naples is a festering pit of disease. You are fortunate to avoid it. Now provision yourselves, see to the horses and find out where that witch has gone!"

\* \* \*

"Stop pacing, Michelle!" Gwyn flicked her hair back and re-tied it with a leather strip. Shouts from sailors and fishermen clamoured in her ears—she tried to block them out. Michelle's fretting added to her irritation.

"How long does it take to get a boat ready to cast off?" Michelle demanded, tapping her fingers on her legs. They were waiting at the end of one of the stone jetties—the lateen-rigged half-galley that would take them to Venice tied up alongside. The captain had permitted them to load their gear but asked them not to come aboard until the ship was ready, stating that passengers got in the way. Gwyn could believe it— there was precious little space between the oarsmen's benches and when those big, burly men weren't seated the deck was crowded.

"They're waiting for the tide," Meric told Michelle. "See the high water mark? It's not quite fully in."

"I know, I know."

"Well, I'm going to stroll down the jetty and back—I want to stretch my legs as much as possible before I'm stuck on a boat for a few hours." Gwyn stood, shooing away a curious seagull.

"Take Meric with you at least," Michelle said.

Gwyn sighed. "Fine. Come on, old man."

For once he didn't banter back. Gwyn flicked a glance at him and regretted her teasing. Her friend looked weary. "Are you alright, Meric?"

He looked at her and smiled. "Aye, just didn't sleep well. I'll be glad when we're away too."

They dodged a captain yelling at a pair of sullen sailors. "Dawn, I said! It's mid-morning you slovenly, slack-arse mongrels!"

"Do you think we're being followed?" Gwyn continued once they were past.

"I don't know. I wish I'd been paying more attention in Ravenna— I'd have knocked the stuffing out of any man that followed us, but I didn't see him. Perhaps Michelle imagined it."

Gwyn froze. "No, she didn't," she croaked, pointing.

Meric followed her gaze. Cesare marched along the docks, black cloak swirling behind, tall Swiss mercenaries flanking him. He had spotted them. His men drew their swords and charged with a roar. "Run, Gwyn!" Meric urged, snatching her hand.

They bolted down the stone jetty. "It's Cesare Borgia!" Meric yelled. Michelle's head snapped up. She leapt aboard the boat and disappeared into the hold. For a moment Gwyn thought she was abandoning them, then Michelle reappeared with two crossbows. "Get on board!" she yelled. "Tell the captain we have to cast off."

"What's going on?" The boat's captain appeared from the tiny cabin at the stern.

"We're under attack!" Gwyn gasped as she hurtled aboard. "It's Cesare Borgia—we have to go, now, please!" She threw all her force of will into the command, praying the captain wouldn't simply dump them over the side and sail off without them to avoid trouble.

"Borgia, eh?" He rubbed his weathered face. "I hate those Spanish pricks. Cast off!" he roared. His crew leapt to the oars. Gwyn scrambled out of the way as Meric caught the crossbow Michelle tossed him. They fired—the mercenaries advancing towards them dropped to the deck.

"Row!" the captain bellowed. Strong oar-strokes shot the boat forward as the last rope slipped from its mooring.

Curses chased them as they pulled away. Gwyn clung to the mast, eyes locked with Cesare who stood at the end of the jetty. Even as the distance grew between them, Gwyn felt his terrifying grip on her soul.

* * *

Chioggia slid away behind them as the oarsmen rowed. Meric escorted Gwyn to the bow, while Michelle returned the crossbows to the hold. Once the galley was underway the oars were shipped and the mainsail raised to catch the southerly wind. Michelle watched the activity, finding the purposeful action reassuring after their close call. When all appeared to be to the captain's satisfaction he beckoned to Michelle. She climbed the slightly raised poop deck to join him. "Why is the Pope's bastard after ye?" he wanted to know.

Michelle hesitated. She didn't want them to seem important—Venice was at odds enough with Rome to see a benefit in holding them prisoner while their value was explored. The captain might try to sell them to the authorities. "Nothing you need to worry about," she replied firmly.

"Excuse me, captain," Meric interrupted as he climbed the short stair. He sounded worried. "I thought you said yours was the only galley making the run to Venice this morning."

"Aye, that's correct."

"So what ship is that?" Meric pointed over the captain's shoulder. Chioggia was growing distant, but they could see a white and red striped sail unfurl and billow, its colours distinct against the muddy grey of the island town.

"That's the Mariella," the captain answered slowly. "Fastest ship in the lagoon." He sounded puzzled, then looked at Michelle and Meric. "I know the captain—he'll carry anyone for the right price. Seems the Borgia bastard really wants you." He spat over the stern rail.

"I'll make it worth your while to get us to Venice before he catches up." Michelle caught his gaze.

"Hrmph." The captain hoicked and spat again. "I'll do my best, but they might catch up before we reach Venice."

They haggled for a few minutes then shook hands on the deal. The captain bellowed orders to increase sail and to re-deploy the oars. He returned his attention to the helmsman beside him and Michelle and Meric hurried past the busy crew to re-join Gwyn at the bow.

"Gwyn." The girl looked at her—she was pale. "The second this boat hits Venice we need to run. It's a warren of alleys and canals—we should be able to lose him but we need to move fast. We'll disguise ourselves and seek passage on a ship to Spain, then jump ahead to just before it leaves."

"I thought you said we couldn't afford to lose time—'cause of the next turning point?"

Michelle grimaced. "We can't, but whatever ship we find won't be leaving until a certain time anyway and I don't plan on hanging about in Venice for Cesare to find us. He's tenacious."

"He's a bloody pitbull," Gwyn put her face in her hands.

"I'm not sure what that is, but, yes. If you say so."

That was enough to get Gwyn to look up. "I forget things are so different in your time." She gave a tiny, rueful smile, then took a deep breath. "Okay. Focus. I won't let myself be caught by him again."

Michelle awkwardly patted Gwyn's shoulder. "I wish we could put him out of action for good, but he's too important for history. We need him to give up the chase before it alters the timeline. I want to be done with Italy."

"I know." Gwyn stood, looking out over the rail. She swallowed hard.

The red and white striped sail was closer.

# *Thirty-Five*

**1493 AD**

As the next few hours passed, there was nothing to do but watch anxiously. The long, narrow isle of Pellestrina clung to the starboard side as the *Mariella* loomed behind them. Several smaller islands came into view as Lido took Pellestrina's place then drifted to the north-east. The main island of Venice was mostly blocked from view by Giudecca, an isle that lay due north. The captain struck a course through one of Giudecca's larger canals and they passed small farms and orchards, as well as various stately homes. The sails luffed as the wind faltered and the captain ordered more hands to the oars.

Down in the hold, Gwyn gestured at their packs. "How are we going to carry all this?" Despite travelling light, it was too much to move quickly without horses or mules.

"Sort," Michelle replied grimly. "Ditch the food—I've got vitamins to stop us from getting scurvy on the ship. Keep a dress.

"I'll take the cooking stuff." Meric frowned as he considered his saddlebags.

"What about the crossbows?"

Michelle pursed her lips, clearly wanting to take the weapons. "Gift them to the captain. He can sell them." Meric nodded and disappeared above.

Gwyn's stomach somersaulted. *It's not like I'm any good with one anyway.* But she would have felt better facing Cesare with a projectile weapon in her hand to stop him from getting too close.

Michelle gripped her shoulder. "I wish we could get revenge on that bastard. I hate having to run."

Gwyn nodded. *Trust Michelle to completely miss the point.* "Okay, I think I can manage the rest."

"Let me help you." Michelle arranged the bags across Gwyn's back and shoulders, tightening leather straps so they wouldn't slip. "Got your knife handy?"

"Yep." It was in a small sheath on her waist.

"Good. If you get stuck, cut the bags loose and ditch them. But I'm hoping we get enough of a head start to lose Cesare in the alleys. I've asked the captain where the larger ships dock—he's given directions but…"

"But what?"

"It's a maze." Michelle jerked a thumb at the so called 'floating-city'. They were getting close. "I've got a map on my computer, but I can't stop and consult it in public, and it might not be accurate. Things change over the years."

Gwyn gulped. "So we might get lost."

Michelle gave another grim smile. "And so might Cesare. We just have to make sure we don't get lost in the same place."

* * *

The boat hit the stone landing. Michelle, Meric and Gwyn exploded into action, leaping from the boat. "God speed!" Meric called as the galley shoved off again, reversing its course to confuse the *Mariella*. The captain waved, patting his now substantial purse with his other hand. Gwyn and her companions tore down the wharf and entered a myriad of cobbled alleyways.

"Should… be a bridge… up here." Michelle gestured. They rounded a corner and saw the bridge—stone steps in an arch with high sides. Pounding over it, they shoved past two women carrying cages of squawking chickens and turned down the next street. "Okay… should be able to walk now."

Gwyn glanced back. "Their ship was right behind us, they would have seen where we went."

"If he's smart, which we know he is, he'll have sent a couple of thugs after us and stopped to hail our captain himself. I hope he doesn't give him too much grief—he did well getting us here."

"It cost us enough." Meric had been put out at the amount Michelle had handed over.

"I've got plenty of funds," Michelle reassured him. "But I don't go shouting that to the world. And we can always resort to you playing cards, no?"

"Aye," he grunted disparagingly.

"Never mind now." Gwyn shifted the strap on her shoulder to stop it digging in. "Which way?"

"We need to cross the Grand Canal and find the main basin. I think it's this way." They hit a dead end—the alley they were on opened onto a small canal. "Crap. Go back."

They asked directions several times, becoming lost near a Church dedicated to Saint Barnabas. "Take a gondola, you fools," one man advised them rudely. "Why are you walking all laden like donkeys? Foreign idiots," he muttered as he returned to hawking his wares.

"At least in Rome it doesn't cost to walk!" Meric grumbled.

Gwyn pushed past several university students to the nearby canal and hailed a gondolier. "How much to take us to St. Mark's?" He eyed them, taking in their heavy packs and flushed faces, and named an exorbitant price.

"To hell with that." Meric dragged Gwyn away. "Come on."

When the end of another narrow street deposited them at the Grand Canal, Gwyn glared pointedly at Michelle.

"Fine!" Michelle threw up her hands. She let Meric haggle and it was with relief they clambered into the long, narrow vessel, balancing their packs on their knees as the gondolier pushed off with his long oar.

"Wow." The beauty of their surroundings distracted Gwyn from her fears. Scores of gondolas crisscrossed the Grand Canal, carrying fabulously dressed Venetians amongst more drably attired commoners. Grand houses overlooked it all. Voices—laughing, shouting and everything in between—carried across the water, accompanied by rich smells—cooking food, fish, the piquant odour of effluent as it gushed forth from sewer pipes. Gwyn gripped the lacquered wooden sides of the gondola. Venice had been on the itinerary for her family's European holiday, but she was receiving a far more authentic dose of the canal city than she ever would in tourist-ridden modern times.

The thought of her family gave her such a pang she gasped. For months she had pushed memories of them to the side, wanting desperately to go home but not daring to let that longing ache interfere with the mission. Knowing that she had to undergo a sea voyage and deal with more turning points before she could return to her own time was enough to crush her.

"There!" Meric called out. Gwyn lifted her head.

The Grand Canal opened out onto St. Mark's Basin, where a forest of masts bobbed and swayed, rooted in the pride of Venice—its ships. Many-oared galleys dominated the water, but the occasional three-masted galley with high fore and aft castles could be seen, and innumerable fishing boats and flat bottomed wherries crowded the spaces between. Their gondola angled left towards the dozens of small wooden jetties that clung to the waterfront edge of a large square.

"Palazzo de Doge," their gondolier grunted. "San Marco back there." Skilfully he slid his vessel up against the jetty and held it steady while Gwyn and Michelle climbed out. Meric heaved the packs up to them.

"Wait." Meric didn't disembark immediately. "Where should we look for captains of the bigger ships? We want to take passage to Spain."

The gondolier stroked his moustache. Meric growled and dug a coin from his purse. "Taverns that way." The man jerked a chin.

Meric hauled himself up, accepting Gwyn's hand to steady him. "Let's find somewhere out of the way to stash Gwyn and our gear."

"Hey!" Gwyn was miffed at being made bag-sitter again.

"Sorry." Meric pulled his own packs over his shoulders. "Michelle is more assertive than you, and we need to move fast."

Gwyn noticed Michelle studiously observing their surroundings and sighed, appreciating that the woman had learnt some tact. "Alright, fair enough. Come on then."

They located a tavern, paid for a private parlour and Gwyn was instructed to stay put. "Have something to eat and save some for us," Michelle pressed some coins into her hand. "We'll try to be back soon."

Gwyn waited. She ordered food—a fishy soup, bread, grilled

zucchini and leeks arrived. The soup repelled her but she forced herself to eat the vegetables. She checked all their gear, she paced, she stretched. Knowing Cesare was somewhere in the city made it impossible for her to relax. He was searching—he wouldn't stop until he'd found her.

"Dammit!" She felt like a caged rat, or that drab songbird she'd joked about all those months ago. Cesare wanted to find her and squeeze until she sang the right song. Gradually dread turned to resentment, then anger. *Why should I be running in fear of my life?* He's *the evil one!* She slammed her fist against a wall then shook it, cursing at the pain but relishing it too. She hit the wall again. "Ow!" The pain made her angrier. The bruises Cesare had marked her with had all but faded, but the grubbiness she felt between her thighs and on her breasts could never be erased, and she hated him for it.

"Is everything alright?" The maid who had delivered the food knocked on the door.

Gwyn's anger evaporated and embarrassment flooded into its place. "Yes—sorry, just stubbed my toe."

"Are you done with the plates, signor?"

"Ah, not yet—my friends will eat when they return."

"I can keep it warm until then." Gwyn passed out the soup tureen and plate of vegetables, averting her eyes as she thanked the maid. When the girl had gone Gwyn sighed and looked about. *I should probably get some counselling or something when I'm back in my own time. I'll have to make up a heap, and damned if I know what to do till then! Just deal with it, I suppose.* She examined her memories, cringing with each one, starting not with the rape but from the first time Cesare had been nice to her and it had made her feel good. *Not your fault!* her brain shouted, but her heart refused to listen. *Fine! If you can't forgive yourself just yet, direct the anger at him.*

It was with a great, shuddering sigh that she opened her eyes. If she faced Cesare again, she had to be ready, and not crumble.

# Thirty-Six

**1493 AD**

Michelle shoved in the door. "Found one. Three days from now, evening tide." She fell on the bread ravenously. "Did you eat everything else?"

"It's keeping warm in the kitchen." Gwyn rang the bell and the maid reappeared after several minutes. She disappeared and returned with the food.

"Hmph, probably asking for food poisoning." Michelle stirred the soup. She didn't bother to sit, instead she stood with her back to the small fireplace, leaning over the rickety table that held the food.

"Well, don't eat it then! Where's Meric?"

"He's not back yet?" Michelle tasted the soup and pulled a face, abandoning it in favour of the vegetables.

"No—I've been waiting for hours! It's dark out there!"

"I hope you used the time to rest. I wonder what this spice is? I don't recognise it."

Gwyn could have screamed at her. "How could I rest? You left me here alone—Cesare could have walked through that door at any moment!"

Michelle stabbed a piece of zucchini with her knife. "Highly unlikely—he was searching the docks."

"You saw him?"

"Yes, but he didn't see me."

Horror gripped Gwyn. "What if he found Meric?"

"Meric can take care of himself."

Gwyn thumped the table. "You two act like I'm the one who needs babying. Meric didn't notice that guy following him in Ravenna. I'm going to search for him."

"Do not go out there, Gwyn!"

Gwyn looked at her scornfully. "I'm going to use the timepiece." She tried to connect. She hadn't tried to use it in any way since Cesare had kidnapped her. It had been useless when she'd most needed it. She hated that she had relied on it when her wits and strength should have got her out of trouble. The sick feeling rose up again and her connection to the timepiece severed.

*Never mind that now. Find Meric.* She slowed her breathing tried again. As she sank into the timepiece, Meric's face came to mind, calming her. She waited as the mental tug wavered then solidified into a direction. Just like when she had located Cesare on the ship and seen him about to go overboard, a vision of danger appeared. "He's being tortured!" Her eyes flew open. "Cesare has him—I told you he was in trouble."

A frown crossed Michelle's face. "Tell me where—I'll go find him."

"No way!" Gwyn snatched up her cloak and flung it on. "Come on!" She shoved past Michelle, who cursed and hastened after her. Gwyn darted between patrons in the tavern's taproom; a man with a large belly got in Michelle's way.

"Gwyn, slow down!" Outside, Michelle grabbed Gwyn and yanked her to a halt. "We need a plan." Her loud voice made Gwyn wince—the quietness of the street contrasted sharply to the noisy warmth of the tavern. She took a deep breath of the fresh air, untainted by the odour of sweat and beer and fish stew.

Gwyn's jaw worked. The chill rising from the nearby canal made her pull her cloak firmly around her and she stamped on the hard cobbles. "We grab Meric and jump away. We take Cesare with us if need be then you can conk him on the head or something."

"His guards won't let us get near him!"

"We have to try! He's hurting Meric!" Gwyn took off again and Michelle ran to catch up. This time they kept walking at speed. They skirted around a couple of well-dressed merchants laughing loudly at a crude joke. "It's not far." Gwyn half-closed her eyes and checked with the timepiece again. The pull from Meric was even stronger. "Just across that—dammit!"

A canal blocked their way. No bridge was in sight. A solitary lamp hung from a nearby home, encircled by the crazed flutters of moths and mosquitoes. "Here." Michelle lit her torch. Gwyn gazed down at the dank, slime-covered stone of the canal walls. The smell of sewage was even stronger than it had been earlier in the day.

"It's low tide—even if you wanted to swim across you'll struggle to climb out," Michelle stated in a low voice.

Gwyn frowned and looked for steps.

"Here, there's a boat," Michelle whispered, pointing. Tied to a post a dozen yards to their left floated a gondola. "Come on, quietly now."

They crept along to the boat—Michelle kept her torch dim. Two yowling cats ran out from an alley, startling both women. Michelle whipped out her knife and crouched, ready to fight. Gwyn stumbled and almost fell in the canal—Michelle snapped out a hand and steadied her. "Thanks," Gwyn gasped, trying to slow her racing heart. They reached the boat.

"Get in." Michelle helped Gwyn down and slid in beside her, then tried to undo the rope that held the gondola fast. "Bloody hell." She took out her knife again and sliced it.

"I could have got that loose," Gwyn protested.

"Your hands are shaking and—we don't have time. Hold on while I get the oar."

They pushed off and paddled back up the canal, crossing to the other side. Gwyn clambered out. The rope was too short to tie the boat but she still held onto it.

"Okay, let me go first and suss out the situation," Michelle said.

"They are *torturing* him! We can't waste time."

"First tell me where they are exactly! Fifty metres, five hundred metres?"

"Oh." Gwyn rubbed her face. "Um, it feels like a turning point. We have to stop Cesare from coming after us or it will derail history again. But I can't leave Meric behind."

Michelle gripped her shoulder tightly. "Gwyn, I don't know how we're going to save him, but we'll do our best. We're going to have to improvise."

Gwyn nodded, biting her lip, then both women froze as a man's scream ripped the air.

\* \* \*

"You are a particularly loyal man, Meric." Cesare toyed with the knife, tapping the blade on the mottled skin near Meric's eye. The eye twitched and watered, but Meric held Cesare's gaze. His torturer's dark eyes glittered; his sweat reeked of excitement. Meric had smelled that animalistic odour on soldiers revelling in the kill. His own blood tasted coppery as it trickled from his lip.

He sat on the grimy cobblestones of a dead-end alley, hands bound behind his back, feet tied together. A split lip and black eye adorned his face. The rest of the bruises weren't as obvious—of the five mercenaries present, only one held a torch. His back pressed against the cold stone wall; Cesare crouched beside him and hovered the point of the knife near Meric's eye. "Are they really worth it, those witches? Worth protecting? I can pay you in riches they couldn't even dream of, you can have all the women you want gracing your bed. Just tell me where Gwyn is."

Meric coughed and spat out a mouthful of blood. "I don't know where she is."

"Don't lie to me!" Cesare snarled, stabbing the knife into Meric's leg. Meric roared in pain. "I will do much worse to you before this night ends if you do not tell me where she is!"

Meric had no doubt. Cesare's pursuit bordered on fanatical, and Meric had no fancy tricks to magic himself out of there. He was just a foolish soldier, one who'd not kept his wits about him and allowed Cesare's men to jump him. His whole body ached. The wound in his thigh burned—it was as though fire blazed from where the knife pierced him. A fresh surge of pain rushed over him as Cesare yanked the knife free and Meric's leg bled heavily. "They went to find a ship," Meric croaked. "I was to meet them at St Mark's." He was going to die. The watch in Venice only patrolled the rich areas—this was a dank side-street; the grimy cobbles were slippery and stank of fish guts. *Just have to lie enough to throw him on the wrong scent. I hope Michelle will realise something is wrong when I don't come back and get Gwyn out of here.*

"A ship to where?" Cesare's nostrils flared. Meric had seen wolves kill a sheep when he was a child looking after the village flock. The way they sniffed the air in anticipation of the kill came to him so vividly in that moment, with Cesare all but twitching before him.

"England," Meric grunted. "We were to book passage to England." *He's a man, not a wolf—he can be tricked, reasoned with.*

Cesare frowned and stabbed Meric's other leg. Meric screamed as more fire raced through his veins. "You could not possibly hope to find a ship and board it this very night. Where did you take lodgings?"

"I don't know! I just had to find the ship and meet them at St Mark's! Michelle was organising lodgings!" His head pounded and felt light. He hoped that Michelle was with Gwyn, safe back at the tavern. He hoped they had found a ship, that they would board and flee and that this ordeal would be over soon.

"You're lying!" Cesare hissed.

"And you're deranged," Michelle declared, striding into the torchlight. The Swiss sprang alert. Michelle held up a hand and said, "Stop!" They paused.

"Michelle, get out of here!" Meric barked in Turkish. "I can't walk— just go and make sure Gwyn is safe."

"Shut up, Meric. If you wanted the girl, your eminence, you should have bargained with me," Michelle said. "I don't take kindly to my property being stolen."

"What?" Cesare stood, frowning. Meric focused on the sheen of blood on Cesare's blade.

"Gwyn, come here!" Michelle beckoned, and Gwyn emerged from the darkness of the alley behind. "You want her, you buy her."

Meric groaned. "What are you doing? Run, Gwyn! Michelle, get her out of here!"

A sinister grin spread across Cesare's face. "What's to stop me from simply taking her?" He twitched his fingers and the soldiers advanced.

"Stop!" Michelle yelled. She raised her wrist and a blinding flash illuminated the alley. Cesare threw his hands up in front of his eyes.

Meric blinked furiously; stars and spots danced on the back of his eyelids. "I will curse each and every one of you if you lay one hand on me!" Michelle boomed.

Vision returned. Michelle stood before them, a frightened-looking Gwyn beside her. Cesare clutched his knife, waving it as if to ward them off. The Swiss shuffled and looked at each other uncertainly, crossing themselves. Meric could smell their fear. Michelle gripped Gwyn's arm. "So, what are you willing to pay for her, Cardinal?"

Suspicion overtook confusion in Cesare's voice. "This is a trick!"

Michelle sighed. "Yep." She shoved Gwyn towards Meric. The girl ducked and rolled under Cesare's outstretched arm. He was forced to defend himself as Michelle attacked.

"You shan't reach them!" Cesare slashed. Michelle ducked under his swing and tackled him. They fell back towards Meric and Gwyn.

Meric shouted, "No!" as Gwyn grabbed his hand then reached to grab Cesare too. Blue haze rose and his stomach lurched. The haze faded and he vomited, a cold sweat breaking out all over him. A thump and muffled groan sounded and Meric peered blearily. Cesare Borgia lay unconscious on the ground before him. Meric's limbs were heavy. His vision blurred and he passed out.

# Thirty-Seven

**1493 AD**

"Meric. Meric, please wake up." Tears rolled down Gwyn's face as she knelt over her friend. She registered Michelle tying Cesare's wrists with the rope from the gondola and knew she should be glad that he couldn't hurt her, but all she cared about was Meric.

Vomit and blood smeared his face. She used her sleeve to try to wipe it clean. The wounds on his legs continued to bleed. Should she bind them? "Michelle, help me! Please—his legs!"

Meric's hand brushed hers. "Leave it, Gwyn," he croaked.

She grabbed his hand. "Meric! It'll be okay. Michelle, don't you have something that can help?"

Michelle dropped to her knees beside Gwyn and ordered, "Tear strips for bandages—we need to compress the wounds." She felt the pulse in his neck and listened to his chest.

"Leave it, I said!" Meric's voice was stronger. Both women looked at him; Gwyn distraught, Michelle grim. "I can't walk and you can't carry me."

"We'll get a boat!" Gwyn interrupted, slicing her tunic for strips. She paused and looked about frantically, noticing for the first time the cold light of dawn. Dew covered the cobbles and there was no sign of the mercenaries.

"Gwyn!" Meric tugged her hand and her attention back to him. "It's too late. By the time you find a boat, then a surgeon—I don't want to spend my last minutes being jostled about like a dying pig." His face was pale under its stubble and his breath clouded the morning air.

"No," whispered Gwyn. She pulled off his glove and clutched his fingers to her lips. His hand smelled of leather and copper.

"If we can stop the bleeding we might be able to save him." Michelle wound the makeshift bandages around one leg. They soaked through immediately. "I have antibiotics that will protect him from infection."

"You... can't..." Meric batted at Michelle's efforts with his free hand. She continued bandaging doggedly.

"Meric!"

He smiled at Gwyn, blood staining his chipped teeth. "I'm glad I got to spend this time with you, little sister. You make life more interesting."

Tears flowed down her face. "You'll be okay," she declared. "Michelle's going to save you."

The cracked smile broadened. Gwyn was aware of Michelle swearing. Her legs felt damp—had she knelt in a puddle? "You saved me, remember? All those years ago. You're a good girl, Gwyn. Be strong."

Gwyn pressed his hand to her face and clenched her eyes shut. "You're not going anywhere, Meric. You're going to be okay." She squeezed his fingers and breathed, inhaling and exhaling with all her concentration. Leather, sweat, blood and metal overwhelmed her senses, everything that was Meric, his essence, his life.

"Gwyn."

Gwyn didn't open her eyes.

"Gwyn." Michelle's hand was tentative on her shoulder. "Gwyn, he's gone."

At that, she did look. Meric's face had slackened, staring eyes half-closed, jaw lolling to the side. The tears renewed themselves and she struggled to draw breath, mouth open and chest heaving. She flung herself on him and sobbed into his neck, then turned to Michelle as the older woman gently disentangled Meric's hand from Gwyn's grip. Michelle hugged Gwyn tightly, rocking her back and forth.

"To show love is to show weakness." The voice came from behind them. Gwyn and Michelle drew apart. Lying on the ground, hands and ankles tied, Cesare watched, his face dispassionate.

"You." Rage flew into Gwyn's heart like a flaming arrow, igniting the tinder of misery and sending all her emotions into a blazing inferno of hate. She snatched the knife she had used to cut bandages and dived at him.

"Gwyn, no!" Michelle yelled and grabbed Gwyn's arm. Gwyn fought ineffectually, spitting every swear word she knew at the startled Cesare. She had the satisfaction of seeing a moment's fear in his eyes before he masked it. She stopped and released the knife. "I'm sorry, Gwyn," Michelle murmured, still holding Gwyn around the waist. "He's too important."

Gwyn took a deep breath. She didn't dare look around. The sight of Meric would cause her to lose control again. Instead she looked into Cesare's dark eyes and summoned all the authority she could muster. "You shall not follow me anymore," she ordered. "I am lost to you." She squared her shoulders and Michelle let go. Gwyn spoke again.

"Go back to Rome, Cesare Borgia, and fulfil your destiny."

\* \* \*

"Only two passengers?" the first mate asked. "Thought ye said there'd be three?"

Michelle shrugged. Gwyn bit her lip and looked away. "Third one couldn't make it," Michelle replied. "Can we come aboard?"

The mate waved them into the skiff. "Sí, the captain is waiting on few more pieces of cargo, but you may as well come and get settled. It will be good to get out in the fresh sea air again and away from this cesspit of a city."

They sat on their packs as they were rowed out to the large half-galley. Climbing the rope ladder in breeches, Michelle was glad they'd maintained their disguise as men. It would take some effort for the sea voyage but would attract less comment than travelling as women without a male chaperone.

There had been no pursuit from Cesare. Michelle had cut his bonds, eyeing him warily, but all his attention had been fixed on Gwyn. He had bowed, then turned on his heel and walked away, leaving them with their friend and the smell of death.

They had to leave Meric—trying to dispose of a body, even respectfully, would have attracted unwanted questions. It had been hard enough to sneak back into the inn at dawn, heavily bribing the maid to ignore their bloodstained clothes and dishevelled appearance. They had washed, changed and left, jumping to just before their ship was due to sail.

Now as sailors shouted and oarsmen heaved, Gwyn and Michelle stood silently in the bow. Venice fell away behind them, unwatched.

Michelle hesitated, then put an arm around Gwyn's shoulders, ready to pull back if her touch was rejected. Gwyn didn't respond for a second, then reached up to squeeze Michelle's fingers.

Michelle breathed in deeply, strangely comforted. The salt air filled her lungs as the thud of the ship's drum beat time for the rowers. The deck vibrated and both women braced their feet to compensate for the swell.

Michelle felt Gwyn's back straighten, and she offered the girl a small smile. "On to Spain."

**Read on for a sneak peek at Gwyn's
next time-travel adventure:**

# Heart and Stomach
# of a Queen.

JODIE LANE

# *One*

**2623 AD**

*The Shift is here.* Owen shivered despite the warmth in the lab. He couldn't really call it a cell—it was larger than his last apartment—but the data displayed on the screen in front of him chilled him more surely than any prison could.

"Ah, Owen." Jaysen Fitz strolled into the lab. "We are in the process of making history, or unmaking it, as it were." He chuckled at his joke. Owen gave a wan smile.

"What… what happens now?" he asked.

Fitz hooked a stool with his foot and dragged it closer. The screech grated on Owen's nerves. Fitz sat, still smiling, his good mood a contrast to Owen's sense of dread. "Now? Nothing just yet. I don't understand all the particulars but my associates assure me that there are a number of turning points in the fifteenth and sixteenth centuries. Once the nexus on those closes on them history will be forever changed and *this* reality will fade away. Thanks to your own projections we have seeded people at appropriate times to… *guide* the future of humanity to a much more fitting destiny."

"Oh." What could Owen say to that? Trapped by these Earth First fanatics, he was dependent on their goodwill to live. Would they kill him now as they had threatened?

Fitz noticed Owen's discomfort and leant forward, clapping the smaller man on the shoulder. "Never fear, Owen! We still have use for you. My scientists are good but they aren't the best. Not like you. You must explain to me sometime how it all works—how the Shift doesn't change things immediately even though it's all in the past to us now."

"Um," Owen mumbled. *Even if I dumbed it down for you, your head would explode, you dirt-grubber.* He didn't dare say that. "It's to do with temporal displacement." Owen's gaze drifted back to his computer, the display of lights overlaid by a multi-coloured wave representing four dimensions. The lights represented turning points—they lay in a channel of blue light. He'd watched one light explode like a tiny sun going nova, shifting the course of the channel, but somehow it had shifted back. He had theorised during his time at the Agency that it would take several turning points to shift the course of history, particularly when they were relatively close to each other, as these were.

In the background, Fitz prattled on about humanity taking its rightful place as lords of the galaxy, with Earth at the centre of this glorious empire.

Owen stared glumly at the lights. Before the Agency had been enmeshed in scandal and all operations suspended, they had multiple Agents dealing with single turning points. This scatter was a temporal and geographical nightmare. How could anyone hope to fix all that?

As he watched, one of the lights winked out. Owen frowned. He checked another screen. His calculations showed the turning point had been there. Had it spontaneously resolved itself? It was possible.

"I'll leave you to it!" Fitz clapped him on the shoulder again. Owen nodded and tried not to look confused, swinging his eyes back to the computer as soon as the lab door locked.

Another turning point winked out. Owen dragged data from one screen to another, speaking algorithms into his self-designed program. He checked the result twice.

It wasn't an anomaly. Somewhere, in the fifteenth century, someone was repairing history.

# AUTHOR'S NOTE

I'm aware how Euro-centric this series is—when I started I had plans to take Gwyn all over the world, but the plot constraints meant I had to limit her geographically. Having said that, it would have been a shame to miss out on the deliciously wicked era of the Borgia Pope.

Renaissance Italy went through incredible cultural and political upheaval, and intertwining of religion and politics makes for a fascinating examination into human character. Corrupt? Yes. Avaricious? Most definitely. But the sponsorship of artists such as Da Vinci and Michelangelo couldn't have happened without powerful patrons. Martin Luther wouldn't have been disgusted into writing his Ninety-Five Theses if the Church in Rome hadn't been so visibly debauched and hypocritical, and so wouldn't have sparked the Reformation.

Whether these are good things or bad is a moot point—they are interesting, and interesting makes for good stories. I loved writing Cesare as a villain—he is complex and intelligent—and the way Gwyn and Michelle both deal with him highlights their strengths and weaknesses. Neither is the ideal Renaissance Woman, though both are incredibly strong in their own ways. I shall enjoy watching them continue to grow in the final book of the series, *Heart and Stomach of a Queen.*

This book is also littered with cameos from notable historical personages. Da Vinci, Machiavelli, La Bella Fornezi, Caterina Sforza, Lorenzo the Magnificent. Each of these characters could have dominated a novel, so I hope my judicious use of them enrichens the story, rather than detracting from the main plotline. Ladies Fornezi and Sforza, in particular, are women I'd love to write stories for their own sake.

A final note—as with all my novels, I have taken great liberties with the timelines. Lorenzo de Medici actually died before the new Pope was elected, but it suited me to keep him alive several months longer. King Charles of France didn't invade until a few years later, and the Rome didn't try to consolidate its nominal rule over the Campagna until after that. But because Gwyn messed up the timeline I was able to cram all that excitement into less than a year, moving armies around in the space of weeks instead of months and accelerating political machinations. As usual, however, my stories are based on historical events, and I really don't have to imagine much to come up with drama and intrigue.

I hope you enjoyed the tale! Please leave a review on Goodreads or Amazon, or you can get in touch with me via my website: www.jodielane.com or through my Facebook page: AuthorJodieLane.

# ABOUT THE AUTHOR

Jodie Lane is an avid amateur historian, combining her love of travel and adventure with fascinating stories from the past. Brisbane based, she studied a variety of modern history at the University of Queensland, and loves to read a wide range of historical and science fiction.

Her travels have taken her all over the world: she has lived and taught English in China and Romania, backpacked through Europe and South America, and holidayed in the Middle East, Central and North America, South East Asia, New Zealand and South Africa. She speaks basic Spanish as a second language and her sport of choice is wing chun (kung fu).

Other short stories include "The Job", "Naughty Zombies" (*Obliquity*) and "The Voice" (*Evil Inside Us*).

You can find out more via www.jodielane.com or like her Facebook page www.facebook.com/authorjodielane.

# BIBLIOGRAPHY

Hale, J. R. Machiavelli and Renaissance Italy. London: The English Universities Press Ltd. 1961.

Haslip, Joan. Lucrezia Borgia. London: Cassel & Co. Ltd. 1953.

Hibbert, Christopher. The Rise and Fall of The House of Medici. London: Penguin Books, 1974.

Yriarte, Charles. Translated by William Stirling. Cesare Borgia. London: Francis Aldor. 1947.

www.ingramcontent.com/pod-product-compliance
Lightning Source LLC
Chambersburg PA
CBHW020007140726
47904CB00018B/1986